Marley's Ghost

Marley's Ghost

Mark Hazard Osmun

Twelfth Night Press
Corte Madera, California

Library of Congress Catalog Card Number: 99-64220

ISBN: 0-9673079-0-2

Publishers Cataloging-in-Publication Data

Osmun, Mark, 1952-
Marley's ghost / by Mark Hazard Osmun. — 1st ed.
p. cm.
Prequel to: A Christmas carol / Charles Dickens.
LCCN: 99-64220
ISBN: 0-9673079-0-2

1. Misers—England—Fiction. 2. England—Social life and customs—19th century—Fiction. I. Dickens, Charles, 1812-1870. Christmas carol. II. Title.

PS3565.S65M37 2000 813′.54
QBI99-891

Manufactured in the United States of America

Cover design and illustration by Wendell Minor

Published in the United States by Twelfth Night Press,
433 Town Center, #606, Corte Madera, California, 94925

Publication date: 2000

2 4 6 8 10 9 7 5 3 1

This book is dedicated to Sally,
for bringing a spirit back to life

and

In memory of Hazel and Jim.

Acknowledgments

This book arrived as a Christmas gift; an idea that, while welcome, came unbidden. I am grateful to my friends, neighbors and mentors who helped me deliver this package by lending me their kind support, advice, patience and affection over the years. I am thinking of Jim Cobb,Thea Reynolds, Tracy Barrett, Margaret Gibson, Laura and John Mesjak, Peter Clark, Chris Walker, Dave Elliott, Kerwin Louis, Cindy Black, and Paul Reynolds.

Special thanks goes to my gifted editor, Ed Stackler, Bob Kenney at Context Marketing, text designer Solomon Faber, proofreader Sharon Dockweiler, and to cover designer Wendell Minor for making time in his busy schedule to work on this project.

Love and thanks also to Joyce West, my sister and conservative advisor, who said, "You should do this."

"...between us and you there is a great gulf fixed; so that they which would pass from hence to you cannot; neither can they pass to us that would come from thence."

– Luke 16:26

"How it is that I appear before you in a shape that you can see, I may not tell...I am here tonight to warn you, that you have yet a chance and hope of escaping my fate. A chance and hope of my procuring, Ebenezer."

– Marley's Ghost, from *A Christmas Carol*,
by Charles Dickens.

Contents

BOOK I. Turner & Marley

Prologue: Fever
Elizabeth's Furnace
Christmas Past
Ushers Well
Hardchapel
Ezra's Ghost
Marley's Dance
Funerals
Steel & Spark
Solace Home
Ghost

BOOK II. Marley's Ghost

Pooka
Brighton
Ruprecht
Solstice
Berchta
Three Spirits
The Brotherhood
The Light-Giver

BOOK III. A Christmas Carol

Marley's Face
Sol Invictus
Scrooge and Marley
Christmas
A Christmas Carol
Author's note

Book One:
Turner & Marley

Prologue: Fever

December 24, 1835
London

Jacob Marley's forehead burned and his eyelids swelled with heat and lay thick and heavy against his eyes, making him fear that perhaps blistering, red coals hovered just above him.

The thought of coals made Marley jerk his eyes open. But he saw only wavering black and orange shadows; light tossed from the dying wood fire in the hearth, dancing across his face and about the bed.

Marley swallowed and licked his cracked, thin, pale lips—aware of the sight he'd become: his face a hard composition of sharply-angled bones and hollow cheeks, eyes narrowed by a perpetual squint from which deep creases trailed.

"No coal," he whispered.

"Mr. Marley? Did you say somethin'?"

A woman's voice. A high Cockney tone floated past him then merged with other sounds, sounds that alternately swelled and shriveled in volume and clarity.

Harness bells glided up from outside the window, followed by the muffled drag of a sled close behind.

Faint voices of carolers rose to the window ledge, singing: "...born on Christmas Day, To save us all from Satan's power, When we were gone astray..."

But the rest of their song dissolved there, like a snowflake against warm glass.

Far away, church bells pulsed, then faded, leaving in their place the solitary beat of the floor clock.

Marley's attention turned to the steady ticking of the clock and, in a minute, his racing pulse steadied. Then the room came into focus.

Mrs. Dilber, the housekeeper, sat on a chair next to the great canopied bed.

"Mr. Marley, you say somethin' 'bout coal?"

Marley recognized the voice. Mrs. Dilber spoke the brutalized, amputated English of the Cockney, stretched and irritating, and yet over the years he'd tolerated it—remarkable, since he tolerated little else.

"All's well. You just stay with us, Mr. Marley. Shall I bring up the coal brazier after all? I don't know why, for all these years, you never used it. So cold up here and wood burning up so quick and expensive and with so much smoke and ash. I'll bring up the braz—"

Marley slowly raised his left arm and shook his head as rapidly as he could manage.

"No. No coal," he gasped with an urgency that made Mrs. Dilber jump.

Marley's arm hovered in the air for a moment longer, then dropped back to the bed. He strained to breathe.

"Well. Very well," said Mrs. Dilber. "Have it your way. You always have. Don't blame me when..."

Mrs. Dilber stopped abruptly. She reddened and dropped her gaze to her lap and smoothed her apron with both hands. A full minute passed before she looked up again.

"Mr. Scrooge will be along shortly," she said before affecting a sudden, merry tone. "I'm sure you two will have plenty to talk about. Won't that be nice? But you could use some warmth in here, I still think. I'll just add a bit more wood to your fire."

Marley closed his eyes again. To his great relief, his eyelids slid coolly back into place, their fire gone. The woman's right, he admitted. It's getting colder.

With his eyes shut, Marley felt invisible. He could hear Mrs. Dilber talking to herself, and yet Marley believed that he no longer existed within the room. Certainly Mrs. Dilber spoke as though alone.

"Fifty-nine years old. I'll be that old myself before long," the housekeeper's voice murmured from the darkness. "It's five o'clock. Mr. Scrooge said he would come at seven. Don't know as Mr. Marley'll last that long though."

Marley listened to the woman's skirts rustle like leaves in a strong wind as she moved across the room. He did not take offense at her remarks. It seemed, in fact, that the woman spoke about someone else, a "Mr. Marley" whom he might know, though only in passing.

"It'll be mighty odd with you dead and you and your belongings gone. Then we'll have eight empty rooms instead of seven. Dust and polish a bit of furniture, clean room by room for ten years and, by-and-by, these old sticks at least come to be old friends."

Marley listened and envisioned the room. He lay in a large bed bracketed by four, thick posts in which carved, wavy-haired cherubs soared, positioned so that they appeared to be holding up the bed's canopy and curtains. Marley pictured the deck of cards lying unopened on the reading table next to a book titled, *Probability Theory*. Authors on book spines came to Marley as he browsed through his mind's library: Malthus, Smith, and Locke stood interspersed between scores of ledgers and numeric tables. But Marley could not remember the significance of any of them.

The sound of something being rousted and dragged made the books disappear. A light, human grunt issued from the direction of the fireplace, followed by the crushing glee of a log dropped onto embers. Orange and red specks of light suddenly exploded across the screen of Marley's eyelids.

He thought he saw the fireplace and the fire in it as plainly as with open eyes. The apron of the fireplace still had its original paving: hand-painted Dutch tiles illustrating religious scenes—Cain and Abel, Moses holding the Tablets, Lucifer being cast out of Heaven, angelic messengers descending through clouds.

Marley imagined a strange, black and white creature coming toward him, but before he could make it out, he heard Mrs. Dilber again and suddenly returned to the present.

"There, that ought to do you," said Mrs. Dilber's voice. "You always needed a good fire. Don't know why you never filled a coal scuttle. I hate seeing you this way—though if you ask me, you never really seemed alive. Never a proper coal heat, never any company that I could see, never a good meal—though the Great Lord knows, I did the best I could with what provisions you kept. The Good Lord gave you such gifts and you wouldn't open even a one.

"Oh my," Mrs. Dilber exclaimed suddenly. "Tomorrow is Christmas. Here now, Mr. Marley. You know what day tomorrow is? It's Christmas. I'd almost forgot. I know you're not much a one for Christmas, but in keeping with the situation, I thought I might place a wreath in the window."

The housekeeper sighed. "It must be the season that makes me take such liberties. A wreath, then? Right. Over there where you can see it. Wouldn't that be nice? I doubt you have the strength to object now. A bit of evergreen and hollyberries and mistletoe. A bit of life in the middle of dark winter, eh? A little Christmas present from me to you."

*****

Marley closes his eyes again. Mrs. Dilber's voice fades until he can no longer hear it. Even the memory of the room disappears, giving way slowly to a panorama at the center of which a moist, grassy field opens to him, its air scented with dust and hay. A bright sun shines, warm and so brilliant that the green of the grass causes him to squint. The field slopes away. Below him, a stream cuts across the meadow and beyond that some woods, thick and dark with summer leaves, writhe in a serpentine, seductive way. A black bird caws from within those limbs. A pond, its waters ivory-black and mysterious, suddenly shakes with the impact of frogs crashing into its pool, retreating from the banks and from the approach of children. The children laugh and shout. Marley, once again a boy named Jake Turner, feels gangly and awkward and free. He holds the hand of his twin.

"Ezra, hide."

Laughing, he tugs the bewildered boy, the image of himself, toward a place of concealment. But Ezra doesn't move and instead looks blankly at Jake.

"Come," Jake says again. "It's hide-and-seek. We hide now."

"No. Just you," says the other.

But Jake tugs again and his brother follows, over a ridge in the field to a circle of rocks where they crouch low. Jake puts a finger to his lips. "Whisper when you talk, so they don't find us," he says.

Ezra nods. Then Jake lies on his back and watches the summer sky, now outlined in rock; he imagines the blue circle of air to be below, not above him; that the earth holds him by his back, suspends him like a bucket over a well, above the pool of blue air, and that, if the earth released him, he would fall down into the sky—and in that moment when up and down reverse and when all things are possible, his orientation changes and he imagines himself falling up instead of down, thrust soaring into the heavens.

"This is what I think heaven is," Jake whispers to his brother. "Just this. Summer. Warm. Just us and no one knows where we are."

Suddenly, a deep voice resonates from behind him, speaking his name: "Jacob."

He stands and turns. Night and winter cover half the field. He turns back and forth: light and summer on one side, darkness and ice on the other.

The low voice says his name again: "Jacob."

He sees a glow behind a dark, winter hill. A large silhouette appears; a great man striding up against the ridge line. Then the figure stops.

Though the boy can only see the outline of the broad-shouldered form, he knows it stares at him and wants an answer.

"Jacob."

The boy shakes with an ill-defined dread.

"Look to your brother," the figure commands.

Ezra lies peacefully in the grass, oblivious amid the warm light of the summer field.

"When the time comes," the voice trembles. "How will you choose?"

*****

Marley woke with a start. Even though blankets wrapped him to his chin, violent chills twisted and wrenched at his bones. Marley shivered then shut his eyes, making all around him dark.

Elizabeth's Furnace

May 24, 1789
Elizabeth's Furnace, Northumbria

Jake and Ezra Turner huddled against each other, their knees pulled up against their small chests, their bony rumps on the hard rock floor of the landing, their backs pressed against the dark, sweating wall of the coal mine. Jake put his arm around his brother's shoulder and pulled him closer so that the other boy's head lay against his breast. With his free hand Jake removed his own cap, then wiped his brow with a grimy forearm and looked upward toward the main shaft.

Scores of miners—men and boys, all exhausted at the end of ten hours underground—congregated in the large room, waiting for the lift to arrive and thereafter deliver them to the world of light and air.

The air in the room, due to the shaft, flowed more easily there than in the rest of the works. But only a few steps deeper into any of the tunnels, the atmosphere closed in, becoming hot, humid and full of the gagging, mixed scents of human sweat, ammonia from the stables, and acrid dust.

Jake shifted, careful not to disturb his brother who had fallen asleep. During these waits for the lift Jake felt more anxious than he did when working deep in the tunnels, holding spikes for the drillers whose nine-pound mauls soared just inches past his head. Being so close to freedom for so long seemed a reckless temptation for the malevolent God. If they could only arrive at the shaft and hurry onto the lift before God noticed, they would have a better chance.

Though they'd been in the mines for three years, Jake still had not grown used to any of it: the dense air, the bent-over postures, the cave-ins, the fires, the dark. And rather than abate, his troubles promised to grow worse soon. More dangerous jobs awaited boys who turned thirteen; and Jake and Ezra had just done that.

Jake swallowed hard and tried to slow his breathing, aware that Ezra might sense his fear and become fearful himself.

Soon Jake found it hard to breathe at all. He imagined himself climbing up the back of one of the big miners, standing on the man's shoulders, just to be closer to the surface—even though that world of trees and open fields and sun twinkled more than a mile above them.

How long before it comes, Jake wondered again. He pulled at his soaked collar. Then he looked at his brother who wriggled himself more tightly against his side.

You're the smart one, Jake thought. He looked at his twin's sandy hair running in light streaks between layers of soot. What are you dreaming about? he wondered.

From what Jake knew, Ezra lived unaffected by the calamity of their situation. Thirteen years old, the both of them thrown into this hot, black pit, and yet Ezra exuded serenity. Even the recent cave-in seemed washed from his mind.

Jake, however, could not forget it. Tunnel Seven.

The shifting rock first creaked and groaned, then a trickling noise rippled in the walls, then the long, squeaking sigh sounded just before the timbers splintered and the walls rushed in on him. Dirt and coal and rock swirled around him like a solid whirlpool, rising up to his chin and filling his nose and mouth and ears and eyes full of cinders and dust. He lay buried for five hours, just his nose and mouth above the crush of dirt and coal. No light. And every few minutes, new sounds threatened from the earth above: squeezing and moaning as the seams eased into new positions. Each time, the boy's heart sped in anticipation of another fall. He'd wrenched his hands frantically, trying to dig them free from his side. Slowly he'd moved dirt and then one arm snaked out from the ground. With it, he'd dug harder, freeing the other arm. He extracted himself finally, long before the rescue party could get to his section.

Ezra, though nearly affixed to Jake's side, escaped the cave-in, thrown clear by the force of the explosion. When Jake emerged, he found Ezra waiting, rocking and humming in an agitated way, his fingers fluttering in the air before him. But with Jake's return, Ezra calmed and soon his expression returned to its soft, slack look: a short grin fixed on nothing in particular. Ezra's fingers, however, continued to ripple and jump as if animated separately from the will of their owner.

Since the cave-in, there'd been talk of another disaster. New, more dense clouds of coal dust raised by the first explosion, now posed the threat of spontaneous ignition. Everyone might be incinerated at any moment without warning.

Jake looked across the room at the biggest of the miners, a timber man named Gren Sully, who sat against the opposite wall, whittling a piece of wood with a large axe.

Sully's forearms seemed wider to Jake than his own torso. The tendons in Sully's arms rolled under the skin like waves as he worked the axe along the wood. Though long and heavy, the axe slid under Sully's stroke like a penknife, leisurely shaving fine scrolls of wood from the piece of scrap timber. The shavings dropped and piled around Sully's feet like curls of blonde hair.

The boy looked at his own wiry arms, then back at Sully's.

Then he estimated their relative heights. Though tall for his age, Jake stood a full foot below Sully. The huge man's back covered a portion of the wall as broad as one of the old bookcases in Jake's former home. Other miners told tales of Sully's strength and Jake himself had once seen the man lift the back end of a coal wagon alone. Jake remembered seeing the great strain on the man's wide, squat face: all his features compressed together as though the tons of coal and years of earth above them had pressed his forehead, brows, eyes, nose and lips together in many compacted seams.

Sully loomed invincible. Immune. No one could harm him or make him go anywhere he didn't want to go. He could leave this mine any time he wanted. If I were like that, Jake thought, I'd pick up Ezra, leave here and never come back. Jake closed his eyes and imagined how it would be: himself a powerful giant before whom rough men cowered.

But as soon as this comforting vision appeared, another voice in Jake's mind spoke: Why doesn't Sully leave? it asked.

The answer, truth of the mines, and of the country in general, came to the boy with demoralizing simplicity: there existed a force even stronger than Gren Sully: money. Money, or the lack of it, buried all miners.

Jake bowed his head and closed his eyes. I will have enough money before long, he thought. I have the cards. I have greedy men who think they can beat me. Even after they lose, they still think it. Let them think it. The laws of probability mean nothing to them.

Then again, what law of probability could have predicted himself and his brother buried deep in a mine? That outcome couldn't even have been dreamed—not even up to the time that father...

Jake wondered if he'd missed anything, any clue. He'd been sitting at the table at home, studying formulas, himself the mathematical prodigy of the Royal Academy.

Loud voices at the front door interrupted his concentration, but he focused harder and made the noise go away. He listened to his own voice whispering:

"Consider a compound of two events. Consider the outcome of tossing two dice numbered 1 and 2; the corresponding random variables are X and Y. Any outcome associated with a joint probability, say pij = Pr (X = i, Y = j) and the totality of outcomes with a joint probability distribution {pij} where i takes on the values of x_1, x_2...of X, and j has the values of y_1, y_2...of Y..."

At nine years old Jake Turner ranked at the head of his class, but doubted whether his father knew it: the man had been so angry and fearful about things then.

Jake rose from the table that night and brought his schoolwork to the bedroom to show his father.

Father sat on the edge of the bed, alone, head bowed, head cradled on the heels of his palms, eyes toward the floor, hidden.

Jake presented the work to his father, grinned and asked, "Is this right?" already knowing the answer.

His father looked up. For a moment not even a flare of recognition lit the man's eyes.

"Is what...?" father asked.

The boy pushed the paper forward and the man looked at it, not comprehending.

How small the chair seemed, how poorly it fit a man of his father's height. The chair should have been bigger so that it would not have bent the tall man's knees back toward himself. Father's face registered pale white, except under the eyes where black half-moons hung like shaded cups. The paper trembled in Father's hands; he shook his head sadly.

Suddenly Father stood, knocking back the chair. He threw

the paper to the floor and shuddered as he looked at his son.

"Is it right?" he shouted. "Is it right? No, it is not right. None of it! What good is it? What possible good?"

The man stood so much taller than Jake that his words seemed hurled from a great height downward, gathering weight and momentum before they hit.

"It is the ruination of us. Only the *great academy* for our genius. Well no more. We're ruined."

The man stopped and stared at his son, tears rimming his eyes.

Suddenly Ezra stood between them, no particular expression on his face, no judgment, no fear, just the endlessly dancing fingers and a side-to-side swaying of his body, the boy looking at their father as if to see, from close-up, what might happen next.

Their father looked at his sons and the man's features suddenly sagged.

He lifted his hands to his face and cried, "Oh my God."

When he removed his hands, his real self seemed to have returned from its inexplicable absence.

Father crouched low and whispered, "Jacob, son. I am so sorry. Please, forgive me."

But Jake turned and ran from the bedroom, through the parlor, out the front door, and into the cold winter night, into an ocean of darkness. He stopped at a well and held onto its rough stone edges, the way one might reach for a life-ring. He bent over the rim and peered down, then straightened up thinking, even as a child, that it would be strange to fill a well with tears.

Ezra caught up with him there. The simple boy lifted Jake's arm and put it upon his own shoulders. Ezra did nothing else; just stood there, swaying, his head against his brother's chest.

After a long time, Ezra spoke. His voice, as always, made a garbled sound, as if his tongue crowded his mouth. He rocked on his heels and, as he often did, parrotted the last thing heard.

"So sorry. Please forgive. So sorry. Please forgive. So sorry. Please forgive," he droned, echoing Father.

Jake woke from the memory only to find that the lift still had not arrived. Ezra dozed, unmoved, still nestled against his brother's armpit.

In the half-light Jake looked across the room and caught Gren Sully's dark gaze aimed directly at him. The giant's head wheeled at a different slant, bending to catch something said to him by another miner, a small, rat-like man.

Sully nodded to the man, then jerked his head in the direction of the main tunnel. He lifted his axe with one hand and gestured with it casually, as one might if holding a small stick. He pointed toward the figure of a man coming up the mine's main road; the man's shape, a flickering silhouette of black against the dim glow of miners' lamps, wobbled along the side of the tunnel.

Sully turned and spat.

Jake turned to look down the tunnel, then looked away. Everyone knew the shape, motion and outline that approached: Badger.

Badger, the short-statured foreman, rolled toward the main room with the reckless air of a drunken jockey looking for a fight. According to the miners, Badger's odd gait followed a mine riot years ago in which several crews tried to kill him.

Badger, though stumpy, possessed a powerful frame and, more important, a vicious temperament. He'd survived the attack with merely a broken leg; and killed two miners in the process before the rest of them backed off.

A quirt dangled from Badger's wrist and seemed to dance while he walked and swayed. In his opposite hand, Badger brandished a thick, black club.

The foreman entered the shaft landing and looked around at the assembled miners. Jake stole a second glance. Badger's forearm muscles spiraled like deck ropes, bulging to nearly the size of Gren Sully's. Badger sucked at his teeth, drawing in air and spittle through large gaps, and pulled back his upper lip in a wince. He stood with his fists on his hips, just to the side of Jake and Ezra, the heels of his boots just a pace from where they sat. Badger's eyes scoured the worn-down crews.

"I just found a nipper fast asleep at a gangway door," the foreman bellowed suddenly, causing Jake to flinch.

Badger looked from face to face.

"No one sleeps while they're in this mine! A sleeping man can't act when there's trouble. A sleeping man *is* trouble... In the winze or at the pit eye, or anywheres inbetwixt, no matter. No one sleeps!"

Badger rocked on his heels, his baton held behind him, a hand at either end.

"We had a firedamp go up in Tunnel Seven—if you gents will recall. Lost a dozen men, a girl, a week of production. There's still dust down there. You keep a watch on your lamps—and no open flames. If the dust fires up... Well, let me put it so: it's a rich vein down here, nothing but fuel. An unquenchable fire. Not something you want; not so close to Satan's parlor. Stay alert. Stay awake."

Jake stared, mesmerized. He'd never been so close to the fearsome Badger. Now he could reach out and touch the man's pant leg; few ever came so close without being thrashed. Jake's heart raced; a vision leaped into his mind: he became an English explorer in deep Africa. A huge, hulking gorilla—

Badger—lumbered into camp. He must remain very still or...

But in his fear and fantasy Jake forgot about Ezra and the fact that his brother, also at Badger's feet, slept deeply: in open contempt of the foreman's explicit command. Jake remembered too late when, with gut-lightening horror, he heard Ezra snore.

In the same moment, Badger's quirt leaped like a viper, then snapped backward, followed by the whirl of the foreman's body raking the whip downward toward the sleeping boy.

Jake reacted instantly. He jerked sideways, swarming across his brother's body, covering the sleeping boy's head with his own and beating the whip to the target. The leather of Badger's quirt cut deeply into Jake's left cheek, but Jake did not cry out or flinch away. Instead, he remained affixed to Ezra, content to intercept whatever lashes might come next.

Badger stopped abruptly. He straightened up and looked down at the bleeding boy as though not expecting to see anyone there at all. Badger slowly nodded to himself and lightly brushed the whip's lashes against his own leg.

"So...Mr. Jacob Turner, is it?" he said.

The foreman smiled crookedly and sighed.

"Mr. Turner, do you suppose I don't know what I'm doing? Do you think I don't know who is to be disciplined and who is not? Perhaps *you* know best, eh? The school boy. Yes. Perhaps, I should consult you before administering the lash. Perhaps I'm not smart enough. Is that it?"

Badger paced, still grinning like a professor toying with a pupil in front of the class. He tapped his baton in his palm, musing.

"You know, Mr. Turner, you're not well-liked here. *I* don't like you. And I'm sure not many of your brethren here like you—certainly not the ones whose money you steal at cards every night. Oh, you thought I didn't know that, did you? No, how could I? I'm not quite as smart as our young genius here, am I? Am I?"

Jake said nothing.

Badger stalked around the boy, like a prosecutor, his hands behind him again, his lower lip pushed forward in a contemplative expression. He walked back and forth, then stopped.

"What did you say?" the foreman demanded suddenly.

Jake shook his head.

A sharp report cracked and the quirt snapped, striking Jake across the eyes. The next strike laid open a portion of the boy's neck. The next caught him across the arms; the next across the belly. Jake rolled to his right but the foreman kept pace, leisurely walking sideways, the lash opening wide streaks in the boy's heavy jacket. One lash caught the top of the boy's right ear, taking a small piece of it. Jake curled into a ball, his head tucked deep against his chest, his hands cupped over his ears while the beating continued.

After two long minutes, the whipping stopped. Badger panted while he wiped his brow.

"So, Mr. Turner, will that arrangement suit you?" he said between breaths.

Jake, on all fours, looked up at the foreman through swollen eye slits. He spat a stream of blood that splattered on his own hands.

"I'll kill you," he cried.

Badger laughed and turned to the assembled miners.

"Did you hear that lads?" he chortled. "Young Mr. Turner has vowed to kill me. I don't know if I can go on. Watch my back, eh?"

Badger then leaned close to the boy and whispered into the bloody ear.

"The coroner don't come 'round when colliers die, Mr. Turner. Keep that in mind, boy," he said.

But Jake heard only a humming, high-pitched noise that grew, then suddenly erupted into a loud, sharp explosion between his ears.

He passed out, dreaming that he sat again at his table studying formulas and probabilities.

Once again loud voices jousted at the front door, but this time Jake listened to them, pulling them back from the ledgers of his young life.

His father's voice clashed with that of another man whose words thundered, then cracked, going from low to high, twice in mid-sentence. The man cleared his throat and growled at Father.

"...Your children are *your* business...There shall be a trial...recover the full amount...you'll know the inside of Marshalsea Prison...you'll like Marshalsea...debtors of your kind..."

The door slammed. Its report made the cottage shake, the sound echoed throughout the structure, shaking the boy. The sound ricocheted from room to room, and did not lessen with time. It grew so loud that it seemed to originate from every room. Then from only one room. Father's room: a loud blast, hollow, ringing; exploding the air inside an ear. Then silence rushed in to fill the raw void.

*****

Jake regained consciousness by degrees. First he heard the rubble-drag of feet shuffling across rock, or perhaps dice cups being shaken, he couldn't be sure which. Then he saw the mine, tilted sideways, men seemingly cemented to the walls by the soles of their feet. It puzzled him for some time. Then Jake understood that he lay sideways on the floor and that the miners stood upright. Jake pushed himself into a sitting position and immediately felt his head throb. He knew he must be bleeding, but before examining his wounds he looked for Ezra.

To Jake's relief, his brother still sat next to him. Ezra hunched down, his arms pulling his knees tightly against his chin and ears; his shoulders cupped around his legs. His head turned sideways and he rocked back and forth. He hummed an uneven melody to himself, but not one of comfort; its rapid rises and falls jittered, grating and unnerving as a rock slide.

Jake moved close to Ezra and, wincing with the effort, put an arm around him and stroked his hair awkwardly. Then Jake pressed some coal dust to his own face to stop the bleeding.

"I'm not hurt," Jake muttered.

The sound of his own voice shocked him. His words bubbled and blurted from his swollen face, the words contorted by their rough escape from his mouth. The effect unsettled, rather than soothed Ezra.

The simple boy kept rocking and humming. Jake shifted his position again and resisted the urge to wince. He tried speaking more carefully this time.

"I'm not hurt," he said again. "Don't worry about me."

Ezra stopped humming. Jake spoke slowly, deliberately, spitting often so that the blood in his mouth would not make his speech any more unfamiliar.

"You mustn't fall asleep here. Do you understand?"

"Mustn't fall asleep. Do you understand," the other boy mimicked.

Jake watched Ezra's face, then he picked up a shard of wood and began to trace precise patterns in the dirt. First he drew a cross, then marked it off in small increments. Below that he traced numbers and mathematical symbols. Then he returned to the cross and sketched in points and rolling lines, bell curves and parabolas.

Jake looked up as he drew, noting that his twin watched

intently, Ezra's eyes appearing sharply focused and switching quickly from the graph to the formula below it and back again.

After Jake finished the drawing, Ezra studied it for several moments then looked at his brother. A soft, small trace of a smile appeared on Ezra's face, as though something had been communicated.

Ezra answered Jake's cryptic drawing by softly whistling the notes of a mournful old folksong. Jake took a breath and painfully managed to sing a verse of the song.

"There lived a lady in merry Scotland/ And she had sons all three," Jake sputtered. "And she sent them away into merry England to learn their grammmaree."

Ezra's face brightened.

"To learn their grammaree," Ezra repeated. "To learn their grammaree. To learn their grammaree."

Jake felt the room spin. He concentrated, trying to will the mine back to stillness. Gradually the whirling subsided.

Ezra too stopped rocking; he spoke without looking up.

"I want to go home, Jake."

This time Jake looked away and did not say anything for a while. He pulled his brother close to him.

"I know," Jake murmured, his mouth nearly swollen shut. "Someday."

They sat closely for what seemed a long time until suddenly the squeal of ropes and wooden pulleys made them jerk their attention toward the shaft where the mechanisms that lowered the lift whirled and hurried into action.

"Deliver us from evil," came to Jake's mind: a frequent line from one of his mother's prayers. Only then did he think to look around the rest of the room, and across it to where Gren Sully had been. The sight caused a surge of dumb excitement to flood through Jake and he missed a breath.

Badger stood before the giant.

"Sully, you and Ferrel here, go down Number Seven and help the new crew shore the drift," Badger said.

Sully did not move. He put aside the whittled timber and grumbled, "I'm done for today."

Badger, who had started to leave, stopped and turned around. He looked down at the floor as if in thought, then smiled, chuckled and shook his head. He sauntered back toward Sully who stood to meet him.

Badger still chuckled and stopped only when his chest touched the belly of the colossal man.

The foreman looked straight up at Sully's chin and said, "Not now, man. Those boys have put me in a mood. I'll say when you're done."

"We've been down here for ten—"

Suddenly, Badger's black club lashed out and struck the timber man behind the knee. The blow arrived so quickly that it appeared Sully had fallen on his knees in worship. But a groan, not a prayer, issued from his throat when he hit the mine's floor. Quickly, Badger grasped the club at its ends and brought it up sideways under the giant's chin, snapping the man's head and causing him to lurch backward over his own legs.

Despite that, Sully wriggled away from the foreman, scuttling on his back, his limbs flailing blindly across the rocky floor like an upended crab, and managed to put several yards between him and his attacker.

When almost beyond the range of Badger's club, Sully found a piece of shoring timber the size of a shovel handle. He seized the scrap brace and scrambled to his feet with the wood held high over his shoulder.

Badger, who had almost closed on his quarry, stopped short and took a step backward, assessing the shift in power.

Slowly, Badger smiled.

"Here now, Sully," he said casually, shaking his head and chuckling. "You win. No need to have tired men working in a mine. I wasn't thinking."

Badger walked over to the timber man with his right hand outstretched. Sully kept the brace poised to strike, but Badger came forward, unconcerned, his hand before him, until he stopped no more than two feet away. Badger stood before Sully, vulnerable as a sleeping child; but calm, his hand extended.

"Sully..." the foreman said. "Gren Sully...Come now." Badger turned his hand palm up.

Slowly, Sully lowered the timber and shifted it to his left hand. With hesitation Sully reached toward the offering. The foreman took the giant's hand in his and shook it as though greeting Sully at a wedding. Badger's smile grew wider as they shook hands; the longer they shook, the more he smiled.

Suddenly, in a movement almost too fast to be seen, Badger moved Sully's arm toward the side, then pushed backward toward the big man's ribs. The move, as intended, created just enough of a lurch to pitch the larger man one step backward.

Sully's feet skidded across a loose pyramid of bricks which lay stacked on the tunnel floor directly behind him. The big man backpedaled furiously across the loose footing, kicking some bricks outward as he fell, grabbing helplessly at air until he hit the ground.

Now Badger wasted no time. He picked up one of the bricks and brought it down with a sickening chop, across the miner's left jaw. A cracking sound like a snapping timber ripped across the room and the giant went limp as an empty water-bag.

From that point on, Badger took his time. Blow after blow

from Badger's boots hit Sully in the ribs and chest and arms and face until, finally tired, the foreman stopped.

Sully lay in a mire of soot and blood. His face bloated into something other-worldly: ballooning so that its identifying features plunged under blood-gorged skin.

Badger caught his breath and jerked his head toward another group of miners. The men moved as if to a silent command and gathered around Sully and pulled him to his feet.

"Take him to Number Seven," Badger said. "The shoring will be completed today."

The crew staggered under the weight of the timberer, but slowly made progress toward the unstable tunnel.

Jake stared, dumbstruck. Sully could not be beaten. But Badger brought him down. Badger.

A crash of wood and grating metal hit the mine floor, making Jake jump at the sound. The lift arrived.

Deliver us from evil. Jake grimaced. Not even prayers leave here, he thought. The lift never arrives soon enough. The mine traps even prayers.

If it had not hurt so much to move his face Jake might have cried.

*****

Later that night, while the other miners slept, Jake rose from his barracks cot. He limped cautiously to the near window, taking care that his movements did not wake his brother. Ezra would often stir whenever Jake moved, as if an invisible cord connected their bodies so that one could not so much as flinch without jostling the other. But this time Ezra lay quietly, his breathing deep and regular, no trace of disturbed dreams or unsettling memories to distort his features.

Jake drew back the coarse cloth that served as a window shade. Smoke from the mines' ever-burning, vent furnaces clotted the night, making the heavens even less accessible. Only rarely would the sooty veil rip, revealing a momentary glimpse of the sky: itself just a paler shade of black, peppered white in places by random stars.

Jake stared at the brightest star he could find. Ordinarily such a star would remind him of Christmas and tales of wise men finding what they sought. But now the star stood as a representative of heaven and so Jake felt bitter toward it. His thoughts took the form of accusative complaints such as: Why did you let this happen? and, Why won't you save us?

But the star said nothing in return; it would not rise to the challenge. It glared back silently, arrogant and indignant as a king improperly addressed by a serf.

Mother believed in you. She thought a savior would come. But I never believed it.

The boy held his ground, hoping secretly that the taunt would make the Almighty react. But nothing happened and the silence went on. After a while Jake began to feel he might have made a mistake. What if God could hear him? What if some worse fate were being prepared for the faithless? He amended his remarks.

"I'm sorry," Jake said, mouthing the words inaudibly. "But if you can hear me, won't you please come soon? Not for me, you understand. But for my brother. He's done you no harm."

Jake watched for a sign in the sky, but soon the furnace smoke closed off any view beyond itself. After several more minutes of silence, the boy turned from the window, returned to his place and painfully lowered himself back into the cot.

He closed his eyes and dreamed of stars that could speak—but they spoke too faintly for him to understand their explanations and he wept in frustration.

In another dream Jake imagined that he woke with a start, believing that he'd only dreamed his life in the mines and that if he could just get out of bed he would find himself at home, his family intact.

With the odd and incorrect certainty of dreaming, he felt the seasons to be reversed as well. If he could rise, it would be Christmas again, the last hopeful time he could remember. Christmas: the way it had been. Everyone would be there; if he could only rise.

Christmas Past

Four years earlier. December 24, 1785
Meadow Bridge, England

Jake Turner's last happy Christmas came and went when he and Ezra reached nine years old. On that Christmas Eve a rare, thick snow covered the croft and the cold night seemed to wrap itself like a great fist around the cottage.

The two boys lay on their stomachs near the hearth. Jake sketched formulas, graphs, tetractys, gnomons, cross-hatched intersections, and angular numerical domains on a slate, while Ezra watched the emerging shapes with rapt interest.

As he worked on the numbers Jake simultaneously took in the smells coming from the cooking fire at the other side of the room. A soft, sweet, comforting scent of oatmeal and barley came from that direction and something else—raisins, perhaps. He could remember raisins from the prior year.

Jake stole glances toward his mother from time to time, seeing if he could discern the ingredients for this season's pudding. His mother leaned forward over a pot, stirred it, inhaled the steam and nodded to herself. Her auburn hair wrapped behind her head in a tight bun, and even as she worked in the warm room, she kept her dark, long-sleeved dress buttoned to the neck. Jake looked closely at her neck, at the small piece of skin just above the collar and below her jawline; a glaze of perspiration there made her flesh shine.

She had worked preparing the food most of the day and

already some of her labors presented themselves. The long wooden table held two bowls of fruit, a platter of biscuits, and a cutting board with a thick loaf of bread upon it; a pitcher of cider and four mugs awaited the family.

In the center of the room a small evergreen stood, candles placed carefully on its boughs. Below the tree lay four small parcels. Holly and ivy framed the whole of it: the threshold, table, and fireplace mantel sported wraps of green leaves and red berries.

Father sat near the fire, watching the boys. He sipped from a steaming mug and periodically tugged some smoke from an old clay pipe. Jake thought his father looked weary and in fact should, having come in not long ago from the fields. But when Father saw Jake looking at him he smiled kindly.

"It's the oddest thing," the man remarked. "Ezra seems to know exactly what you're doing. I swear, it's the only time he seems...calm."

Jake did not know how to answer that. He knew Father had not meant anything unkind. But part of the boy wanted to correct his father who seemed to believe, like the others believed, that Ezra understood nothing and possessed only a freakish genius with music. The truth, however, could not be articulated—though that didn't make it less true.

To the world Ezra appeared as a simpleton. His hands constantly fluttered before him, like struggling birds on the ends of strings. He had a way of staring steadily and unselfconsciously at people who interested him, even strangers, that clearly made those people uncomfortable. Ezra's speech, when he spoke at all, came slowly, thickly, and often he only repeated what someone else had just said. Other times he spoke out of turn, interrupting others with starkly irrelevant statements. To the world, Ezra played an idiot who could perform music extraordinarily well.

No one besides Jake could know the truth. No one else could speak the secret language he and Ezra shared: a secret language not only of twins, but of twin geniuses. Their language resided in the ethereal realms of frequencies, vibrations, musical intervals and arithmetic ratios. Objects, thoughts, feelings, philosophy, the rational, the irrational—everything conceivable or even inconceivable to normal thinking—could be expressed in their exchange of numbers and music; and expressed far more precisely and profoundly than conventional language allowed.

Jake could not explain this to his father, nor to anyone, for that matter, other than Ezra. By definition the plane on which the two boys communicated existed beyond the understanding of normal people and existed only for them.

"He understands," Jake said, without offense.

"Well he certainly appears to," Father conceded.

Mother crossed the room bringing her husband another mug of steaming punch. He took the drink in both hands, the mug nearly disappearing behind the broad wall of his fingers.

"This one should take the chill off you," she said. "You shouldn't work so late out in the cold."

"Thank you dear. Aye, it's cold out. When I came in I thought I'd never get warm. It's like the cold just tries to suck the life right out of you, and then you hobble back indoors, stamp your feet, hug yourself and still the chill lingers cold on your coat like ice, like some layer of frozen dust that you must brush away before any real warmth can get to you."

"Well this should take care of that," Mother said, returning to the kitchen fire.

A blow of strong wind outside the cottage made the door frame shiver. The concussion arrived with a high-pitched whistle that slowly faded into a low, strained moan. The boys looked anxiously toward the door.

Father laughed and blew a great wreath of smoke above his head.

"That would be Kari. She's the wind, the first of the frost giants," Father said, winking at the boys.

Jake knew this to signal an imminent story. He made a notation on his slate and pushed it aside. Then both boys looked at their father.

"Do you know," Father began, his voice dropping ominously. "Do you know what makes Kari cry like that?"

Ezra stared at his father while Jake shook his head, no.

"Not many do anymore," Father said. "So I'll tell you. Kari mourns the winter land, the loss of warmth, the loss of sun, the loss of spring and summer when life is abundant. She mourns the loss of Brigid."

"Who is that?" Jake prodded.

"The goddess of spring and light. She warms the earth and makes the fields grow high. And, oh, she is beautiful to behold. Spring is in her light step and her radiant smile. Her long, golden hair shines like sunlight and is so long that it reaches her ankles. Her lips are the color of roses and her eyes are green as spring grass. All who see her fall in love. The earth itself yields up its bounty to please her, and she, in turn, embraces the land and all of us. You've felt her yourself, have you not? When the summer sun warms your face?"

Jake nodded. Ezra looked at Jake and nodded more vigorously than his twin.

"Jake's slate," Ezra said, apropos of nothing apparent.

Father went on.

"So, you might ask: where is Brigid now? I'll tell you. She's a prisoner of the old ice hag—Cailleac Bheur. Locked away in the far northern mountains of the world. Oh, Cailleac Bheur is a fright. She's an old hag: very short, just under four-feet high, but broad as our wagon.

"She wears just a single, black animal hide which only covers her shoulders and chest. Her hair is all clumps of dark, frozen mats. Her eyes are red-rimmed and bloodshot. Her nose is flat and runny. Mucus freezes on her bristly upper lips so that she has to flick at it with her thick fingers to break off chunks."

Jake wrinkled his nose at the imagined picture. He noted that his father cast quick glances periodically toward the kitchen as if expecting to be rebuked at any second by his wife. But Mother moved from pot to pot evidently unaware of the story.

Father took another pull at his pipe and went on.

"Bheur's skin is pale blue and mottled with a dark purple web of veins. Her feet are bare, covered only by coarse, pig-like whiskers and the same sort of hair covers her legs, and arms, and upper back, neck and face. She waddles, like she's trying to hold something between her legs. In her mouth there's just a single, hooked, spiked tooth. Her lips are cracked. Her tongue is grey. And she reeks an overpowering, rank scent that would make you pinch your nostrils together."

Jake and Ezra edged closer to their father, as though to see the picture more vividly. Father grinned at the boys.

"Bheur envies Brigid for being all that she is not. For being warm and beautiful and enjoying the love of the people. So Bheur spies on Brigid, biding her time, looking for the moment when she might capture the Lady of Spring. And that time always comes. It happens when the people start to take Brigid's gifts for granted; when they start to think the sun will always be there as their right. When the people forget to adore Brigid, she weakens, her power fades—and that's when Bheur strikes."

Father jumped from his chair suddenly and the boys shrieked and rolled over each other trying to escape from the imagined hag. Father laughed and waited for the boys to return to their places.

"The old crone leaps out of hiding," Father said. "Her powerful, hairy arms crush poor Brigid around her little waist and then the old beast drags the sweet princess away to the north. When they are far away Bheur imprisons Brigid within a wall of ice this thick."

He held his hands as far apart as they would go.

"Deep in her mountain. And that's where Brigid is now, frozen solid. And that's why it is so dark and cold these nights. And that's why the wind cries her name. Can you hear it? Brig-id. Brig-id."

Ezra laughed and mimicked the cry, his fingers rippling wildly in front of his face.

"Brig-id. Brig-id. Brig-id."

"Spring always comes back," Jake insisted.

"Do you think so, son? Who can say? Maybe it won't this time. How does Brigid escape, trapped under so much ice? Eh?"

Father waved his arm, gesturing toward the tree and the holly over the threshold.

"That's what all this is about," he said. "These are left-overs of the old magic ceremonies once used to recall Brigid. The yule log in the village started out as a signal to remind Brigid where we were, and that we missed her. The tree here is to remind us of her power to make things grow. The lights, the songs, all of it, is really meant to awaken Brigid from her cold slumber.

"Without her, it would be an endless winter and we would be at the mercy of the dark and cold and the restless spirits that roam about."

"Ghosts?" Jake said, now more enchanted.

"Ghosts and worse. Why on nights like this all kinds of

things scramble about."

"Like what things?"

"Well there's Odin and Ruprecht with their band of Jolerei, the lost and hungry souls of Yuletide. They hunt in the winter snows with packs of ravenous dogs.

"And there's Berchta: an old woman who rides a huge horse across the skies trailing behind her a sad band of elves, fairies and the ghosts of murdered children. She seeks vengeance on—"

"That's enough."

Jake's mother bustled over to her husband, regarding him with a severe frown.

"Jonathan Turner. I won't have you filling these boys' heads with your pagan nonsense; not to mention blasphemy," she said. Then, turning toward the children, "Boys, your father has enjoyed a bit too much warm gin punch and is just talking to hear himself. Brigid, indeed."

The big man smiled sheepishly.

"Aye, listen to your mother, boys. I'm just spinning yarns," he said. But then he added, "Still, you know, Rebecca, the pagans lived here first and they believed as devotedly in their ways as you—as we, I should say—believe in ours."

Mother threw up her hands and huffed.

"You'll have these children believing in fairies and pookas next. A lot you believe in anyway. I know you're a doubter and yet you go on and gargle a gay air and become very poetic and misty when talking about customs come Christmastide."

"True. But, my dear, even non-believers can envy the customs of those with faith."

Mother stared hard at her husband. He looked down and chuckled to himself, then looked at the twins.

"I'm only teasing. Listen to your mother, boys. She is the steady one." Then, turning to his wife, Father said tenderly,

"Merry Christmas, my dear."

Mother's stern look melted immediately.

"Merry Christmas to us all," she affirmed, planting a light kiss on the man's cheek. To her boys she said, "And just so there's no confusion. The tree is a symbol of the everlasting life we shall inherit because Christ was born this night. And the presents that I've seen you staring at all day, those are merely symbols of Christ's gift to us: redemption from our sins."

Ezra bobbed up and down eagerly.

"Symbols of sin. Symbols of sin," he chanted.

"No dear," Mother said patiently. "Symbols of hope."

Father stood up and clapped his hands.

"Ezra, my boy," he called. "Let us make some songs. Shall we? Some Christmas songs. What say you to that?"

Ezra leaped to his feet and scurried to the small pianoforte—the Turners' only luxury—and took his place at the keyboard. Only when at the piano—and when following Jake's calculations—did Ezra's hands cease their agitation. Now Ezra's fingers caressed and gently dusted the keys, lightly touching the perfect arrangement of thin black bars set against thick white ones.

Father leaned close to his son and hummed softly in the boy's ear to indicate which song he'd like.

The music followed immediately, Ezra playing, Father and Jake singing, Mother looking on, keeping time with her feet.

"God rest ye merry, gentlemen/ Let nothing you dismay/ Remember Christ our savior was born on Christmas Day/ To save us all from Satan's power when we were gone astray/ Oh tidings of comfort and joy…"

When they finished the song, Mother remarked, "'To save us all from Satan's power.' There boys, that's the meaning of Christmas: salvation."

Ezra played that particular passage again. "From Satan's

power," he babbled.

The phrase reminded Jake of their weekly trips to the kirk where the weighty, but energetic Parson Cowens spoke so unrelentingly about the devil that the boy had come to associate the stone church more with hell than with heaven.

During the sermons Cowens himself seemed, to Jake, somewhat demonic: dressed in a black robe, a fierce grip on the shoulders of the pulpit, near-frenzy in his words, flecks of spittle escaping his mouth at certain times.

Last week the parson read directly from the Bible, but the topic had been the same one.

"'...I beheld Satan,'" Cowens read. "'As lightning falling from heaven...And no marvel, for Satan himself is transformed into an angel of light. Therefore it is of no great thing if his ministers also be transformed as ministers of righteousness...'"

Jake's extraordinary memory cataloged all the readings. One from Revelation gripped the "boy" in him, the part of him that gravitated toward anything gruesome or horrible.

Parson Cowens had read, "'I stood upon the sand of the sea, and saw a beast rise up out of the sea, having seven heads and ten horns and upon his horns ten crowns, and upon his heads the name of blasphemy...And the beast which I saw was like unto a leopard, and his feet were as the feet of a bear, and his mouth as the mouth of a lion: and the dragon gave him his power...'"

Though Jake pulled no meaning from the reading, the images intrigued him.

When Ezra finished echoing the carol and the line, "Satan's power," Jake turned to his father.

"Is Satan a dragon? The parson said he was."

Father looked toward the cooking area.

"There, did you hear that?" he chuckled toward his wife.

"And you're worried about them believing in fairies and pookas."

"That's enough now," Mother declared, using a vaguely menacing tone.

Father turned back to the boys. "Ezra, let's do another song. Jake, you choose it."

Jake chose "The Wife of Ushers Well," a grim folk song selected not for its words, but for its simple, perfectly-proportioned musical structure. In its arrangement, the music rested on Pythagorean harmonic ratios and also possessed an openness that would allow Ezra room to maneuver, embellish, and impose upon it the special syntax of the twins' own language.

Jake began singing without first announcing the tune, but Ezra quickly supplied the music from the fourth note on. While he sang, Jake swooped his arms through the air like a conductor, drawing imaginary loops and curves which Ezra watched with the same keen focus he'd given to Jake's calculations—and indeed, the shapes Jake traced in the air formed the complex geometries of the twins' private dialect. Ezra's musicianship provided the other half of the dialog as they discussed topics known only to themselves—the morbid lyrics of the song holding no more relevance to their discussions than bookshelves might hold to the contents of the books upon them.

The boys laughed during the performance, delighted by their ability to communicate the difficult intricacies otherwise locked in their minds. Their music/numeric language provided their only true outlet. Only through that cryptic channel could the boys lift the terrible isolation imposed upon them by their respective genius—genius that pulled them away from the games and company of normal children.

Jake sang:

"There lived a lady in merry Scotland/ And she had sons

all three/ And she sent them away into merry England/ To learn their grammaree.

"They had not been in merry England/ For twelve months and one day/ When the news came back to their own mother dear/ Their bodies were in cold clay.

"'I will not believe in God,' she said/'Nor Christ in eternity/ Till they send me back my own three sons/ The same as they went from me.'"

On the second round, Mother interrupted.

"That's hardly a cheery carol. Where did you learn that?" She glanced sharply at her husband. "What goes through your minds? I wonder. Ezra dear, please play something a little brighter. A reel, if you please."

Mother hummed a bar from a lively reel, unaware that she'd selected a piece—"Sir Roger de Coverley"—far more suited to fiddles than pianos. Still, Ezra picked it up.

Jake sat quietly nearby on a stool and watched Ezra's hands—as fascinated by their movements as Ezra had been of his drawings and calculations. Ezra's fingers skipped across the board, moving lightly as bees, hovering and dancing to the very music they themselves created. His hands flew without error to every key at precisely the right moment. The music jumped and bounced and soon Father and Mother locked arms and whirled themselves in reckless circles around the room. Jake stood and clapped out the time and watched his parents dance until the kettle sang in the kitchen, announcing dinner.

*****

After dinner—a hearty meal of roast mutton and potatoes and a rapturous treat of raisin pudding, Father stood and nodded deferentially to his wife.

"Bearing in mind the real meaning of Christmas," he said.

"We shall now move to the tree and look toward our gifts with grateful hearts."

Jake rose soberly, holding himself back lest he betray an eagerness bordering on impiety. Ezra, on the other hand, flew from the table—a whirl of arms and rolling fingers—and ran toward the tree, arriving there agitated as a jay.

"Grateful gift tree. Grateful gift tree. Gift tree," Ezra chanted.

Father knelt down at the base of the tree and selected Ezra's gift first. He handed a narrow package to the boy who tore at it—though ineffectually—making the ribbon's knot tighter rather than looser.

Mother stepped in and opened the package for her son: a simple tin whistle. Ezra's eyes widened as he examined the finger holes. After only a few moments inspection, Ezra began to pipe out the same reel his mother had requested earlier.

Mother received a wool shawl. She looked at her husband with soft, wet eyes, kissed him on the cheek and wrapped the garment around her shoulders.

Father received a new bible.

A short, slender package remained under the tree.

Jake imagined how he might feel if he received a toy like the ones he'd seen in the shop windows—say, a wooden tumbler or the figure that was mounted on springs and bounced out of a snuff box and was dressed in a black gown, with rope hair and a red cloth mouth, or the toy donkey with skin made of real hide, or the Jacob's Ladder made of little squares of red wood that flipped and clattered over one another, creating pictures.

How did children play with such things? It might be interesting to have one, just to see.

Jake opened the package. At first he thought he'd received a ruler. But this one had more lines and numbers and a gauge that slipped along its length.

"It's called a slide rule," Father said. "The man where I bought it said it calculates..." He hesitated, recalling the term. "Logarithms."

Jake studied the device much the way Ezra had examined the tin whistle. He pushed the gauge from number to number, and read the different values along its line. Clearly, the slide rule could speed up complex multiplications. Jake wondered if he could outrace the device to an answer. He felt that he could; in any case, it would be immensely fun to try.

"Thank you, Father. Thank you, Mother," he said, embracing them both.

"You'll have great use for this device, Jacob. All mathematicians use it. Especially those at the Royal Academy."

Father let the phrase hang for a dramatic moment before continuing.

"Which brings me to a momentous announcement," Father beamed. "Jacob Turner, having excelled beyond all normal ranges for anyone his age—or any other age—in mathematics, of all things, and I, having procured a generous advance against next year's harvest, can proudly announce that next month Jacob shall be able to attend The Royal Academy of Mathematics here in Meadow Bridge."

Jake did not know what to say. Only men—gentlemen, in fact—attended the Academy. He could not picture himself among them and yet, he knew he'd received a great honor, and would be able to indulge his greatest personal joy and learn from great men. Where his father had found the money remained a mystery to him, but money itself was a mystery then.

"I will study there?" Jake asked, unsure if he'd even heard correctly.

"Yes," his father said. Father's voice then took on a solemn tone. "You'll be a famous man someday," he said. "You will go to university, something no one in our family has ever done. And from there. . . "

Jake looked at his mother, expecting to see a soft light of pride and approval in her eyes. Instead he saw concern contract her features. Clearly she had been surprised herself.

"Jonathan," she said. "He's only nine years old."

Father nodded, seeming to have expected this.

"Rebecca," he implored. "What Jacob can do is so far beyond his years. Just as Ezra's music—" Father paused, then went on. "It would be a disservice to Jacob not to have him fulfill—"

"The cost," Mother said, incredulously. She had lowered her voice but Jake heard her anyway.

At this point Ezra returned to the others and, seeing the numbered rule, snatched it from Jake and gleefully, rapidly, pushed the gauge back and forth along its track.

"Ezra," demanded Father. "Give that back to Jacob before you break it."

Ezra continued to play with the device.

"He won't break it," Jake asserted. "I trust him. You won't break it will you, Ez?"

Ezra grinned and squinted at the small numbers.

Father turned back to Jake.

"Well, Jacob, what say you?"

Jake hesitated. "I don't know. I like learning," he offered.

"You were born for this, son. I believe the Academy was put in our county just so you could attend it. I swear I believe that."

Mother sighed.

"But there are no children there," she protested. "No one his age."

Father nodded and sighed also.

"There are no children his age *anywhere*, my dear."

"There is one right here. Exactly his age. What about Ezra?"

Father looked across the room toward Ezra, who continued to pump the gauge up and down the rule, seemingly oblivious to the discussion.

"All the more reason," Father said. "Jacob must do very well indeed, for I don't know who else will care for Ezra when we're gone."

"And the money? You never spoke to me of debt."

"An advance is all my dear. An investment in the boy. Nothing ventured, nothing gained."

At that Mother relented. She sighed and reached over to pat her husband's large hands, then she smiled tenderly at him.

"You have great faith after all," she said. Then she kissed him lightly on the cheek and turned to Jake.

"You shall be a great man, one day," she said to the boy.

Father stood to his full height and stretched.

"There," he said in a relieved tone. Then, turning to Jake, said, "What say I find the cards and we play a round or two of Forfeits. I may win one from you yet."

"A man of great faith, indeed," Mother mused.

*****

Jake and Ezra slept peacefully that night until suddenly both of them jerked upright in their beds as though yanked by their shirt collars.

Jake breathed heavily; the air around him felt massive and close, smothering. The room seemed to have grown smaller during the night. Jake threw his blanket aside. He experienced a strange feeling of unspecified dread, a premonition of confinement, of being squeezed into a dark place.

Ezra had also thrown his covers aside and also pulled desperately for air.

No words passed between the boys, but when their eyes met they both jumped up and hurriedly threw on their clothes, boots and jackets and ran from their room, through the cottage and out the front door into the open, cold night.

They ran no more than ten yards before stopping; the odd panic having vanished as soon as they gained the outdoors. They stood in snow up to their boot-tops, snow that ran in pure rolls across all the farms as far as they could see; snow that, lighted by stars and only a sliver of a moon, took on a beautiful shade of glowing, light blue.

The boys scrunched their gloveless hands inside the sleeves of their coats and looked at the stars. So many stars glimmered in the night that the sky seemed to lack room for them all, forcing some stars to come down to the earth, where they touched the tops of the distant trees on the horizon.

"It's not so cold," Jake said.

Both boys stood quietly for several minutes, the only sounds coming from their cloudy breaths.

"How did the Wise Men know what star to follow? There are too many. Were there fewer stars then? I doubt it."

Jake spoke in English, rather than in their secret language, since he only wanted to hear himself speak, fill a place in the vast void that hung above them.

"Why did they think a star would lead them to a savior?"

Ezra made a moaning sound like rushing wind and then turned it into a name. "Brig-id," he murmured in an eerie voice. "Brig-id."

Jake laughed.

"I suppose Brigid is a savior of a sort. When you think about the stars, about the infinite number of them, about infinity itself, about infinite possibilities in an infinite realm, then I suppose there might be such things as saviors," he mused.

Ezra shuffled his feet. His fingers churned inside the sleeves of his coat. After another few minutes the boys turned around and walked back to the cottage.

Ushers Well

June 7, 1789
Elizabeth's Furnace, Northumbria

Two weeks after the beatings, Jake and Ezra labored alone at the end of Tunnel Seven, loading picks, axes, spikes, hammers, bracing and the rest of the shoring crew's equipment and supplies into a wagon for transfer to the next repair site. The passage had been reshored, but mining had not resumed and, for the time being, the tunnel echoed its silence and desolation like that of a crypt.

Jake urged Ezra to work quickly, so that they could finish the job and flee this particular tunnel and return to the company of others before panic set in.

Jake avoided looking at the walls. In the inconsistent lamplight, the black walls of the coal seam shimmered and, in Jake's mind, suggested a wave of black water. He feared—irrationally and in spite of himself—that just behind the walls, just inches from where he stood, a swollen lake trembled with its own mass. In Jake's fears, the subterranean lake pushed hard against the wall, straining, just moments away from bursting through to crush and drown him and his brother at the same time.

Jake kept his eyes locked upon the floor and the cart, never raising his head higher than the cart's sideboards, unless to check the glow of Ezra's lamp. Because he wouldn't look up, Jake almost had to step on a tool before finding it. Then he would squat down, pick it up and retrace his exact route back to the wagon.

Jake completed his last tour of the site, taking small, quick steps. He hummed a nervous medley of folk songs to soothe his nerves and heard Ezra join in. Jake started to smile at this, but his face still ached from Badger's beating and he shortened the smile to a grin.

Suddenly four boots appeared in Jake's circle of light. Jake cried out and jumped backward, nearly dropping his lamp. But he held on to the light and lifted it higher and, in spite of his other fears, looked across the tunnel at the wall before him.

Two men stood near the wall. One of them, small and thin, had a pointed face and prominent front teeth, like a gnawing varmint. The other towered against the wall, monstrous and horrifying. Jake's lantern trembled. The big man's face wavered in the shadow-light, pale and mottled with bruises that appeared in varying shades of purple and black with yellow-green at their edges.

"Gren Sully," Jake whispered.

The big man stepped forward into the center of the light.

The lamp fell from Jake's hand.

"Christ, boy," Sully growled, picking up the lamp and placing it on the wagon. "You'll have us all lost in the dark. You're not afraid, are you?"

Jake swallowed, half believing that the sounds came from a ghost.

"Well?" Sully demanded.

Jake swallowed again. "You've not been seen in two weeks," Jake stuttered. "We... We all thought you were dead."

The big man limped noticeably as he crossed to Jake. "Well, I'm not."

In spite of his initial shock, Jake found himself growing pleased and excited by the prospect of speaking directly to the big man. He'd rarely heard the man speak and imagined that Sully, like storybook giants, only spoke in booming monotones. But Sully's voice moved methodically, evenly, clearly, and in a low register.

The thin man piped up.

"He ain't dead by quite some lengths, as some has come to know."

"Shut up, Ferrel." Then to Jake: "You're the one Badger thrashed aren't you? The one who plays Three Jack Maul, wins all the time?"

Jake nodded. Ezra moved into the light and stood at his brother's side.

Sully regarded the boys for a few seconds.

"Fine," Sully said at last. "This tunnel isn't finished yet. There's a side-tunnel back a bit. I need someone small and nimble to string a rope for me."

Sully looked at Ezra.

"But I don't need you both." Sully turned to Jake. "Just you."

Jake didn't move.

"Ferrel. Tell him you'll watch over the other one." He turned back to Jake. "There now: your brother is in good hands. Right? If you can't trust your own comrades, it's a pitiful world you're in."

Jake hesitated.

"I suppose," he said. "But, well...is it safe?"

"We'll find out," Sully said.

"It's just that... I was here when—"

"All the better, boy. You'll keep your wits about you."

Jake looked at the enormous man in front of him.

"I suppose," Jake said. "But I've never left Ezra alone."

"He won't be alone. Mr. Gordy Ferrel here will watch over him." Sully's tone took on a faintly threatening aspect.

Jake turned toward his brother.

"If I go with Mr. Sully for a little while, will you be all right?" Jake asked.

Ezra looked from one man to the other to Jake and back. Jake grasped Ezra's shoulders and looked directly into his twin's eyes.

"Do you understand? I won't be gone a minute," Jake said. "You stay with this man. His name is Ferrel. I'll be right back."

Ezra weaved his weight from one foot to the other. "Promise," he said.

"I promise," Jake replied and kissed his brother on the forehead. Then he turned to the timber man and followed him into the darkness.

*****

Sully held the lamp so high that its light fanned out over a wide swath of the tunnel, leaving only the broad area of his shadow unlit. Jake walked just in the wake of the light, to the timber man's side, looking closely at the walls, at the new timbers, and at the seam itself, searching for any clue of instability, or for anything familiar from the day of the collapse.

Black dust still hung in the air along with something that smelled like rotting meat. Every so often, Sully would stop and listen. Jake heard only drops from seepage landing in unseen puddles, sounding like fish picking insects from a pond. Faintly, other sounds meandered toward them from other parts of the labyrinth: squeaking trolleys, clanging hammers, and faint shouts sinking softly into distant tunnel walls, losing their meanings in the journey.

Neither man nor boy said anything until Sully broke the silence.

"You threatened to kill Badger," Sully said. "Did you mean it?"

Jake stammered out a laugh.

"At the time, I did. Not that it matters. I couldn't kill anyone, even if I were able. And I don't suppose I'd have much chance with him anyway."

"He's a murderer, that one," Sully said, as if to himself.

From time to time the boy stole looks at Sully's wounds. He touched his own face, remembering his own beating. Jake had that much in common with the big man.

"I only got the whip," Jake volunteered.

"Aye. The club is worse," the timberer conceded. "Badger was mad by then."

The boy leaned around the giant's side to see if Sully wore any look of blame. But Sully just rolled forward without expression.

"Are you still hurt?" the boy asked.

"Not now," Sully said. Then he changed the subject. "You say you were here when it caved?"

"Yes."

"A firedamp?"

"I think so."

"It was a bad job. Gas or no. It wouldn't have happened if my men'd shored it. You a butty?" Sully asked.

"Sometimes."

"How is it?"

"I don't like it."

"No," Sully agreed. "Especially not holding them spikes, I guess. One bad blow, one miss, they crush your skull, eh?"

"I suppose."

"The way you'd like to crush Badger's skull, eh?"

"No," Jake insisted. "I just want to leave here."

"That's a good idea."

When they came to a turn in the tunnel Sully's lamp went out and darkness rushed over them like a tide. The boy grabbed toward Sully and caught the man's belt.

"Don't worry," Sully said. "It's not much farther. Hold my hand."

They walked a dozen or more paces in total blackness. Jake thought about suggesting they relight the lamp; then the man stopped.

"We're here," Sully said. "I'll light the lamp. You hold onto this."

Jake felt the man's huge hand on his, lifting it upward and placing it on a cold metal rod. By touch, the boy recognized the metal as a drilling spike, set loosely, projecting from the wall at a right angle. Amazing, Jake thought, that the big man had not walked into the spike.

Jake waited in silence for the lamp. But no light and no sound came to him: no grate of flint and steel, not even the breathing of Sully nor the slide of his feet against rocks.

"Is this a dangerous part?" the boy asked. But no answer returned. "Is this where the ropes go?" he said again. "Is it safe to strike a light here? Can you hear me?"

Still no sound returned.

Jake held more tightly to the spike and began to move himself along it to find the wall and better orient himself.

The feel of the spike changed. After a foot or two, he felt wetness on the steel, something warm and viscous. The sudden and unexpected change in texture caused him to release his grip and lose the spike in the darkness.

Jake crouched down, close to the tunnel's floor. He withdrew his tinder kit from the pouch on his belt and struck a spark—risking, he knew, another gas ignition. In the brief flicker, he thought he saw the lamp, perhaps a yard away on the ground. In darkness again, he crawled toward the spot, groping until his hand banged against metal. He concentrated then, imagining the scene before him: the glass, the wick, his flint, steel and tinder material. He arranged everything in front of him according to the picture in his mind. He pretended that light already filled the room. Then he set to work. He struck at the flint until he raised a flame and then he transferred it to the lamp.

Jake held the lamp off to one side and turned toward the wall. A paralyzing chill gripped him as he stared at the sight ahead. Then he heard himself scream.

The body of Badger hung against the wall, not five feet away. The foreman looked down at Jake with eyes wide open, glazed and desperate. His chest glistened, dark and soaked. A six-foot drilling spike pinned him like a moth to a board; driven through his sternum and into the rock beyond.

Jake stood motionless, still as an unspoken word. He looked at his hands and the front of his work jacket, smeared with the foreman's blood. He could hear his heart. Badger's eyes stared wide open—horror enough—but suddenly, strangely, a more terrible thought came unbidden to the boy's mind: what if the body that hung on the spike only *pretended* to be dead; what if it could spring back to life?

A voice within Jake screamed for him to run, but he stood transfixed. Run where? To the lift where everyone would see him, see the blood on him? Run where?

The flame in the lamp stuttered, then died, pushing the boy into total darkness again. He wailed once, then clapped a hand to his mouth, afraid that the ghost of the impaled foreman might hear him.

"Follow me."

Jake jumped at the sound and tripped, fell, then scrambled to his feet again.

"Who's there?" he whispered.

"Follow me."

The voice belonged to a girl. It moved through the darkness to a place somewhere in front of the boy.

"There are caverns and passages only I know," the lisping voice said. "Follow my words. I'll lead you out of this place."

Jake did not hear the girl take any steps, but he clearly heard the high, nasal lilt of her voice. She sang an old song he knew well.

The girl's voice trilled: "There lived a lady in merry Scotland/ And she had sons all three/ And she sent them away into merry England/ To learn their grammaree..." The Wife of Ushers Well.

The voice glided over the hills and valleys of the music; a gentle motion, like a bird riding warm drafts. The song moved away from Jake and began to fade and sound hollow, then it stopped.

"Catch up," the voice demanded.

Jake took a step forward in the dark.

"That's better," it said.

The singing resumed and Jake followed, blind as the dead.

*****

Jake crawled in the darkness along ever more narrow passageways with only the girl's singing to keep him from being crushed by the panic of closing walls. He crawled, it seemed for hours. But just when he felt ready to scream out loud, the loose dirt walls took on the cold, hard feel of rock and stone, and began to widen.

Cold, fresh air braced Jake's face. His fingers searched along lines of well-ordered rocks, finding seams he could use as climbing rungs. Slowly, he inched upward in the dark, realizing along the way that he was ascending the side of an old, dried well.

Jake climbed without slipping and finally emerged. The moon and stars greeted him and lighted a clear, night sky. Jake breathed deeply. He pulled himself fully from the well's collar then sat on the earth and looked at the vast, moonlit field around him. He smelled wet hay and the lemony aroma of wildflowers.

He rested for awhile, taking in the soothing balm of the outdoors; but it didn't last. The vision of Badger's body returned. Badger's ghost might pursue him yet. A renewed panic seized the boy. He leapt up and ran until dawn.

Eventually, Jake slowed to a walk, but he kept moving for two days and nights until he no longer remembered his name nor why he travelled at all.

The third morning smelled of cool spring. Jake heard his feet shush along a rough trail. His legs felt soft, boneless from all the walking and he marvelled that they held him up.

Dimly, Jake remembered hearing the ragged, baying of dogs during the night. Animals pursuing him. Far-off echoes, memories of their howls and yelps still lingered. Then those faded and only the impression of hounds and imminent pursuit remained.

Slowly, the lightening sky and the fecund smells of barns and mulch made the world come back to him. Jake sensed newly-cut wood and sawdust. Smoke from a distant chimney carried an autumnal scent that mixed in an odd, but pleasant way with the scents of new flowers. Jake breathed the air slowly and deeply, thinking of it as something stolen—an earlier memory, of playing in the fields with other children.

He barely opened his eyes; just enough to see his feet skip small pebbles in front of him. He followed the stones for a time, thinking of nothing.

At the rise of a hill, Jake looked up in the direction of the trail. A church spire lanced the sky and marked a small village. Jake hesitated.

Smoke rose from only one chimney. Jake could see no sign

of people stirring yet. He could wander the streets for a short time perhaps and scavenge food and water before anyone saw him.

The smoky scent made him think of food. He reached into his pocket and found a piece of paper he'd grabbed somewhere in his flight. The paper announced dock work near London. Jake bit off a corner of the handbill, chewed it and swallowed it. Then he leaned back against a rock and closed his eyes.

This won't do, Jake thought. Perhaps no one will believe I did it. Perhaps I can go back. Perhaps it isn't too late. Jake imagined how he might go about it, return to the mine, clear himself, look after Ezra.

Jake froze, shocked fully awake. Ezra.

As if waking suddenly from unconsciousness and finding himself in a strange place, Jake looked in horror at the expanse of land around him; land now empty of the one soul on earth who knew him and could speak his language, their language; the one soul without whom he could not speak, the one soul he must always protect and love. Empty of that soul, the land around him seemed to go on forever: hollow and vacant of any soul at all.

Jake turned around and started to run back along the trail. Then he stopped, confused. He looked at the hills and farms stretching out in all directions. He'd been in a dazed state of panic-exhaustion for an unknown amount of time. His thoughts jangled into one another, a mixture of recriminations and practical questions. You abandoned him. Coward. How long have you been running? Which way is it back to the mine?

Jake looked toward the village again. Hunger and thirst seared his stomach and throat. I'll go there first, he thought. Drink water. Maybe someone will lend some bread. Someone can direct me back.

The trail curved down from the hillside and ended at the beginning of a cobblestone lane that coursed between several rows of small, thatched, whitewashed buildings. An odd structure stood in the town square, but the boy could not see it distinctly at first.

Jake continued past a lumber yard where scraps of wood lay about and the syrupy smell of cut wood lingered. Once past the yard, Jake saw the odd structure in the square clearly.

It stood exactly in the center of the street: an open frame made of three thick, roughly-planed timbers nailed at right angles. The two supporting posts rose about nine feet tall; a cross beam sat atop the posts, spanning the five-foot gap between them. Wood shavings and scraps formed a trail between the structure and the lumber yard.

Suspended from the center of the cross beam, its toes no more than eighteen inches from the ground, its head only twelve inches from the top, hung a bloated corpse, its hands tied behind its back, a heavy cord around its blackened throat.

Jake stared at the hanged man and backed away.

The dead man's tongue pushed outward, thick and mottled, squeezed out of its mouth by the rope. The eyes bulged wide open and glared from their sockets.

"It's a bad way to go."

The voice made Jake start.

"Ho! No need to fear. He's a dead man now; can't do no harm."

A heavy-set man with a thick moustache covering both his lips approached Jake. The man wore a workman's apron. Gold sprinkles of sawdust powdered both his moustache and the hair of his arms. He jerked his head in the direction of the hanging.

"We could've built a contraption much higher, used a lot

of play in the rope. You see, that way he could fall a bit first. The jerk would break his neck and he'd die quick. But that costs a little more. This way, it just strangles them—slowly."

The man spat and kicked some wood shavings over the expectorate.

Jake's mouth caked dry and pasty, and felt as though his tongue might stick to it, or that his windpipe might become sealed if he tried to talk. He managed a hoarse whisper.

"What'd he do?" Jake said, gesturing at the hanged man.

"Killed his wife," the carpenter snuffed, looking the boy up and down.

The man studied Jake for several minutes without saying a word and Jake began to feel uneasy. The man spat again.

"Your face is black," the man said, moving to within inches of the boy.

Without asking leave to do so, the carpenter placed a finger on Jake's forehead and ran it down the boy's nose; then inspected his fingertip.

"You're filthy. More than most," the man said, licking his finger. "This tastes like coal dust to me. It's streakin' down your face. My. Your eyes look like teeny, little, red spider webs. I bet you've been travelling hard."

"I'm thirsty," Jake whispered.

The man did not say anything nor point to a well. Instead, his eyes narrowed at the boy.

"A man came through here the other day. Said a boy killed a miner. Said we should watch for him. Said there's a reward for catching that boy."

Jake felt a chill wriggle down his back and felt his blood pulse against the sides of his throat. He said nothing and glanced quickly past the man toward the road.

"Something interesting out on the highway?" the man asked.

The carpenter's voice took on a snide tone. He drew a work knife from his belt and ran his thumb along its edge. Then he put his face so close to Jake's that the boy could feel the prick of the man's whiskers and smell the rank scent of sour whisky on his breath.

"You won't even make it to the road before I put ten cuts in you," the man said. "You come with me now. Don't make me cut you."

The carpenter snatched Jake's upper arm.

"Here we go," he said.

"Wait," Jake stammered. He forced a laugh.

"You've mistaken me," the boy insisted. "Here, look! I have a note from home. I walked here from Newcastle. I'm supposed to be apprenticed here at this very mill."

Jake dug into his pocket with his free hand and pulled out the folded notice he'd tried to eat earlier. He showed it to the workman.

"Here," Jake pleaded. "Read it."

The man stopped. His eyes narrowed again. He took the paper from the boy.

To unfold the paper, the man let go of Jake's arm but stood close enough to catch the boy if he ran. Slowly, the carpenter unfolded the paper: one turn, then another.

Jake marveled how the mystery of a folded page could hold a man tight as a noose: both hands holding the paper; the eyes watching it unfold; but more important: the attention focused only on the page itself.

At exactly that moment—the carpenter looking at the notice of work in London—Jake struck. He kicked hard at a point between the man's legs, the swing of his foot so swift that it lifted both him and the workman off the ground. The workman dropped into a heap.

"Bastard!" the man screamed.

Jake ran.

As he rushed away he could hear the man rising quickly to his feet, too quickly. Heavy steps soon rose behind him, growing louder and closer, then all at once, Jake crashed into the ground, the full weight of the carpenter plunging upon him.

The man wrapped an arm hard around Jake's throat and winched his legs, heavy as anchor chains, tightly around the boy's body, pinning Jake's arms to his sides. Jake struggled for a minute, then gave up.

The carpenter breathed heavily for a long time, then finally spoke.

"I wonder when they'll hang you," the man whispered nastily into Jake's ear. "Right away. Or after a long time in prison."

Hardchapel

December 27, 1796
Hardchapel Prison, London

The animal sounds of men in the cellars—groaning, hissing, barking threats, howling their madness, weeping, stuttering their chills—all those sounds shuddered off the walls that surrounded the twenty year-old Jake Turner, but he sat on a hard ledge and ignored them.

He stared into the dim light at a spot on the far wall and concentrated on the pain in his right hand. He'd struck an inmate with the knuckles of that hand; hit the man in the skull, knocking the prisoner unconscious, but the knuckle had cracked and the hand swelled. It mended, but it still pained him. Jake Turner focused on that pain, not wanting to avoid any of it.

He'd been in Hardchapel Prison seven years, entering at age thirteen. The last four years he'd spent in the cellars, where those without money go to suffer.

Unlike the upper levels of the prison, where debtors and criminals of means could buy comfort, the cellars reeked misery. Blocks of damp stonework, rising twelve-feet high, defined the long, common cell meant to house a hundred prisoners, but which in fact held triple that number.

The only light in the underground room trickled in narrow streams of dirty grey from a grate in the ceiling. Rows of coarse, rope hammocks holding human forms drooped from iron rings along the walls. A sour stench of old, soiled straw rose from the floor: a thick, foul scent of sweat, ammonia, excrement and decay.

In a year, he'd be twenty-one; old enough to hang. But Jake rarely thought of hanging or of his age. Half the time Jake thought of himself back in the mines and would even brace against the walls in the position of a butty holding a spike, awaiting a hammer's blow.

He suffered least during his mine delusions because they implied a proximity to Ezra; of being close enough to speak with and protect the boy.

But when made aware of his actual surroundings Jake embraced its miseries, trying to inhale and fill himself with all the pain they offered: the icy rattlings of his own knees, the churning claw of hunger, the throbbing ache of bruises, the screaming helplessness of boredom. Even so, he felt the punishment was insufficient, considering his crime. He knew himself as a coward and a traitor: one who deserted a brother.

Sometimes, when lucid, Jake imagined ways to escape. Always he stood guard, wary and waiting for an opportunity, or for an attack, the next struggle for rations, the next attempted theft of his shredded blanket. Surviving long among men—among the savage animals called "mankind"—one had to be fierce and much more cunning than the other brutes.

Now Jake stared ahead, grinding his aching knuckles into the stone until the pain overwhelmed him.

A bobbing light—the glow of a lantern—descended the far stairs, then approached. Jake tensed his legs, ready to spring, it might be Gren Sully and he might catch the man unawares. He could bury a four-inch chip of stone in the giant's neck if he could surprise him. But no, Jake remembered, Gren Sully worked at the Furnace. Sully lived in the mine, not here.

The light stopped in front of Jake and hovered, blotting out his vision of the men behind it.

"That's him," said the turnkey's voice.

"Bloody hell," said another voice. "I'd not have recognized him. He looks like a bloody wolf. A bloody, mangy, fucking wolf."

The man chuckled and the lamp moved closer to Jake's eyes.

"A pale wolf at that. Someone suck your blood out, sonny?" the unknown voice hissed, stretching its S's.

"I wouldn't get that close, if I was you," the turnkey said. "Those crazy eyes are trying to find you. He's a killer, you know."

Silence for a second, then: "I'm not worried. I've got this."

"Well, if you think you're fast enough to get a shot off," the turnkey said dubiously. "But I'll be going now."

"Leave the lantern," commanded the other man. "Set it over there."

The light moved away from Jake's face. After a few moments, his eyes adjusted and he could make out the features of the remaining man.

"You don't know me, do you?" the man said.

Jake saw a man of medium height and light build, a man who would not survive an unarmed fight. But the man's aspect—a half-sneer, slitty eyes, greasy coils of black hair, a thin, tautly-muscled neck, the sibilant voice and venomous expression—evoked the image of a viper and Jake instinctively edged back.

"I watched you play cards here once," the man said in a leisurely and also threatening way,

"Must be four or five years ago. Back when you were on the upper floors. Do you remember? You were remarkable. You always won. Always took the money. Of course, that was your mistake. You never let the others win. You never let them believe there was a chance of them winning. You must do that, you see, or well... as you know: they'll stop playing. Then you end up, well, with no money and in a place like this."

The man grinned as though he enjoyed seeing Jake with no money and consigned to the cellars.

"No matter. They've forgotten about you now. And I have a proposition: you will play a card game. I will bet on you. If you win, I will see about arranging, oh, a bit more food for you and perhaps a blanket or two. You can still play can't you?"

"Who are you?"

Jake tried to sound menacing, but his voice only scratched along, dry and gravelly.

"Snelling. Mr. Snelling to you. You can still play, still win, can't you?"

Jake nodded slowly.

"Good. I don't know why I didn't think of this before. You'll beat Bill Worthy for me. A bit of cash for me, a bit of comfort for you. Then perhaps skin a few more marks, at least until they catch on again—or until they hang you, eh?"

Snelling chuckled and grinned. Then the grin slid into a sneer.

"Get up," he commanded.

*****

Without knocking, Snelling opened the door of the top-story cell and pushed Jake into the chamber first. Jake took one step, then stopped, amazed by the bright afternoon sun pouring in through the window, by the lavish room and by the unseemly people in it.

The large cell, now a well-furnished apartment, hosted a motley core of hard men and their women, all of whom shone in the sunlight and in the red heat of a crackling fire.

Jake recognized some of the men from his brief time on the upper floors: prisoners—murderers, rapists, robbers—not simple debtors. These men, despite their crimes, lived well here away from the cellars and the impoverished inmates.

Some of the men clutched themselves against the women and sprawled on couches and pillows in various stages of undress and passion. Other guests, sated or more interested in money, played dominoes and cards. Still others clustered around a great serving table and dipped from its steaming tureen and speared pieces of beef from large platters.

A rotund gentleman, standing near the table laughed loudly: a booming laugh that embraced and enfolded everything within the room. The laugh rolled across the women, the tapestries, the recamier, the sleigh bed, the quilts, the armoire, the bookshelves, the fiddle, the keg of ale, and seemed to add life to everything it touched.

Jake stared at the festivity, astonished and resentful, but the revelry did not last long: abruptly, all activity ceased and all eyes turned toward him. The laughing guests quieted and stared. Many frowned. Bits of cloth and rags—and fine napkins recently stolen from the host—suddenly pressed themselves against many noses. Diners lowered their plates and mugs. Libertines untwined.

"Smells like a cess pit," someone muttered.

Snelling addressed the large man who had laughed.

"This is him," Snelling said, angling his head toward Jake.

The round man, who gave no sign that he noticed Jake's smell, bowed graciously.

"Bill Worthy," he said. "Your obedient host."

The man walked directly to Jake, ignoring Snelling, smiled kindly and held out his hand.

"Welcome, Mr...?"

Worthy paused, waiting to hear Jake's name.

Snelling answered.

"He's Turner. Jake Turner."

"Welcome, Mr. Turner," Worthy said, without so much as a flicker of an eyebrow.

"Mr. Snelling tells me you're quite a card-player. Mr. Snelling is willing to risk twenty pounds on that conviction: you and I, at any game I choose. Do you think you can?"

Jake said nothing.

Worthy rolled his eyes.

"My good lord, I apologize," he said. "My manners are poor. You are, no doubt, like any gentleman, desirous of the opportunity to relax and, em, wash up."

A murmur of agreement circulated among the guests.

"Molly?"

Worthy winked and gestured toward one of the prostitutes.

The woman, dark-haired and heavy-set, lifted the hem of her morning gown and curtsied playfully. She danced over to Worthy and presented her hand.

Instead of taking just the one offering, Worthy took both her hands in his and delicately kissed the rough fingers of each.

Jake puzzled over the time the man spent kissing the prostitute's hands. He watched Worthy's plump lips—thick, pink slabs of flesh—delicately pinch each of the woman's fingers, enveloping them, one-by-one. Worthy's lips reminded Jake of pudgy cushions, as did Worthy himself. Worthy could be a finely-stitched cushion: his girth puffing against the waist of his fine wool trousers, his waistcoat stretching its wings to hug his middle.

"Molly," Worthy said, gently. "Would you and Bess be so good as to show our Mr. Turner where he might freshen?"

"We'd be glad to, I'm sure," the woman smiled.

She waved at a smaller, younger, red-haired girl.

"Bess, would you help me, dear?" she laughed.

The girl disengaged herself from one of the men, smiled and took Jake by the arm.

Snelling stepped up.

"Mind what you're doing," he said to Worthy. "That boy's a killer. I'd not send him off alone with women. I'd not be near him myself, except for this."

Snelling patted the pistol in his belt.

"Not to worry, Mr. Snelling," Worthy said. "These ladies can take care of most men."

Snelling shrugged and stepped back.

"When you're done," Worthy said to the older woman. "Please find new clothing for Mr. Turner. Then kindly return him here—no worse than you found him."

Molly wriggled her brows at Worthy as she took Jake's other arm and turned him toward the door.

"We'll return him good as new," she winked. "I promise you that."

*****

The women led Jake down a corridor of upper-level cells, walking several paces in front of their charge with their backs toward him, evidently unconcerned about Snelling's remarks. Occasionally Bess, the red-haired one, would look over her shoulder and smile at Jake, but for the most part, the women seemed to trust him to follow like an untethered, but predictable, horse.

The girl who'd smiled at Jake shouldered a wool scarf to make up for her lack of more substantial clothing. Besides the scarf, she wore only a slip of a dress, made of material so thin that whenever they approached a lamp, her slender outline became visible through the garment. She looked frail to Jake, her body's silhouette more like that of a boy's, but the oddly pleasing arrangement of her pale eyes, long, red hair, and peculiar smile, moved him, then just as quickly, raised feelings of apprehension.

Jake did not know these women, nor, for that matter, the man who commanded them. The girl's kindly look, the way it made him—however strangely and briefly—want to speak to her, could easily ensnare him somehow, distract him, catch him off guard. Life in the cellars taught Jake to suspect the motives of all humans, women included, especially when met on unfamiliar ground.

On the other hand, moving from the cellars to the upper levels of the prison improved his lot dramatically. As long as he remained above ground, he'd follow his escorts.

The dark-haired woman, Molly, sashayed ahead, whistling a bright tune, her wide hips swaying across the corridor in time to the song. She never said a word and only once acknowledged that anyone followed her: that, when she jauntily tilted her head to the right to indicate an impending turn down a new hallway.

At a closed door, Molly stopped, produced a key from her apron, opened the lock and ushered Bess and Jake inside, following them and closing the door.

Inside, the room stretched forty feet wide and twenty feet deep, part kitchen, part laundry. To the left, a strong fire burned below a large iron pot that hung in the hearth. Near the fire several pheasants dangled from strings and slabs of dried pork rested on hooks. Cleavers and knives lay about a table upon which sat yet another platter of beef.

The floor slanted unevenly downward from either side of the room toward the center, forming a channel that led to a grated drain. Next to the drain sat a large, round milking stool and next to that stood a huge metal tub resembling a horse trough—though double that size. Dark water filled half the tub.

Molly looked around the room as if taking inventory, then turned to the girl.

"Dear, would you fill three buckets from the pot and set them near the tub?" she asked pleasantly. "Now where is the lye? 'Master Turner,' is it? Take off your clothes. Bess, when he's done, throw his clothes on the fire, please. And Master Turner, you can then take a seat on that stool."

Without waiting for compliance, the woman walked to a bank of shelves and began sorting through small boxes of cleaning powders.

Jake made no move to undress.

Molly selected a box from the shelf and turned back toward the tub.

"Yes?" she asked, looking at Jake with a puzzled expression. "What is it?"

"I'll do it myself," he said, surprised again at the hoarse sound of his own voice.

Molly put her hands on her hips and chuckled; her large breasts moved loosely under her gown.

"Oh, you're not shy around the likes of us are you?" she cooed.

"I don't take orders. Especially not from women. Nor from men either," he added.

Bess, filling buckets from the cauldron, paused to watch the exchange. Molly grinned and smiled knowingly.

"Oh that's it," she said, sounding sincere. "I understand perfectly. I didn't mean to be rude. Forgive me. It's just that, you see, I'm eager to start. Mr. Worthy would be very cross with Bess and me if we didn't take good care with you."

Molly paused, lowering the box of soap to her side. She looked at Jake with widened eyes.

"You will help us won't you? You won't put us at odds with Mr. Worthy?" she asked.

Jake hesitated, then, without showing embarrassment, pulled off the rags that comprised his clothing.

Molly smiled and started to thank him for cooperating, but as soon as his shirt came off, she stopped.

Bess put a hand to her own mouth to cut off an exclamation.

Molly spoke first.

"My, somebody did you some harm, didn't they?" she said in a matter-of-fact way. "Oh, look at those scars, welts, bites..."

She lightly ran her fingers across the wounds, old and new. Jake stood still.

"Badges of courage," she said. "That's what they are. You don't have to tell us. We know how it is."

The woman brushed Jake's hair once then resumed her directions.

"The breeches, please, Master Turner. That's it. Now sit on the stool if you please. Bessy, ladle some water from the tub into the bucket to cool it, then slowly pour some of it over him; give us something to work with."

Jake flinched at the first shock of water—not that it scalded or chilled, but he had not felt water on his body for so long that the novelty of it startled him. As the water ran down his neck, back, chest and groin, Jake became aware of his own fetor. The water seemed to unlock for the first time—to him—the thick, rank smells his body had accumulated over time. Aged sweat and waste combined in a dizzying stench that caused Jake to turn his head away, but to no use. He glanced briefly at both women, ashamed; but neither woman showed any notice of his foulness.

After dousing Jake, Bess remained nearby, seemingly

unconcerned about getting her own clothing wet. She regarded him without flirtation or judgment; she looked at him the way one might look at a wounded friend who needed stitching.

Molly meanwhile, soaked some rags in a solution of caustic soap and water and began to sponge Jake's back. When the harsh mixture reached his sores, he cried out, but remained sitting.

"Aye, it hurts at first. I know," Molly said. "But there's nothing to do about that. Has to be harsh to kill all them pests. Now close your eyes."

She nodded for Bess to pour more water, and Jake did as instructed.

"And kill them it will," Molly continued.

Jake kept his eyes closed, unable now to meet the women's faces. Shutting his eyes amplified the feel of the circular motions of the older whore's strong hands pushing the stinging soap across his back, under his arms, across his stomach, down his thighs. The whole experience of anyone's hands on him—in anything but a violent way—made him wonder if he'd ever felt such a thing in his life.

Jake's penis began to harden. He moved his arms nearer his lap and kept his eyes closed, hoping that somehow the women would not notice his state.

Before this, Jake had experienced no sexual encounters of his own. His exposure to the act had been indirect. During his early years on the upper floors he'd noticed women visiting the cells. When he first heard their yelps and cries of passion, he'd taken the noises to be part of everyday assaults, struggles over money, the settling of arguments or demands. Even later when Jake saw a trouser-less man pressing upon a still-dressed woman—the man's face locked in some silent snarl, his hideous rump thrashing amid the swells of the woman's skirts—even then Jake thought of it as a fight.

Later, during a card game, the boy told the other players what he'd seen. Raucous laughter erupted around the table.

"That's right sonny," one man chortled. "It was fight true enough. Only there's a bit more to it than that."

The players roared again.

Eventually, as the night progressed, the older men filled in the details—as they saw them—for the boy. As Jake came to understand it, sex meant power, dominance, and physical release; in that order. During his time in the cellars, he saw nothing to contradict that view. On the rare occasions when a flash of sexual energy hit one of the cellar wretches, an attack on a weaker inmate would follow and the sounds of the rape would pierce the souls of those who still had theirs.

But now the soothing, rubbing motion of the old whore suggested something different. Jake listened to the women's voices; they did not moan or sigh, they simply talked.

"Did you ever groom a horse, Bess?"

"No. You?"

"Oh, yes. Seems like a long time ago. You can soak them and they still look dry. But then you can skate the water right off their backs with a stiff board, like this."

Jake felt the woman run the edge of her palm up his spine and heard the sussurrus of water rush up his back in the direction of the girl.

"Oh see what you've done," Bess' voice laughed. "You've wet me. Be careful," she warned. "I've got the buckets."

Jake heard Molly chuckle, then he heard her sniff the air around him.

"The lye's done its work," Molly said. "Now for something more fragrant. Something from the Indies. Bessy, help me with this, would you?"

Jake heard sucking sounds coming from both sides of him.

He opened his eyes. The women, their dresses drenched, rubbed orange cakes of soap in their hands, working up thick, clove-scented lathers. Molly's blouse clung to her front, encasing the swell of her heavy breasts like a second skin. The lower portion of Bess' gown pasted itself to her small, upper thighs and gathered at the mound of her sex.

Jake barely had a moment to marvel at those sights before four hands glided around him from all sides. This time the soap inflicted no bite. Instead it moved in long, sweet-smelling ripples down his back and sides, then up again in slow circles. An oily sheath gathered on his body from neck to ankle.

"You've a hard body, Master Turner," Bess remarked.

Jake looked into the girl's eyes. Bess smiled briefly, then held his gaze with a more serious look.

"And you've hard eyes, too," she whispered.

Then Jake felt two hands suddenly encircle his penis from opposite sides. One hand made rotating motions around the shaft, the other stroked the underside, just below the head. His whole body stiffened and he moved as if to rise, but then sank back. His breaths turned into short huffs. He closed his eyes again.

At one point the uppermost hand disappeared and Jake opened his eyes. He saw the large figure of Molly step across him, lift her skirt and lower herself onto him, guiding him inside her. She placed her hands on either side of the stool to support herself then began to rock slowly forward and back. The lower hand, Bess', remained wrapped around him, making twisting motions that now caressed both Jake and the woman above him.

Jake's chest pounded. He looked from face to face for an answer to the feeling that rose within him: a feeling of pleasure and fear, a pleasure so intense that he feared his body might split apart.

Molly pulled away her blouse and pushed her nipples into Jake's mouth. Then Bess leaned in, and using her tongue, took Jake's mouth away from Molly's breast. Her tongue ran around his, then pulled his tongue into her mouth and sucked at it. She kissed him hard throughout the act until, suddenly, Jake's whole body quavered, his head jerked backwards and he cried out.

*****

When the threesome returned, only Worthy, Snelling and Tannin, the jailer, remained in the apartment. Worthy stood at the window, looking outside through the heavy iron grate in the direction of the walled courtyard below.

The open window allowed fresh, unseasonably mild, December air inside. From the yard below the thump of hard balls hitting the courtyard bricks could be heard as prisoners played rackets in the few hours lent to them by the sun.

"Look at the steam rising from their heads," Worthy remarked. "See which players are breathing hardest. You wouldn't bet on those, would you Mr. Snelling?"

Tannin cleared his throat and Worthy turned from the window.

"Ah, Mr. Turner," crowed Worthy, sounding delighted. "You all look much improved—and newly-dressed I might add." Worthy nodded at the new breeches, fresh white shirt and tan coat that the women had found for Jake; he also noted the change of clothing on the women. "Welcome back all, and my thanks to you ladies. I trust you're all feeling refreshed?"

"I'd say so," Molly laughed. Bess smiled and moved to the table and poured a cup of tea.

Jake looked at the men without comment. Whatever had happened in the other room, he needn't share it with this band. He was not a fool.

Despite his pleasure, Jake made himself remember that the women had been working not for him but for Worthy. Worthy and the women had their own motives. He would not be fooled; he would not drop his guard. The women were whores. As for Worthy... he would see.

"Please take a seat. I was just watching the men in the yard, while our good jailer pondered his next move," Worthy explained. "I simply cannot understand what it is that makes men bat balls about."

Tannin placed a 5-4 domino on the speckled tree of bones on the table, then leaned back in his chair, a satisfied grin rippling his fat cheeks. Worthy stepped to the table and examined the move.

"A drop more beer, Mr. Worthy?" the jailer asked.

Worthy continued to inspect the configuration of dominoes.

Tannin insisted.

"Don't hesitate at the price," the jailer said. "This one's a gratuity from myself to you."

Worthy smiled indulgently.

"I did not hesitate over price," Worthy mocked. "I'll make up for your prices, however outrageous, by the end of our game. On the contrary: your use of the word 'drop' paralyzed me. I took you literally for a moment. Pour me a full measure, man. Pour."

Worthy's huge laugh erupted again.

When the torrent of Worthy's laughter subsided, Tannin held up a hand in protest.

"You must be sympathetic to my circumstances, Mr. Worthy," he said in a miserable tone. "Many jails don't offer liquor anymore. I must go to quite some additional expense to transport good beer and porter in here without causin' tongues to wag. Why I'm at some risk as it is of losing everything—just to keep me residents happy, contented and peaceable."

The jailer, a man nearly as rotund as his host, widened his eyes as he spoke, affecting an air of innocence and sincerity; but instead he achieved a look that made the women snicker.

Tannin frowned.

"The crown made a mistake, if you ask me—interferin' with a jailer's right to sell beer to the residents. I'm in earnest. It's bad enough that they started mixin' the common criminals with the debtors. We had a tidy system before. Now we could lose control of the whole lot of them—especially without the incentives."

The jailer looked at the two women.

"But the powers haven't said anything about the ladies yet," he conceded. "At least we still have that."

"A prison revolt across the empire if they banned that traffic, I'd think," Worthy agreed, glancing at Jake. "The crown would be going too far, if it took that tender mercy out of the equation."

Worthy placed a 6-5 tile amid the lanes of dominoes.

"Molly, darlin,' would you be so good as to fetch another plate; our guests look faint to me and I think the meat would do them some good. Another platter should be ready by now. Down in the snuggery."

The woman mocked an even deeper curtsey than before, then trotted out of the cell, running her fingers through Worthy's hair as she passed.

Tannin said, "You're ever the gent, Mr. Worthy. The best priso— best resident, of my watch."

The jailer ran a thick hand across his mouth, already anticipating the roast beef that Worthy's cooks prepared every weekend.

"You are the gent," Tannin repeated. "Now then, here's my play."

The jailer placed a 5-5 on the table, but still had five tiles left. Worthy had one to go.

"No sir, *you* are the gent," Worthy declared. "You have paved my street with gold: observe."

Worthy laid down his last tile and beamed.

"Now let's count up your liabilities, then we eat."

Tannin pulled at his wispy beard.

"Lord in heaven. How does it happen? Every day. Every game. Miracles are hatched from your arse, Mr. Worthy. You dance with the devil, I'm thinking."

Molly soon reentered the apartment, carrying with her a platter of sliced beef, still snapping with the heat of the kitchen fire. She forked layers of the meat onto several plates. Tannin clapped his hands and rubbed them together briskly.

"You're blessed," Tannin said to Worthy, and pointed to his own head. "Blessed with the goods up here. Aye, kill me if I'm lyin'. You are the cleverest of the lot I've seen and I've seen a lot."

Worthy bowed slightly.

"You're too kind, sir," Worthy replied. Then he turned to Jake.

"Eat. Please," Worthy begged. "We have soup as well."

Snelling, who had taken Worthy's place at the window snarled.

"He don't eat till he's played."

"Are you tired of rackets so soon, Mr. Snelling?" Worthy said. "I would have thought you'd be mesmerized by a ball striking a wall, over and over, for a much longer time."

Snelling sneered, his slick, black moustache rising on one side.

"Bettin' rackets is more excitin' than snaggin' shillin's from an innkeeper," Snelling hissed.

He turned to the jailer then and feigned a respectful bow.

"No offense, Tommy."

The jailer looked at Snelling briefly, then got up and took his plate to another part of the room.

Snelling moved behind the chair that Tannin vacated, but did not sit.

"I wager on sportsmen now," he said. His eyes became slits. "That way, bettors can't cheat."

Worthy sat and sipped from a mug.

"Indeed," Worthy said into his ale.

Bess shoveled more coal on the grate, then closed the window shutters.

"Gets cold fast," she said.

Worthy ignored Snelling.

"Here, Mr. Turner. Enjoy some food," he said.

Again Snelling protested.

"After he plays, he eats."

Worthy frowned. "If he wins, you get my twenty pounds. What does he get? A share of the winnings?"

Snelling's face contorted.

"Bloody hell, man. A share? No. I've promised him food. And a good blanket."

At this the company fell silent. Snelling looked from face to face.

"He gets the food whether he wins or not," Snelling protested.

Worthy spoke in a measured voice.

"Here, we eat when and what we want," he said. "I'm not bound by your ways, Mr. Snelling. And I'll not have a hungry man in my apartment."

Worthy gestured toward the meat and the soup bowl.

"Please, Mr. Turner. Let me help you to some chowder and meat. Don't protest. I'm having some myself and I won't eat alone."

Worthy cast a menacing look at Snelling.

"Not a word," he warned.

Worthy ladled out soup and forked over great, wet hunks of meat onto Jake's plate.

Jake sniffed at the food cautiously, then took a bite. Then he took another and another. He took the pieces of beef in his hands and ripped off as much as his mouth could hold, hardly chewing before swallowing and biting again. He snorted in the effort to both swallow and breathe. Jake then grabbed the soup bowl with both hands and thrust his face at it, tilting it toward himself so quickly that much of the hot fluid leaked down the sides of his face, down his neck and chest. But he didn't flinch from the heat and loudly gulped the bowl dry.

Worthy lifted his own bowl of soup and tilted it and sipped from its edge. Then Worthy ladled more soup into his guest's bowl and began to talk.

"Mr. Turner, you will find me a man who is direct," Worthy said. "I hope you don't mind...I like to know whom I am playing. I am told you killed a man. Is that so?"

Jake glared across the table.

"No. It's not so," he said flatly.

His voice came out surprisingly clear and without the low accents of the cellars.

"Then why are you here?"

Snelling interrupted.

"He murdered a mine foreman when he was only thirteen. They didn't hang him though—the locals didn't like the foreman. The magistrate put him in here till he dies or till he's old enough to hang, which in either case is not that far away."

Snelling turned toward the jailkeeper and spoke sarcastically.

"Meaning no disrespect Tommy—but when one lives in the cellars here, being dead can't be too far off."

The jailer frowned, then his face sparked with recollection.

"Oh, aye. I recall him," the jailer said. "The killer boy. He's tried twice to escape. We had to whip him. We should never have mixed the felons with the debtors."

"I killed no one."

Jake's hard voice silenced the others. Finally, Worthy spoke.

"You worked the mines?"

Jake nodded.

"Where?" Worthy asked.

"Elizabeth's Furnace."

"Oh, up north. I've never been there, myself. Tell me: how did you come to be such an accomplished gambler that the cautious, and compassionate, Mr. Snelling is willing to risk his money on you?"

Jake looked at Snelling, who glared at Worthy.

"Numbers," Jake said. "I can calculate probable outcomes."

"Calculate..." Worthy repeated. "You gambled in the mines?"

"Yes."

"Did you kill anyone over a game?"

Rage simmered in Jake's chest.

"I say again," he repeated slowly, biting off each word. "I did not kill."

"Of course," said Worthy. "I beg your pardon, truly."

Worthy pointed toward welts, visible on Jake's neck above the collar.

"How did you come to be bruised?"

Jake looked off for a moment, then faced Worthy again.

"There's fights in the cellars—who gets the hammocks and who gets the shelves, who does what—that's how it is."

"Don't you have family? Anyone to visit you? Anyone to

bring you food and such things?"

Again Jake looked away. He turned back to Worthy abruptly.

"Are we to gamble or not? If so, tell me the game and let's get on with it," he said.

"The amount of the wager, again, Mr. Snelling?"

"Twenty pounds."

"That's a bit high for you, isn't it? Twenty pounds would probably make good all your past losses to me, no?"

Snelling's face stretched into a thin smile.

"That's right."

"Are you good for it?" Worthy asked. "After all: twenty pounds. You wouldn't want to wind up in a debtor's prison, would you?"

Both Worthy and Tannin laughed.

Snelling threw a cloth bag at the jailkeeper.

"Here it is," Snelling yelled. "Tommy, you hold the stakes."

Worthy held up his hand.

"Count it please, Mr. Tannin," Worthy said pleasantly, smiling at Snelling's furious expression.

The jailer opened the purse, counted the various coins and notes then nodded to Worthy.

Worthy grinned, pulled out two notes from his waistcoat pocket and handed them to Tannin.

"There's mine," he said. "It's a wager. Now then, Mr. Turner: what game do you like?"

"Three-Jack Maul."

"In that case, we shall play Rails. Do you know it?"

Jake shook his head, no.

Worthy smiled and replied, "Then I'll explain."

*****

The game, Rails, moved simply and quickly. The players

anteed a crown apiece, then received five cards each, face down. Whomever did not deal, bet; then the dealer turned the top card from the deck. If the bettor held a higher card of the same suit, he won the pool; if not, he showed his hand to the dealer. In that case, the money would remain in the pool and the dealer would bet on his own hand against the next card drawn.

Jake watched the cards, dispassionate and single-visioned as a monk. He placed bets without feeling, the money no more significant to him than beads on a string—this, despite the glares and nervous pacing of Snelling across the room. Jake showed neither glee nor despair in winning or losing hands.

When his turn to deal came, Jake shuffled and distributed the cards as though in a trance, staring at a point beyond Worthy's head, barely looking at the cards themselves until the deal ended. Then he would assemble his cards and read them slowly, like one poring over scriptures, looking for hidden meanings or answers to age-old riddles. Thereafter he would examine the cards remaining on the table and prepare his bets.

After a half-hour of play, Jake owned nearly twenty pounds of his opponent's money.

"Mr. Snelling," Worthy laughed. "You have indeed found a talent here. I thank you for bringing him to my attention."

Snelling started to smile at the beginning of Worthy's sentence, but then frowned, feeling that he'd made a great mistake, but not knowing what.

"Let us play one more round," Worthy said, happily shaking his head. "Just for the benefit of our jailer—I shall educate him by narrating how it is I've lost. After that, Mr. Tannin, you may turn over the stakes of Mr. Snelling's side bet to him and Mr. Turner, of course, will keep the actual winnings."

Hearing that the boy would keep the money, Snelling took a step toward Worthy, but then thought better of it.

Worthy dealt and Jake bet a crown. Worthy turned over the top card in the deck: five of diamonds. Jake lay down a seven of diamonds and took the pot. Then Jake dealt and Worthy bet—this time five crowns. Jake revealed the top card of the deck: nine of diamonds. Worthy laughed and groaned at the same time, and turned over his hand: ten of spades, the queen of hearts, the jack, eight and two of clubs. The players anteed again and as Worthy dealt, he talked to the jailkeeper.

"You see what he's doing, Mr. Tannin? He's counting the cards. You can tell by the way his eyes move. Watch them. He's memorizing the cards. I am impressed. He says he's never played the game, and yet he is playing it perfectly."

"And how is that, sir?"

"Intelligent betting in this game is simply a matter of keeping track of the cards to determine whether the chances of winning are better than the chances of losing. It's about lessening your risks."

Worthy grinned at the boy.

"Isn't it, Mr. Turner?"

The young gambler bet to match the pool. Worthy turned over the six of spades from the top of the deck. Jake pulled the seven of spades from his hand.

At this Worthy erupted in a barrage of laughter.

"You win. You win." he gasped. "I concede. Oh great day. Mr. Tannin, please pay Mr. Snelling."

Worthy laughed until Snelling had collected his winnings, then he wiped his eyes and took a deep breath.

"Now, Mr. Snelling," he sighed. "You will have to excuse us...Mr. Tannin and I have things to discuss with the young Mr. Turner."

Snelling curled a fist.

"Here, now. The bastard comes with me," the thin man snapped.

Worthy's brows jammed together like one befuddled by an obscure science.

"He comes with—With you?"

Worthy turned to Jake.

"Do you wish to leave, Mr. Turner?"

"Not particularly."

"Then there you have it," Worthy said, clapping his hands together. "I am much relieved. For a moment, Mr. Snelling, I thought something was amiss."

Worthy rose from his seat. Suddenly his great girth did not seem an impediment to action, but rather an ominous potential force. Snelling stepped back.

Worthy said, "Good evening, Mr. Snelling."

His voice sounded strangely different: dismissive, threatening, cold and bleak as a wind in an empty churchyard. Snelling hesitated, then turned quickly and left.

Worthy followed and closed the door to the apartment. Returning to the table, he rubbed his palms together in satisfaction.

"Mr. Tannin," he announced. "Prepare to understand some marvels."

Worthy's face split into a grin.

"Now then, Mr. Turner: would you explain to Mr. Tannin your analysis of this game, what you thought after hearing its rules and how, therefore, you came to play it so well? Explain, for example the last series of bets."

By now, Jake had already swept the cards together and put them back in a single deck. He thought for a moment, then spoke as if reciting an old prayer.

"I bet first," he said. "There were forty-seven cards whose locations I couldn't guess. The top card of the pack was equally likely to be any of them. In the first round, I received the ace of spades, seven of spades, jack of hearts, six of hearts and seven of diamonds. That left three hearts, seven diamonds and thirteen clubs that I couldn't beat—twenty-three—leaving twenty-four cards in the deck that I could beat.

"The odds rose slightly in my favor. So I bet, the five of diamonds came up, I won. Mr. Worthy then bet. The nine of diamonds appeared. He lost and had to reveal his hand. He had the ten of spades, the queen of hearts, the jack, eight and two of clubs. I could eliminate the queen of hearts, the nine of diamonds and three clubs from the list of those I couldn't beat. On my next bet only forty unknown cards remained, eighteen of which I could not beat. The odds favored me: twenty-three to eighteen. I bet; I won. And so on. It's not a complicated game."

Worthy beamed, his cheeks full and red.

"Not complicated when you think about it, eh, Tannin?"

Worthy's eyebrows fluttered merrily.

"But it's how *fast* he thinks about it that has me inspired," Worthy continued.

The jailer smiled slyly and cocked his head.

"Ah. What is it? What's that look I see in your eye, you old rascal, you old fox. Let's have it," Tannin cajoled.

"All in good time, Mr. Tannin. All in good time. First, since Mr. Turner was good enough to share a trick with us, I think it only fair to share a trick with him."

Worthy turned to Jake.

"Mr. Turner. Did you know that a clever man can make indebtedness a profitable venture? No, you probably did not."

Worthy took a long drink of ale, extracted a handkerchief from his coat pocket, wiped his lips and leaned back in his chair.

"I'm not one to be unnecessarily modest," Worthy continued. "So I don't mind telling you, Mr. Turner, that we have a rare and brilliant arrangement here. To wit:

"Once upon a time, I visited the magistrate to help a woman of Molly's acquaintance, out of some difficulty. Arriving early, I listened to the proceedings of various cases, one of which caught my attention. It involved sentencing a deeply-indebted crofter. Hopeless really—what with the madness of Debtor's Laws.

"A debtor, as you might know, is secured in prison until he can pay his debts. But how can he raise the money to pay the debts while he's in prison? Especially a crofter, for God's sake. What is he to do, plant crops in his cell? Herd sheep in the yard?

"Then I learned something interesting. The magistrate informed the creditor—as a matter of course—that he, the creditor—would be responsible for the crofter's upkeep in prison. Extraordinary, I thought."

Worthy drank again and again dabbed at the corner of his mouth with his handkerchief.

"I know what you're thinking—having been among the pathetic, freezing, starving wretches in the cellars—no offense—you're thinking that creditors, in fact, do not pay for the upkeep of debtors.

"Ah. But that is only because the letter of the law is not enforced. So, being a stickler for the letter of the law, I said to myself, what if a debtor selects his creditor carefully and has some forceful advocates outside the prison walls? Advocates who would see to it that the creditor lived up to his legal obligations? What would happen then?

"Well just this: time goes by. Every month the creditor is presented with new bills from the jailer—from a man like Mr Tannin, in fact. The creditor must pay, or else *he* becomes a debtor, eh? Before long, he realizes that these bills will soon outstrip the original debt itself and he is out double his money and more. What's he to do?

"Negotiate. I, that is to say, the politic debtor, pays shillings on the pound; or is forgiven outright, and released from prison. The original debt, meanwhile having been invested wisely, is retrieved and becomes pure profit for the debtor and his associates."

Worthy grinned proudly. He reached out and drew the dark-haired prostitute toward him.

"Is that not the way it works, Molly, my girl?"

"Poppycock," the woman whispered to him.

"Nay, it's no poppycock," said Tannin. "Mr. Worthy is a man of extraordinary vision. In just the four months since he's been here, he's—"

Worthy waved for him to stop.

"There are flaws in the system," he said. "Consider, for example, the amount of time wasted in jail.

"I said to myself surely prison could be put to some corrective use. Well, as you might know, Mr. Tannin has a thriving economy right here in this establishment. But it is hampered by the fact that many of our customers are without funds of any kind. Am I not right? Mr. Tannin can sell various services—food, water, blankets, a roof...not to mention the extras..."

Worthy held aloft his beer and rocked the woman on his lap to illustrate his point.

"...but only to them that can afford it, and that's less than half the population here. A rising tide floats all boats, Mr. Turner. So it called for encouragement of income-producing activities for the residents. That meant liberal commerce between residents and visitors.

"And *outside* excursions for some residents—such as myself. Mr. Tannin, in his generosity, allows me to 'go abroad.' Instead of sitting here—comfortable as it is—instead of sitting here, doing nothing, waiting for a debt to mature, I can go out and in a matter of an evening or two, incur more debt. If done properly, we can stagger our impositions so that our debts mature on a daily basis."

Jake could barely believe his ears. If he'd heard correctly, Worthy managed to exploit the state, the wealthy, and the poor all at the same time.

Jake jumped up, thinking to shout and curse the men, but instead he sat back down.

Why not exploit them all? Hadn't it been a wealthy man, a creditor, who caused his father's death? Didn't the state keep him separated from his brother? Didn't the criminal poor in the cellars attack him and steal his blankets? Why not bugger them all?

Worthy drew his chair closer to the jailer's and spoke in a tone of conspiracy.

"Mr. Turner never played Rails. Imagine how he'd fare on a game he knew. Mr. Turner here is a young man of extraordinary talent. Well, we knew that when Snelling proposed the bet. But Jake here," Worthy looked up. "May I call you Jake? Jake has been handicapped by his environment. One: he does not know truly how to gamble. Gambling is about making money, not about playing well. I could fix that overnight. Two: his skills are too well-known here to be of any use. Three: even if he could gamble here, what would he make from this sorry lot? Shillings really."

The jailer shrugged.

"Yes? And so?"

Worthy looked astonished.

"'And so?' you say? And so, my good Tannin, I propose to take him abroad."

Worthy looked at Jake.

"What would you say to that, me buck?"

"Abroad?" Jake said.

"Just a few brief trips outside these walls," Worthy explained. "We'd play hard men for real money, a lot of it."

The jailkeeper flushed and hopped from his chair. Tannin paced quickly across the carpet as though every step burned his feet. He swatted the air in front of him.

"You're not taking him out. He's a killer. He's tried to escape before. He'd be gone in a heartbeat."

Worthy caught the jailer and placed an arm around the man's shoulders. He spoke in a soothing voice.

"Thomas, Thomas," Worthy cooed. "The lad is not a killer. Did you not hear him say so yourself? No, I mean it. I know what a killer looks like. I've seen enough. I can see their hearts through their eyes—and though there's little heart left in this one—small wonder—still, this lad didn't kill a soul. Second: he won't try to escape. He'll be making such a wonderful living this way—a far better living than he'd have on the run. He's not stupid, he'll see what's best. Third: the education I'm offering him is something one doesn't run from."

The jailer pulled away.

"Oh, he'll run all right," Tannin said, nodding his head vigorously. "They're going to hang him next year probably. Oh, he'll run."

"No he won't. I'll see to it."

Worthy looked at Jake who had not moved from his seat.

"You won't run. Will you, Jake?"

Jake did not answer immediately.

"Run? No."

Worthy turned quickly to Tannin.

"There you see?"

"He doesn't leave," Tannin said.

Worthy stepped away from the jailer and poured himself another mug.

"Thomas," Worthy said, after taking a long draught.

"Since we've been in business, how much has your income increased? Especially in this," Worthy patted the keg. "This—illicit—liquor trade?"

The jailer shook a finger at Worthy.

"Now Billy, that's not fair. That's not right."

Worthy returned to the jailer and put his thick arm across the man's shoulders again, but this time held him uncomfortably close. He spoke in a near whisper.

"I don't play fair Thomas. I'm not rich enough to play fair. But don't worry. All is well. You shall be well-compensated. Mr. Turner here shall be born again. I shall make a gambler of him. We shall all become famous. Mark my words."

*****

The death blow came suddenly, but Jake Turner did not even flinch when it struck, even though it speared the life out of the player seated to his left. Instead Jake remained seated at the card table and kept his eyes on the killer, a saw-toothed, griseous, white-stubbled, old man with a face like a dried-out field.

Mick, the dealer, lay on his back dead, still in his chair. He had accused the old man of cheating and had been refusing to pay a bet when the blow came. With stunning swiftness, the old man's awl caught the dealer in the chest and knocked both the dealer and his chair backwards, nearly into the coals on the low grate, and caused two hoggish-looking women, who had been standing nearby to scatter off to the opposite side of the room, closer to the counter and to men more interested in them. But other than those, few in the dank tavern even looked toward the shadowy, corner table.

Worthy, masquerading in a threadbare overcoat, patched breeches, a moth-eaten bowler and gloves without fingertips, caught Jake's eye then nodded, evidently reassured by Jake's indifference to the gruesome scene.

The old man crouched next to his victim, pulled out the awl, wiped it clean across his pant leg, then rifled the dead man's pockets. After finding a knife, two cards, and fifty single-pound notes, the old man summoned the proprietor.

"Corky. You take good care of this one, eh? Move along now," he called.

A short, round man in an apron scurried over to the body and dragged the chair out from under it. Then he took the body by its ankles and, puffing for air, dragged it toward a dark, back passage.

"Corky, you keep the bugger's extras," the old man said. "For your trouble. Happy New Year."

Then the old man laughed, revealing a gummy mouth punctuated by six, black and brown, splintered teeth. He spat on the floor and used the back of his large hands to wipe his wet chin.

"How could I cheat anyways," the old man said. "He never said how I cheated."

The old man took his seat again.

"You can't cheat at this game—so long's twelve jacks turn up at the end. Right? Now where was we?"

"Mr. Turner's deal I believe," Worthy said.

Jake looked around the tavern as though bored with the game. Soot and tobacco smoke coated the walls black; packed-down dirt and splintery, unsecured planks defined the floor. Brown, liquid sewage from Monmouth Street crept under the threshold and meandered across the floor between the card players and the bar, but no one paid any attention to its stream.

One of the whores who had been looking at the table, caught Jake's gaze, then looked away.

Jake saw himself in the dusty glass behind the counter. His

copper hair hung tamely, cut and newly-washed. He wore clothes purchased by Worthy in Rosemary Lane, London's "shoddy shop" district where ragged, stolen garments, boots and bedding could be obtained even by the very poor. Jake's patchwork included coarse trousers, an old, grey wool shirt, a tattered, hooded cloak, and boots with loose soles. He kept the hood of the cloak up even while he played.

Worthy nodded toward his protege to resume the deal.

Jake shuffled three decks of cards and then dealt them around the table with the same slow, indifferent rhythm he'd displayed in Worthy's Hardchapel cell. As they left his hands, the cards seemed to float to each man: first to Worthy, then to the old killer—called Bones—then to a small man called Twitcher.

Twitcher, snatched up each card as it came to him, gave each a quick look, closed his eyes tightly as if trying to memorize it, then laid it down again. Each time he did so, the muscles on the left side of his face would spasm, causing that side of his moustache to jump like a horsetail. Twitcher stuttered when he spoke.

"What about M-Mick?" Twitcher said to the old man. "They'll find his b-body. The Charlies will come around, Mr. Bones; we gotta hide you. You d-don't want to go b-b-back to Newgate."

"Shut up, Twitch," the old man sneered. "The Charlies don't come 'round. Not these days. Not here. Corky'll handle it, so quit your whining. You don't see this boy here looking worried, do you?"

Bones jerked his head in Jake's direction.

"What's your name, boy? Turner, is it?"

Jake looked at Bones.

"That's it," he said.

The old man leered at Jake, who stared back. After a while,

the old man spat and dropped his gaze to his cards.

"You're a cold one, sonny," he said. "You don't think twice about a man dyin' at your feet, do you? The dead don't bother you, eh? You only jumped a bit. Ha."

The old man looked at Jake again, moving his gaze up and down Jake's body.

"You got wide shoulders, boy. Hard forearms. What're those blue scars on your hands?" Bones demanded.

Jake ignored him.

"You don't play cards for a living, do you boy?" Bones insisted.

"What now?" Jake's voice registered impatience.

"I want to know how you make your livin'," Bones said, smiling in a way that suggested bad intentions.

"Mills. Farms. Docks. Wherever. What is it to you?"

Worthy quickly raised his mug.

"Gentlemen. To our departed guest. And to the spirit of good fellowship and clean competition that is within us all. Another round?"

Worthy signalled to the barmaid.

"Now let's get to it," he added, gathering his cards.

Bones frowned and looked at Worthy.

"Don't know why you're so quick to play. You've lost a bloody fortune, you have. Look at him, Twitcher. He doesn't mind a bit."

"M-Maybe he's the King in disguise, eh, Mr. Bones? Ha. Right, Mr. Bones? He's the m-mad King. Out for a night. He can afford it. Eh?"

Twitcher raised his brows like a dog inviting a pat on the head.

"Yeah, right enough. He's a real courtier, there. We're sitting with right royalty."

"Three-Jack Maul. Open your bid, Mr. Bones," Jake commanded.

Three-Jack Maul, a miner's game, took its name from the speed with which three men could hit the same spike in rotation. Winning depended on predicting and betting on the number of jacks held in each hand. One could, in theory, keep track of every card played and calculate the odds, but the pace of play made that difficult. Most players relied on luck and guile.

Bones won. Though small stakes, he laughed and slapped his hands together, rubbing them hard. Twitcher won the next, somewhat higher stakes. Worthy drove the bidding higher and then higher again.

"You're a foolish man," Bones said to Worthy. "You never win these. I've watched you. You bid up and up and always you lose. I'm not complaining, though. Bid on."

Several rounds of bidding flew by, currency gathering in the center of the table like a pile of autumn leaves. Throughout the night's bidding Twitcher jerked around in his chair. Bones began to shout out his bids.

"Show. Show." Bones called out after one bid. "Show."

The players showed their cards and counted. Worthy held three jacks, Twitcher five, Bones three, Jake one. Jake's guess exactly.

"Every time you bid us up, this pup wins," Bones complained, jabbing his finger in Jake's direction.

Then the old man stopped speaking altogether. Jake watched the man's eyes roam from Worthy to himself to Worthy again.

"Quite a coincidence," Bones said to Worthy after too long a silence.

The old man's hand slipped to his side and he spat on the floor again. Twitcher moved his chair a hop further from Worthy; the scrape of the chair's legs on the floor sounded like a screeching gate.

"Mr. Bones," Worthy said, his tone sweet and consoling, like that of an undertaker. "Before you contemplate some violent act, I should recommend that you look under the table, for at this moment, I am holding a cocked and primed pistol aimed at a point between your legs."

The old man's eyes widened, then he grinned.

"I doubt that," he said and bent to glance under the table.

At that moment, Worthy lifted the old man's full mug and, lunging across the table, brought the vessel down hard on the back of the killer's bent spine. An immediate snapping sound—like wood breaking in a fire—burst from the man's neck. Bones fell under the table.

Twitcher jumped out of his chair. Worthy eased back into his and smiled innocently. Twitcher looked from Worthy to Jake, then turned and fled.

"Did you see that? Oh, I love people," chortled Worthy. He rocked forward and began herding the stakes into a pile.

"You see, lad," Worthy beamed. "It takes all kinds to make humanity. And these are the kinds: Stupid—such as the dead, I think he's dead, Mr. Bones here."

Worthy stopped raking the money to count the categories on his fingers.

"Cowardly, such as the one what just left; and the Lazy, Foolish, Mad, Treacherous, Murderous, and... Larcenous.

"Now the Larcenous, that would be us."

Worthy moved over to the fallen Bones and removed from his pockets the fifty pound-notes originally taken from dead Mick and added them to the pile on the table, then returned to his place.

"We are what you might call nature's way of keeping the others in check. If we do it rightly, we'll deprive the dangerous ones—kings to beggars—deprive them of the means to do more evil than they do. You take my point?"

Jake thought of the types of people he'd encountered over the last seven years. Sully: cowardly, murderous and treacherous. Bones: stupid and murderous. Worthy: larcenous no doubt, but now add murderous and treacherous to it.

"I suppose," he said.

Worthy smiled broadly. "And our recompense is, well..."

Worthy spread his arms wide before the table.

"Not a bad night, my buck. Not bad at all."

"We're lucky to be alive," Jake said.

"My yes. Aren't we? The world is a beautiful place," Worthy replied, seeming to mistake Jake's point.

Worthy pulled all the table money together and began counting and arranging it.

"But you know," Worthy said. "This life is not for the likes of you or me. It's just a rehearsal—for real money.

"You've seen those smooth gentlemen in their clean finery entering the 'Change? Well, they're no different from this rabble we've been thrown amongst. In their souls they're murderous cutthroats; same as any here. They just shear more lambs—and fatter ones too—than we do. One day, my lad. One day."

Worthy sighed as he counted. When finished he pushed an assortment of coins and notes toward Jake and pulled another pile toward himself.

"There's you and there's me."

Jake slapped a hand on top of Worthy's.

"There were one hundred, fourteen pounds; you've only given me fifty-five."

"Only...? Well, I... Are you sure?"

"Two more."

Worthy made show of recounting his stack.

"Good Lord," he said. "An incredible facility, lad. My miscount. My miscount. So sorry. I say, you were born to make money, my boy. My word, I believe we'll skin Old Scratch alive before we're done. With your skill and my experience. Yes indeed... Well, we should be going back to the Hardchapel."

Both men stood up and moved toward the back door. Then Worthy stopped, pinched his lip between his thumb and forefinger and looked at the younger man closely.

Jake did not return the gaze; instead he looked at the floor, tracing the trails of blood. He thought of how Mick looked: the shock and surprise in his eyes when Bones smacked the awl into his heart. Was it pain or an anticipation of hell that created his expression? Badger had the same look when he hung on the spike.

"Did you really have a pistol?" Jake asked.

Worthy opened his coat, revealing the curved, wooden handle of a dueling piece.

In a blur of motion, Jake snatched the weapon out of Worthy's belt and pointed it directly at his mentor.

"I'm not going back with you," he said.

Worthy stepped back. Slowly a smile fanned across his face. He shook his head, then spread his arms out wide.

"You don't need to point that at me. I'd not force you to go back—not if you didn't want to," Worthy said calmly. "I am a little surprised, however, I must say, that you don't want to return. You've just seen how much money we can make. At this rate you could *buy* yourself a pardon."

Jake kept the pistol level.

"That's as may be," he said. "But I have a brother in the mines. At least he labored there seven years ago. I must find him and get him out."

Worthy nodded.

"Well," he sighed. "I can't say as I blame you. Your heart is in the right place. But you run a considerable risk now. They might hang you this time just to keep you from being such a bother."

"Perhaps."

"Let me ask you this: let's say you find your brother—or not—what then?" Worthy raised his brows and shrugged his shoulders at Jake. "How will you live? What I'm suggesting is that whatever happens, we could still operate our, em, business together."

Jake shook his head.

Worthy insisted.

"It's not as though we'd be gambling forever," he said. "I have plans. With the right amount of money, we can buy ourselves into real business: wear those fancy linens and join the true cutthroats. I swear it. I can see it. It will take some time, but—"

"What will happen with Tannin? Will he hunt for me?" Jake interjected.

"What? Oh, Tannin."

Worthy thought for a moment.

"He'll be upset, but I can calm him down. We'll pretend you never left. There'll be no pursuit for a year at least... But what do you say to the other; to my proposal?"

Jake looked down briefly but did not lower the pistol.

"I see no reason to trust you," Jake said.

Worthy laughed.

"I'm not asking you to trust me," he said. "Trust your experience, your knowledge, what you've seen. Weigh the odds, the chances. Then trust your judgment."

"I'll never return to Hardchapel," Jake said.

"Good idea," Worthy said with a sly smirk.

Then Worthy reached into his waistcoat and pulled out a card.

"If you do return to London. Go to this address. Ask for Molly. She'll get word to me—discreetly—that you're back."

Jake lowered the pistol.

"Goodbye," he said.

Worthy held up his hand.

"Just two more things. One: if you are to keep my pistol, you should know that it doesn't fire unless the hammer is pulled back, powder is in the pan, and it's loaded."

Jake looked at the weapon. The sharp, flint-edged hammer rested harmlessly, like someone asleep, against the steel of the frisson.

"The other thing is that you need a new name."

Jake pursed his lips and nodded.

"I would think that your new name should reflect your strengths," Worthy offered. "Calculation. Gambling. Three-Jack Maul. Something like that: Jack Maul, Jake Maul... here's what: Jacob Mauley. No, Marley. Jacob Marley."

Ezra's Ghost

January 30, 1797
Elizabeth's Furnace, Northumbria

Jacob Marley. On the long journey north, Jake Turner repeated his new name as though it were some latinate prayer or chant that, if echoed often enough, would become true. Jacob Marley.

He reached the outskirts of the mining village around mid-afternoon: the sun had already fallen behind the western hills, its final shafts of light reaching only the highest of the dark clouds overhead. A half-mile away, across the coal fields, lanterns swayed from poles; their uncertain lights all that could be seen of the village. Dark clouds moved across the sky.

As he neared Elizabeth's Furnace, Marley summoned the memory of the first time he'd ever seen the mines and how frightened he, Ezra and even his mother had been. He tried to remember exactly when the Furnace started to poison him, change him. Perhaps it began even before they'd left Meadow Bridge. Marley recalled the eve of their departure; their last night in their own cottage.

Sheets and blankets spread across the floor by the fire; other than those and the one table left unsold, no furniture remained in the home. Near the front door, two large trunks held the compressed lives of the family.

Mother ambled from room to room like a wandering

ghost. Her hair pulled so tightly against the back of her head, that Jake imagined her eyes might not be able to shut. She held an open Bible in her hands, but rarely looked at the pages. The hem of her black dress coasted along the wooden floor, a broom of crinoline underneath. Her lips moved. She prayed. She insisted that the boys pray also—at least three times daily—but after the first few days of that Jake ran out of things to say, things to ask for; none of them could happen anyway. Father was dead and despite Mother's opinion, Jake knew that Lucifer did not fire the pistol.

Mother prayed over their last meal in the cottage. She stood at the end of the table, head bowed, eyes shut tightly. The boys stood also, but their eyes looked at the boiled potatoes and at the bowl of peas before them.

Mother pressed her hands together so hard that they trembled. She said, "Bless oh Lord, these, Thy gifts, and us to Thy loving service. Keep us ever mindful of the needs of others..."

Normally the prayer ended with, "In Christ's name we pray," but this time it went further.

"We are in Your hands," Mother added. "You work in mysterious ways; Your purposes are unknown to us. We humbly beg You, Lord, for Your tender mercies."

God is a frightening thing, Jake thought. People do not even plead so fearfully to their landlords.

"...Let us not forget the sacred bond of family. Please keep us together, well and safe. Look on, with mercy, he who was taken from us by ruinous accident..."

No accident, Jake whispered to himself.

"...Keep my sons under Your protection. Make our way safe and in accord with Your grand design. If it be in Your will. In Christ's name we pray. Amen."

Rebecca Turner lifted her head and nodded, signalling the boys to serve themselves and eat. They ate standing, using spoons, the only utensils left unpacked. Mother herself did not eat, but instead watched.

When the boys finished, she rose and went to the hearth and sat on the bedding on the floor, her legs drawn up, and stared into the flames. Jake and Ezra came to her side.

"Sit closer," she said.

She drew Jake next to her and Ezra lay down with his head on her lap. They said nothing for a time and Ezra soon fell asleep. She stroked his hair.

"So clean now," she said, mostly to herself. She stroked the sleeping boy's cheek. "So smooth."

She leaned forward and inhaled deeply from her boy's hair. Then she straightened up and looked into the fire again.

"Tomorrow we shall go to Northumbria," she said, still looking into the flames. "There's work there. We can all get work. There are mines...and work around the mines..." She paused and sighed, then she said, "God is testing us."

"Why?" Jake asked.

Her answer came mechanically. "His will."

Then she looked directly at him and touched the side of his cheek. She kept her hand there and said, "Jacob, you must promise me something. Promise me that, whatever happens, you will stay by your brother, watch over him. Promise me." She said it with such urgency that it frightened him.

"Yes," Jake said.

"Promise."

"Yes, mother I do."

Then she looked off again. After a time she spoke absently, almost to herself: "You are your brother's keeper."

Later, when only embers remained in the hearth, the small family lay bundled together on the floor. Jake could feel the warmth of his mother's body and he wriggled his feet outside the coverings to cool himself. He felt her stir.

"Mines are underground," Jake said.

"Yes."

"Is that where Lucifer lives?"

She did not answer right away. Then she said, "No. He is elsewhere."

His mother didn't last a year in Northumbria. He remembered staring at her hands when she passed away, thinking how quickly they had changed in that place. The beautiful hands: full, smooth, unmarked, gracefully tapered; the hands that had held him, patted his back, combed his hair, tied his boot laces, washed him, fed him, pulled him on walks, had become withered as if sucked from within, leaving just bones and a scarred covering. They'd become streaked with blue scars; the result of working on the breaker line, separating coal from slag barehanded and having coal dust enter the wounds. Her hands weighed nothing. They'd been stolen.

Mother was wrong, Jacob Marley thought. Satan is right here.

Marley advanced to the pithead of Elizabeth's Furnace and looked at the broken winding gear. The wet snow around his feet slushed aside in muddy craters. The circular track left by the horses had become a soggy trench. Marley pulled up the hood of his ragged cloak and moved about the windings.

One of the two massive support struts lay on its side. The main drum, axle and turning arms dipped at severe angles, burying a third of the assembly in the mud. Marley examined the broken frame. The strut, thick as a large tree, had snapped like a twig. The whole apparatus looked like a colossal, broken, turned-over spinning wheel: the drum twenty feet in diameter; the forty-foot long turning beam, once pushed by horses, now embedded. Along the ground near the axle, lengths of heavy rope emerged from the beneath the wheel.

Marley followed the ropes to the pithead. There they rose, still threaded over the tower and pulleys above the main shaft as though they might once again lift men and coal. He came to the eye of the pit. Layers of wooden planks and oilskin, held in place by twenty-inch timbers, sealed the shaft tightly.

Marley looked down at the covering for a long time. Then he raised his head and looked again at the confusion of broken beams and wooden cogs. In dusky silhouette, the black outlines of the timbers took on a frightening aspect, suggesting a collection of crosses or gallows arranged in a wasteland. Marley could almost picture the bodies. He shuddered and turned toward the distant lights of the village.

At the border of the pit, Marley approached an outbuilding. A light flickered from the other side. Marley pulled his hood tight around his face and moved more slowly. At the corner of the building, he stopped and listened. A man hummed a song.

Marley looked around the edge of the building, then stepped into the light. The man who had been humming looked up and, evidently frightened by the sudden appearance, shouted. Marley jumped backward and the man, now on his feet, wailed, "Don't take me!"

"I mean you no harm," Marley said quickly. "I was just passing."

"Oh my heart." said the man. "Lord, you gave me a fright. I thought you was a ghost." He put a hand to his mouth and rubbed his grey whiskers.

"I was just having a look," Marley said.

The old man stamped his feet as though trying to revive the flow of blood, then moved back toward his fire.

"Oh, that was a scare. Don't know why they need a watchman anyway," he said. "Nothing to watch. It gives me the chills—and I don't mean the cold nights, though they are cold enough. It's all them dead below. Like standin' a night in a graveyard."

He looked at Marley as though the younger man might be a ghost after all. He took a hesitant step forward. Marley could smell whisky on the man's breath.

"Say now," said the watchman. "What *is* your business here? There's things in this shed. You're not thinkin' of stealin' somethin'? Picks and powder? Lamps and...and things?"

"No," said Marley. "What dead?"

"Eh?"

"You talked about the dead below."

"Why the—" The watchman stopped and began to nod his head in a knowing way. "You ain't from here are you?" he said. "You an inspector?"

"No."

"Well, we just had the biggest fire in any Northumbria pit," the watchman said. He crooked a finger and jabbed down at the ground. "Half mile below," he said. "Blew out fifty pillars of hard coal. Look about you. See how the land is sunk. Killed two hundred men."

Marley hadn't thought about it at the time, but now he recalled how the land around the winding gear sagged lower than the rest of the field, dipping, forming a shallow bowl. Now he understood. The entire pit had fallen, causing even the surface land to drop. That's what had cracked the winding frames.

"When did it happen?" Marley asked.

The watchman pulled out a small flask and proffered it to Marley, who declined. The old man took a sip. "A fortnight ago," he said. "A terrible thing. Sometimes I hear their souls crying in the wind." The man sipped again and shivered.

*****

Marley left the pit and walked across the broad field toward the lights of the village. The ground underfoot sucked at his boots as if to pull him underground. He stopped halfway across the field and thought about what he would do.

A remanent of Hadrian's Wall projected just ahead, its irregular stones now graded smooth by a layer of snow. Beyond it and to the right lay the workers' barracks: crude hovels of mud, rock and thatch. Further up, the beerhouse still stood, a place which, following days of high production, would be full of drunken men, shouting, gambling at cards, fighting and gambling on the fighting. Light shone through the beerhouse window; a shadow or two passed before it, but Marley couldn't know from this distance how many men now drank there—much less, which men, nor what they might know about Ezra.

If they catch me, they can hang me, Marley thought. Just let me find my brother.

Marley inspected his clothing again. Mostly he wore what Worthy had found in Rosemary Lane: the trousers, which seemed on the verge of unraveling, the coarse shirt, the hooded cloak. To this he'd added a work coat so thickly caked in black grime that it looked like cracked leather rather than wool, and a shapeless, dusty hat. He felt confident that he looked like a miner—except for the hood. But the hood Marley could not do without. He adjusted the covering over his hat, then climbed through a crumbled gap in Hadrian's Wall and made his way to the beerhouse.

*****

Inside the small, mud shack nearly twenty men sat around several small, plain wood tables. Some played cards; others spoke in low tones. No one shouted, argued, laughed, or challenged anyone else. A result of the disaster, Marley concluded.

The men sat and drank and said little, if anything at all. Smoke, from both the hearth and the men's pipes, filled the hovel and wafted among the black bows and bunting fastened to the thatchwork in memory of the recent dead. Marley moved along a wall unnoticed, hood up. He stopped near a table where four men played cards.

Evidently, the miners had not worked in days. Their skin, washed clean of soot, shone pale as the undersides of snakes, colored only by blue dots and lines: the poisoning effects of ingrained coal.

"Eight jack," said one of the men holding cards. Marley moved closer; his shadow fell across the table. The player sitting with his back to Marley turned in his chair. He had a narrow, hatchet face and bucked teeth.

"Say, sprager! Move! You're cutting the light," he said.

Marley edged aside, but the thin man continued to look at him. Marley turned and walked toward the hearth.

"Wait now!" the man called. "Come here. Do I know you?"

Marley stopped. His pulse quickened and he felt suddenly chilled. He slowly returned to the table.

"Pull back that hood," the miner demanded.

Marley now recognized the face. The sharp nose, its line now a **Z**, had been broken in several places since he'd seen it last, but Marley remembered. Gordy Ferrel, Gren Sully's lackey. Marley slipped the hood off.

When the hood dropped, Ferrel's mouth opened. He let go of his cards and rose.

"Oh dear God. Am I seein' a ghost? Christ in Heaven. You should be dead."

Then he addressed everyone in the beerhouse. "Look lads. It's our own fool back with us." He turned around to Marley again. "How'd you survive it, boy? Speak fool."

Another voice said, "It's so."

Another said, "How'd he get out?"

All the miners now spoke at once.

"How'd you get out boy?"

"Make him speak, Gordy. Make him speak, you know how."

"Maybe a room survived. Maybe he got out the furnace drift."

Marley could not speak. The room began to turn and he put a hand to the back of a chair to steady himself.

Then Ferrel stepped in close to him, grinned, and grasped him by both ears and slowly pulled his head down to his own eye level. Ferrel spoke in a low voice, his lips barely moving.

"Haven't I told you, it's rude not to speak when you're spoken to?" he said. "I've told you that how many times? Remember what happens to rude people?"

Ferrel made a fist, the middle knuckle protruding, and tapped it against Marley's sternum.

"Come now, fool. Don't be rude. How did you survive? How did you get out of the pit? Tell us, Ezra."

Marley's legs wavered and he lost the feel of the chair-back. He struggled for air. But then, he managed a sound. In a monotone, he said, "Don't know."

Ferrel hopped and threw his hands in the air. "There boys," he crowed. "You see ol' Gordy can make the dumb speak." Then he turned back to Marley. "Now, idjit: Are there any others alive? Tell us. Did you see anyone else?"

Marley could only shake his head, no.

The miners now pressed in around Marley. Some reached out to touch him, as though to assure themselves that no phantom stood among them, or, through touch, to borrow some of his luck.

Ferrel began to inspect Marley closely. First the face and head, then the clothes.

"No burns," Ferrel said. He sniffed Marley's shoulder,

smelling the old rags. "He's even been washed," Ferrel declared to the house. Then he turned to Marley again. "Someone's taken care of you, haven't they? Risen from the dead and washed too. How is it you're not dead, boy? You were at the gangway. I saw you there. You were told to stay there."

"He not always does as he's told," said a deep-voice.

Ferrel looked around. "He does when I tell him," he said. "Did you leave the doors? Did you leave the pit before your shift was up? Is that what happened, boy?"

Marley shook his head again, but this time did not stop shaking. Ezra dead? If so, nothing mattered. The room faded; its sounds buzzed together.

Someone said, "It's a miracle. Gordy's group was the last out. No one else could have lived."

Another voice said, "Well this one lived. Gordy's right. He probably ran off early like he's done before. Where'd you run off to this time, boy?"

"It's no miracle," said someone else. "He escaped; that's all. It happened, so it's no miracle."

"I think he ran off before the blow."

"He should've been at the gangway," Ferrel said.

"What? And been killed?"

"He couldn't have knowed it was going to blow," Ferrel replied. "Could you, idjit?"

A large man in the back who had been listening the whole time now spoke. "You won't find out much from him. He's simple-minded. Let him be, Gordy."

Another miner said, "Still, I suppose someone should report it."

"Tomorrow then," said Ferrel. "We'll see what the boss thinks. You missed us, eh pet? He probably wandered off before the blast. Then out wandering and begging the past week. That's what we'll find out, I'll bet on it."

"That could be," said another man. "Who'd notice him? He was probably out of the pit before even you, Gordy."

The large man stepped forward through the group. He looked hard at Ferrel. "Let it be. Leave him alone." Then he looked at Marley. "Would you like some tea, lad?"

Marley's head continued to shake slowly from side to side.

"You see what I mean?" said Ferrel. "Rude." Then he took a step toward Marley. "Boy."

"Leave him be Gordy," said the big man, putting a hand on Ferrel's chest. "That's enough."

Then one of the men who'd been at Ferrel's table spoke. "He'll keep, Gordy. Never mind now. An idiot was gone; now he's back. Cheers, Gordy. Deal the cards again."

Ferrel spat on the floor, then stepped back to his table and slowly took his seat. He looked at Marley over his shoulder. One by one, the other miners moved off, speaking in low tones. Soon Marley stood by himself.

Ezra dead? That possibility and others raced around Marley's mind like bats in a sealed cave. Marley felt as though he'd been struck in the chest. He'd become his brother, for just a few moments; felt for himself how it must have been: to be considered a deformity, a curiosity, an object of ridicule. Marley blamed himself.

And Ferrel. Ferrel must have known of Sully's plan back then.

Marley's legs came back to him and he moved along the wall to the doorway of the beerhouse. He looked one last time at the miners, then slipped out and headed back toward the pit.

*****

Late that night, Marley stood in the shadows near the beerhouse and waited until he saw Ferrel emerge. Ferrel swayed slightly in the doorway, then pulled his coat collar tightly around his neck and plodded up the empty muddy lane toward the workers' barracks. No moon lighted the sky and Ferrel stumbled once across a wagon rut. He walked carefully after that, keeping his head down, regarding his feet and the muck around them. Marley followed.

Ferrel neared the barracks when Marley overtook him and blocked his path. Ferrel stopped and looked up.

"Who's there?" the wiry man challenged.

Marley moved forward silently, ominous as a solstice spirit coming to take the damned. He stopped within an arm's length of his quarry. He could hear Ferrel's breathing accelerate.

Ferrel peered forward.

"Ezra Turner. Is that you?" he said. Marley did not answer.

"Hold there boy; you're not comin' under my roof," Ferrel said, emboldened. "Get gone to your own heap, if it still be there. Or go to them that takes you when you runs off."

Marley pushed a heavy iron drilling spike to the base of Ferrel's throat, pressing it upward against the man's Adam's apple.

"Come," Marley said.

"Wh— who is this?" Ferrel stuttered.

Marley's voice turned cold and precise. "Turn. Walk toward the pit," it said. "Or this goes through your throat."

Marley pressed the tip of the iron bar harder into the hollow of Ferrel's neck, causing him to cough.

"I've no money," Ferrel sputtered.

"Go toward the lamp," Marley commanded.

A small flame, low to the ground, wavered in the distance. Marley prodded the man toward the light, allowing him to turn toward it before nudging the point of the spike against the back of Ferrel's skull.

They walked in silence until they neared the lantern.

Then, before they entered the circle of the lamp's light, Marley spoke again.

"Stop. Do you see that keg?"

A small barrel sat, end up, just within the circle of light. Ferrel nodded.

"Sit on the keg," Marley said.

Ferrel sat, facing the lamp's glare. Marley moved to the light, picked up the lantern and set it down near Ferrel's side. Then he backed away a step and removed his hood.

"Ez—" Ferrel stopped before the name left his mouth. "No. . . " he said, slowly. "You're not Ezra. No, you're the brother. The killer. You're the boy what killed Badger."

"Not a boy now. And you know I'm not a killer," Marley said. "But I'll be a killer soon enough. That should please you."

"It was you in the beerhouse."

Marley held the spike in one hand and stared silently at Ferrel.

"If you kill me, they'll hang you," Ferrel said. "You won't get away this time."

"They won't hang me," said Marley, his voice hard and monotonous. "We'll both be dead."

Marley took the spike and tapped a place on the keg between Ferrel's legs.

"Powder."

He pointed with the spike to a length of cord running along the ground. "Here is the fuse. Tonight we'll learn how it is to die in a blast."

"You're mad," Ferrel said. He started to rise, but Marley thrust the spike against his chest and pushed him back.

"You can't do this," Ferrel's voice quivered.

"Then you have nothing to fear."

Marley lifted the cover from the lamp, exposing the flame, then placed the fuse on it. Sparks immediately scattered from the cord and sputtered along its length, spitting fire at the trembling man.

"You'll die too." Ferrel cried, his eyes on the snapping cord. "You won't do that."

"I'm already dead," Marley declared.

A scent of excrement emanated from the other man. Ferrel started to sob, his voice high and quick.

"Please. Sully made me fetch you. I didn't know what he planned. I'm sorry for it. Please. Don't do it. Stop the fuse. Please. Oh, God stop him!"

"Where is Sully?" Marley said slowly.

"Dead. Dead. Died. The Black Lung...The fuse!"

Marley stood still as a guard, the spike poised against Ferrel's neck. He watched the man gag once as the flame entered the keg.

A series of sparks flickered and jumped around the rim of the keg, followed by a momentary glow within. Then the fuse went out.

Ferrel looked up, his whole body trembling. Marley looked at him and said, "Wet powder...You won't die tonight after all."

Marley lowered the spike.

Ferrel looked blankly at his fouled trousers then up at Marley.

"What did you say?"

"Now you know how you'll be when death comes," Marley said. "In terror. You'll weep and wail and beshit yourself. You'll fear the devil."

Marley drew closer to the man's face. "Every day that passes brings you closer to hell," he said. "There's no way you can stop it."

Marley turned from Ferrel and then, with awful force, spun around with the butt end of the spike foremost, catching the sitting man full in the sternum with a harsh, splintering sound. Ferrel fell backwards into the mud and moaned and coughed.

Marley stepped to where Ferrel lay. He looked down at the man, then raised the spike high and, in one violent motion, drove it deep into the ground, missing Ferrel's body by an inch.

Marley looked down at the miner and spat. Then he turned and began walking south, back toward the road, toward London and toward brothels and taverns, Bill Worthy and money.

Marley's Dance

December 21, 1799
London

Jacob Marley stood at the open doorway of Bill Worthy's office at The Imperial Trading Company. Worthy had not yet finished with the clerk, so Marley hesitated before entering. He watched and listened as Worthy dictated a list. In mid-sentence Worthy paused and abruptly paced across a thick Persian rug, stepped past an unopened shipping crate marked with Chinese characters, then looked out the window toward the street below. He withdrew a handkerchief from his waistcoat pocket and rubbed a clear circle on the glass, peering into the darkness.

"Three in the afternoon and already dark as Satan's bum," Worthy remarked, turning from the wet pane. "Now where were we?...Ah, yes. Read the list back to me."

The clerk, a dark-haired boy in his teens, stood near the center of the office in the midst of Worthy's ever-growing collection. A straw throne whose back fanned upward in the shape of a spade occupied the far corner of the room. Next to the throne sat a globe-stand on which an ivory ball, three-feet in diameter, displayed carved elephants, snakes, and men in turbans parading around its equator. A teak scabbard, also elaborately carved, leaned propped against a tall water pipe, its hoses poised like the tentacles of some new creature. Six painted, Oriental vases and several unopened, wooden boxes with names like Shanghai, Calcutta, and Sumatra burned into their panels cluttered the opposite wall.

"Yes, sir," said the clerk. "Mr. Carlson: Virginia tobacco, one pound; Mr. Martin, one barrel whisky; Mr. Pell, Holy Bible, leather covers; Mr. Batten, hogshead dark ale; Mrs. Langdon, silver tea setting, oriental silk robes, satin bedcovers; Mr. Puttman, letter of introduction to Mrs. Langdon; Mr. Sanders, letter of introduction to Mrs. Langdon; Magistrate Thornton—" The boy stopped and looked at Worthy.

"Yes? What is it?" said Worthy who had just eased himself into the straw throne.

"Opium, sir?"

Worthy stretched and yawned. "Afraid so, lad. Sad habit but the Magistrate insists and we do what we can. Keep it under your hat though. There's a good lad. Go on."

The boy read the remainder of the list, concluding with: "Mr. Wallace, riding boots, Italian; Mr. Russell, currency."

Worthy nodded. "Good," he said, slapping his hands against his belly. "Bring the list to me."

The clerk handed the paper to Worthy and stood nearby, watching the fat man review the names and gifts.

Worthy had been right, Marley admitted: little separated the workings of successful businesses from any of the Hardchapel enterprises.

When Marley returned from Northumbria, Worthy had been as good as his word. The two embarked on a campaign of fund-raising larceny: swindling gamblers at cards for high stakes. Worthy invested the proceeds in the right places, made the right bribes, connections, bought the right information, extorted the right people and within a year, they'd achieved positions in one of the more prestigious firms in the city.

But for all the success—not to mention freedom—that Worthy had delivered, Marley never voiced gratitude.

Gratitude seemed akin to brotherhood—something Marley could no longer embrace; instead Marley strove to extinguish such sentiments whenever they arose. In their place, Marley looked to find fault with Worthy in both significant and petty domains. Marley cultivated resentment of such things as Worthy's ostentatious style: Worthy seemed to choose his clothing in order to prove his legitimacy and success; he wore clothing immodestly, like a person wearing medals in public.

Worthy's satin waistcoat, woven with gold threads, now reflected the flames of the hearth in his office. Great plumes of scarlet silk—his scarf—ballooned around his throat. Streaked with thin lines of gold, Worthy's fine woolen coat and trousers matched the scarf and shone as brightly as the vest.

"Let me see, now," Worthy said to clerk. "We have the lord mayor, both Houses, the banks, customs, the auditor, the beadle, warden, assessor, courts, and, of course, Mrs. Langdon. I'll deliver Magistrate Thornton's package myself and Mr. Russell's. As for the rest, you take two boys and a wagon and get about delivering these goods this afternoon—'Compliments of Mr. Worthy,' remember to say that and 'Merry Christmas' and so on."

Worthy grunted and pushed himself out of the straw chair. He stretched, then dipped his fingers into the pocket of his waistcoat. Fishing out two coins, he stepped to the clerk.

"Here now," Worthy said, taking the boy's hand. "A little something for yourself." He pressed two crowns into the boy's hand and winked.

The clerk looked at the money, then back at Worthy. He began to stutter some thanks, but Worthy cut him off.

"Not at all. You'll look after me one day, I'm sure," he said.

Marley cleared his throat.

"Ah, Jacob," said Worthy. "Didn't see you there. Come in. Come in."

Marley stepped aside to let the clerk out, then entered.

Worthy gestured Marley toward a chair, but did not sit himself. Instead he turned, careful not to upset any of the goods littering his office, and stepped to the fireplace. There he put out his hands and sniffed at the sweet wood smoke.

"Cheer and goodwill," he said. "Christmas. That's all well and good...Except that this time of year they *expect* gifts. Devalues the whole art of the bribe." He shook his head and smiled. "Ah, well. Merry Christmas, Jacob."

"And to you," Marley said, his voice cool.

Worthy chuckled. "Well Jacob, it *is* a merry Christmas at that, eh? Would have been hard to picture us in these straits just a few years ago, hmm? Not bad, I dare say. Wealth rejoices."

Worthy crossed behind a large, mahogany desk, its dark wood polished to a high gloss, its surface cluttered with a motley collection that included playing cards, dice, a stack of blank paper, a pen, and a platter of meat and bread. At the side of the desk a serving table with three crystal decanters held various amber liquors.

"Would you care for...?" Worthy asked, lifting one of the bottles.

"No thank you, no," said Marley. He waited until Worthy had poured himself a glass, then said, "I expect you are concerned."

Worthy raised his brows, then lifted his glass in a toast and drank it off.

"Yes?" he smiled. "Pray tell. Concerned about what?"

Marley walked back to the office door and closed it.

"*I*, for one, am concerned," Marley said.

Worthy sat at his desk, waiting.

Marley shifted in his chair and looked at the various objects on Worthy's desk.

"Well, what concerns you?" Worthy prodded.

Marley eyes came to rest on the playing cards. He gathered a handful of them and shuffled them in his hand, wondering how to begin. After several moments Marley flipped a card at Worthy.

"Spades," Marley said, naming the suit. "Spades: tools, toil. We've worked hard to get where we are."

He threw out another card.

"Clubs," Marley announced. "Violence. We've done that too."

Another card flew from his hand.

"Diamonds. Ah, diamonds. Our rewards."

Marley looked up at Worthy, then went on.

"We are where we wanted to be. Successful. Legitimate. Secure. We no longer have to cheat or even take great risks. So my question to you is why are you putting us in jeopardy? For what?"

"My dear boy," Worthy chuckled. "Whatever do you mean? 'Jeopardy.'"

"The books," Marley said. "I've examined them, of course. A great number of vouchers were written, by you, to a Mr. H.R. Lancaster. These are not, however, recorded elsewhere and the company has no records of doing any business with anyone of that name."

Marley paused, then held out his hands, palms up and shook his head incredulously.

"They'll find you out. You'd throw everything away for a few pounds more?"

"A few *thousand* pounds more," Worthy corrected. "After a time, it mounts up," he added.

"It's not a joke." Marley exclaimed. "Why steal from the company? It's already giving us more than we need—and without any risk."

"Do sit, Jacob," Worthy said peaceably. "Calm yourself.

No need to become conservative all of a sudden."

Worthy interlaced his fingers across his waist and leaned back.

"Life is risk," Worthy resumed. "That's what makes it enjoyable. Look here: A few years ago we were fleecing the riff-raff. Now I'm a member of the board of nothing less than Imperial Trading. And you, you're the wizard of the accounts—and that's no small leap for a lad of twenty-and-three. In five years, you will be richer than Midas. Mark me.

"Now, did all this happen because the board took a liking to me? Liked the cut of my jib? Thought I showed promise? Thought I looked like an honest gentleman? Not bloody likely. In fact, they'd all like to see me hanged."

Worthy poured again from the crystal bottle and moved the glass beneath his nose before taking a sip. "I can't say as I blame them. They're all criminals at heart, you know. Most are criminals *in fact*. Wilkins is a deserter. Snedrick's a pederast. Bagwell's an addict. I know. I've got the proof on them all. That's how we come to be set up so nice."

Worthy gestured toward the desk, the food, the decanters, flicked at the scarf below his chin, then waved his arms generally at the whole office.

"They set me up because I can bring them down," Worthy said, now leaning forward toward Marley. "They fear me. But at the same time, they've come to need me. I help this company. I fix things. Special cargoes arrive—no questions asked at the dock. It's taken care of. Imperial Trading thrives. Our profits were never higher—tell me I'm wrong; you know the ledgers. Everyone's happy. Now, if I keep a little bonus for myself, who's to begrudge it?

"Remember, Jacob," Worthy said, holding up his hand in a warning gesture. "Companies don't last forever. When this one goes away, I shall be on my own island in the Indies, drinking rum and watching the waves. A man could do worse."

Marley shook his head, objecting. "All the same," he said. "This is exactly the sort of thing they need to put you away. And would I be far behind? You amaze me."

"Posh and rubbish, lad. Gammon and spinach. You can take care of the books. Jacob Merlin, wizard of the accounts. You're a prodigy, you are. Work the numbers, please. You know how to do it. Put a bit of this here, a bit of that there. Use your imagination. Square it up. Don't you think you could? You'd do it to save your old mate, wouldn't you?"

Marley looked at the large, hollow globe of ivory. Through the holes of its carvings he could see another carved, hollow sphere, and within that another, and within that, yet another.

"It will take some time," he said.

Worthy clapped his hands loudly and stood up. "There's my partner," he said.

Marley stood also and turned to go.

"Wait, Jacob," said Worthy, coming around the desk. "There's more to be said."

Worthy caught Marley at the door and guided him back toward the center of the room.

"You know, Jacob," he said, reaching his hand up to the taller man's shoulder. "There's something I've never said to anyone that I'm going to say to you."

Worthy paused—whether for dramatic effect or for reconsideration, Marley could not tell.

"I trust you," Worthy said at last. "Yes, it's true. You're not a thief at heart. And you can keep a secret."

Worthy stared into Marley's eyes. "You know, some people must watch what they say. But not you. You never say anything. You rarely speak to anyone. Not even to me and I'm your only friend. I trust you, Jacob. And I'm going to prove it to you."

Worthy went to his desk, unlocked a drawer and returned with several small books. "These are the records of my personal accounts—banks, numbers, names, everything. You keep these under lock and key. If they ever do put me away, you go get this money. You'll buy my way out. I'll show you how—if and when the time comes. Would you do that for me? Could I have your word?"

Marley could not think what to say immediately.

"Are you sure you—"

"You're the only one I trust."

Marley looked down and flushed. He struggled not to feel honored or flattered.

"Well, yes then, of course," Marley said. "If you're quite sure."

Worthy smiled and slapped Marley on the back. "There's a good fellow." he said. Then he raised his right index finger in a cautionary gesture. "And I won't forget you when the time comes, neither," he said, winking. "I haven't so far, have I?"

Marley shook his head.

"Then it's settled." Worthy declared. "We shall celebrate. A visit to Mrs. Langdon's tonight. There's a new girl there you should meet: Ariel. My, my."

Marley suddenly frowned and his voice took on a tone of alarm. "Not tonight." he said. "Did you not arrange..."

"Oh my word, yes." Worthy said. "Forgive me. In all the excitement I'd forgotten. Your investigators. That is tonight. Yes, it's been arranged as you asked. They're quite good, actually. Do a good bit of work for me from time to time."

"Good," Marley said.

Worthy looked at him. "If you don't mind me asking, Jacob," he said. "You've not spent a penny since I've known you. You should have quite a bit by now. Enough, certainly to hire these men for some time...What dirt are you digging?"

Marley looked at the weaving in the rug and said nothing.

Worthy laughed.

"There you go. Fair enough. The best way to keep a secret is to keep it to yourself. Keep yourself to yourself too, eh?" Worthy laughed again. "Next week then?" he said. "At Mrs. Langdon's?"

"Yes," Marley said. "Next week."

Marley stepped toward the door, but stopped when Worthy called to him again.

"You held back one suit, Jacob," Worthy said.

"Pardon me?" Marley replied.

Worthy flipped up a card, the jack of hearts, and displayed it in his hand.

"Hearts," said Worthy. "You held that one back."

*****

That night, in the shadows of a dark archway on the outskirts of Saffron Hill, Marley waited in the cold and remembered how it had been as a child to go from a clean cottage to a place like this.

Saffron Hill's old buildings were so poorly constructed and maintained that they seemed to be held up only by the tightly wedged rows of other crumbling buildings. Little air or light reached this squalor. The denizens enjoyed no safe water supply and no drainage. The common sewer festered stagnant: dead fish, cats and dogs floated in its foul pools under the windows of tenants. Even the neighborhood courtyard gasped, inches deep in sewage.

Marley pulled up the hood of his cape to shield himself from the chill and to block the noxious smells. The old garment came from a small, secondary wardrobe he maintained—hooded capes, threadbare, high-collared jackets, broad-brimmed hats, knitted caps that covered the ears and could be pulled down low to the eyes. Now, in the archway, only the outline of his hood and the steamy, periodic bursts of his breath gave away his existence.

Marley stomped his feet to keep warm and hunched lower within the cape. Then he straightened up. Two men approached, their boots clattering on the pavement. The men came down the rise in the road and stopped at the arch.

"Evenin'," said the man closest to Marley. The man's neck, thick as a bull's and bare, rippled when he spoke. His eyes stared level with Marley's. His chest and shoulders reached so wide that Marley could barely see the other man behind him.

"Good evening," said Marley.

"Would you be a Mr. Smith, what knows a Mr. Worthy?" the first man said.

"I am," said Marley.

The big man stroked his thick, dark beard. "Billy said you might be in need of our services."

Marley nodded and, at the same time, the man's partner moved into view. From his looks—those of a gentleman—Marley would have expected him to be the spokesman; but instead the thin man kept silent, his hands in the pockets of a long, tailored coat.

"I'm given to understand that you find people," Marley said.

"Find people. Find out things about people. Find out things about things about people," the big man grinned. "That's what we do all right." The big man turned to his colleague. "Ain't that right?"

The other man stepped forward, tipped his short-brimmed, bowl-shaped hat, replaced it, and cleared his throat. His words snapped out, clipped and clear, each word enunciated precisely.

"My name, sir, is Raleigh Holmes. My associate—Mr. Simms—and I are indeed in the information business. Our clients pay us to discover information that concerns them. We do not become involved in the meaning, consequence nor implications of providing that information. We do not judge. We are discreet. As you know, Mr. Worthy referred you to us and, I presume, he would vouch for our tenacity and for our respect for our clients' concerns."

Holmes twisted the ends of his bushy, black moustache, then resumed. "Before we discuss the particulars, let me be blunt—you will find me to be honest, but blunt. I do not for a moment believe your name is Smith; but that is your affair and is not important to us. What I want you to know, however, is that you will not have fools working for you. Second, conducting business clandestinely, out-of-doors, in the chill of night, is something we will do if you insist, but would prefer not. My card," he said, handing it to Marley.

"We'll see," Marley said. "I am interested in the whereabouts of a miner. His name is Ezra Turner. Understand this: I want only the information; no one is to know that Ez— Mr. Turner is being sought, nor by whom."

"Particulars if you please," the gentleman said, withdrawing a small notebook from his coat.

"He worked at Elizabeth's Furnace. There was an explosion there three years ago. It is believed that Turner died in the catastrophe. But that can't be. He is still alive."

"How do you know that?" Holmes asked.

Marley looked at the man without speaking, then said, "I just know."

"When was the last time you saw him?"

"I didn't say I saw him, or that I even knew him for that matter."

The gentleman put his pencil down.

"Tell us what you can, then."

"The last time he was seen alive, he was twenty years old. They say he ran off from time to time; stayed with other people."

"Kin?"

"No. He was working on the day of the explosion and was not seen after that. But he may well have run off early or something else..." Marley's voice trailed off for a moment. "He was simple-minded," he added. "People would remember him. He was also a musical prodigy. It was God's one compensation to him." Marley stopped, suddenly aware that he may have said more than he should.

Simms coughed. "People disappear like dust in the mines." He snapped his fingers.

Holmes frowned at his colleague. "Go on," he said to Marley.

"That's all."

Holmes stopped writing for a moment. "What did—does he look like?"

Marley cleared his throat and gave the investigator a physical description of Ezra Turner. "...similar, I suppose to myself," he added.

"Anything else?"

"No."

"Why do you want to find this man?"

"That's my affair," said Marley.

"Very well," Holmes said. "Where can we reach you?"

"You can't. Leave word with Mr. Worthy. He will arrange whatever meetings are necessary between us."

Without another word, Marley turned and left, moving quickly through the darkened streets of the slum.

After feeling certain that the men had not followed him, Marley slowed and began thinking about the arrangement.

On the one hand it gave him hope; on the other hand, what would the investigators find? Ezra did not die: Marley believed that, felt that, knew that to be true. But he knew nothing else. For all he knew, Ezra might despise him now. No, Marley thought, pushing the notion aside. Ezra does not know how to hate.

Marley decided not to return to his apartment and instead walked randomly through the city, looking up only to avoid collisions with objects.

The streets that night alternated in silence and sound. Marley's bowed head took in the noises, but not the sights; he looked only a yard in front of him at a time. He walked down one cobbled way and heard nothing but the clip of his own hard soles. Then, passing into another neighborhood, he heard many sounds: women shrieking, some in anger, some in what sounded like fear, their voices hoarse barks; garbled sounds of arguing drunks intruded along with a thud and a cry that died in the damp air. The sounds bounced around him, but did not seem to include nor affect him.

Despite his freedom and position, Marley remained a fugitive. He knew that to become invisible to the world, he had to make the world itself disappear. Though not an easy trick, he managed it. Isolation for him became a practical penance.

After more than an hour of walking, Marley heard the sounds of a tin whistle jumping between the notes of an accordion and a fiddle. He looked up for the first time and took his bearings. No vagrants, no prostitutes littered the street; no loiterers at all. Most of the buildings huddled closed for the night, their shutters pulled firmly across their windows. Only one place, a tavern filled with people bouncing in jig-step to the music, lighted the street.

Marley stopped across the lane from the dancers and watched the party taking place behind the glass. The tavern's light threw the dancers' shadows onto the stones, nearly reaching Marley's feet. They whirled. The shadows spun carelessly.

Involuntarily, unknown to him, Marley's foot began to keep time with the music. Almost without realizing it, Marley drifted across the street to the corner of the tavern's segmented window and pressed his face so close to the glass that it fogged and he had to withdraw slightly to clear his view.

The dance had no form. Men and women flew about in all directions, in no structure, and one could not tell who belonged with whom, if any did at all. Each dancer seemed to have his or her own idea of what steps best suited the music. Some held one leg aloft, twirling a dangling foot before them while skipping on the other; some locked arms and spun in dangerously quickening loops; some sashayed together polka-style, skirt hems whirling free as flags.

"Merry Christmas," someone said. "Come in."

Before Marley realized it, a man dragged him inside; a big man with a red beard and a roaring laugh. Marley turned to protest but the man thrust a glass of whisky into his hand before he could speak.

"Cheers," said the big man.

Marley half-heartedly raised his glass, then withdrew to an unoccupied bench in a corner, keeping the hood of his cloak up around his face.

Marley watched the orbits of the dancers from the safety of the corner and noted the simple adornments around the room: wreaths and evergreen garlands, green, white and red candles, red berries strung together and draped from the roof beams. A short, thick log blazed on the fire, its heat and the heat of the dancers' bodies warming the whole tavern. Marley had not realized until then how cold it had been outside. He set his glass on the floor and leaned against the wall and watched both the musicians and the dancers.

At the center of the floor, in a coarse, white dress and with a wreath of berries around her head, a girl played the part of Brigid, the goddess of spring. She pranced around the men in the room, giving them comically exaggerated leers.

The other dancers—young and old, men, women and children—flew about with a primitive energy, laughing at themselves and admiring the movements of others. The careless fling of skirts and the constant laughter seemed to Marley to be the same expression: exclamations of freedom, and fearless foolishness. It seemed as though the real spirits of the people had emerged from hiding and now clung to each other in a wild, spinning embrace.

Marley's chest ached and he looked away.

When the music stopped, the girl who played Brigid dropped herself recklessly onto the bench next to Marley.

"Ah. That was a lively one," she declared.

Her brow dripped with sweat and she fanned herself with one hand. With her other hand she pulled her bodice away from her breasts to cool herself. She leaned back against the wall and extended her legs fully in front of her.

Marley glanced at the girl and accidentally met her eyes: they flickered a startling, mischievous, bright green.

She smiled, then looked back to the dance floor, caught her breath, then looked over at Marley again, this time with a mock frown.

"Here now," she said, rising and pulling Marley's cloak off his shoulders. "It's bad luck to wear a coat indoors, especially at a Christmas feast. You must be roasting. Besides you won't feel the good of it later."

"I'm in comfort, really," Marley said, but left the garment on the bench where she'd dropped it.

"Whose kin are you? I don't think you're from around here," she said.

"None. I was pulled in, actually. I really shouldn't be here."

"Nonsense," she said. "The more the merrier, you know. I'm Jenny Thompson."

She held out her hand to Marley. He held it briefly, then released it. Marley hesitated, then said, "I'm Jake McGuire."

The girl smiled again in a friendly, rather than flirtatious, way. She leaned back against the wall and looked toward the dancers and musicians.

"I think I shall dance all night," she announced, stretching her arms high above her head so that the back of her hands scraped lightly against the wall. "Music this good mustn't be wasted."

"I don't think music is ever wasted," Marley said. "Even on those who only listen."

"You might try a dance, Mr. McGuire," the girl said. "You look so serious. It might do you good."

"It has done me good already."

The fiddler at the back of the room nodded to his companions and launched into a spirited reel called "Mary's Wedding." At the first note, the girl began tapping out the time with her feet and clapping her hands. When the verses began she stood and sang along.

"'Step we gaily on we go/ Heel to heel and toe to toe/ On and on and on we go/ On to Mary's Wedding.'"

She took Marley's hand and pulled at him.

"Come, Mr. McGuire. Join the dance."

Marley tried to get up, but his body wouldn't move. He sat mesmerized, paralyzed by the intimacy of the people before him. He could neither explain nor deny it. Still, he could not force himself to stand and he sank back to the bench.

The girl did not let go of his hand but instead followed it back and sat next to Marley, her look changing from eagerness to concern. Marley did not know what to say and so he shrugged.

The girl shrugged too, then turned his hand over, palm up.

"Let's look at your future," she said. She pulled Marley's palm into better light and brought it close to her face.

Marley watched her as she examined his hand. She held it at several angles, trying to see it more clearly. She squinted, following a particular wrinkle. Then she put his hand down, patting the back of it before she let go. She did not say anything.

"So?" Marley asked after a pause.

"Hmm?"

"What did my palm tell you?"

"It said that you shall be very famous one day."

"Did it?" Marley said.

Just then a man in work clothes, his sleeves rolled halfway up his arm, called out, "Jenny. This is our dance." He held out his hand to her.

"Now don't go away," the girl whispered to Marley. She took the other man's hand and waved as she sailed back into the dancing sea.

Marley watched her spin around the floor for a few minutes. Then he left.

*****

Marley arrived at his cold loft after midnight. He lit two oil lamps, started a small flame in the hearth and, after the room warmed, removed his ragged costume and placed each article in a trunk lying in a corner of the bare wood floor.

Marley's room occupied the top level of Imperial Trading's counting house. He had been permitted to convert what otherwise would have been attic storage into a place of his own for a small rent paid to the firm. Marley, hoarding money to finance the search for Ezra, sought out the situation and Worthy had arranged it, pointing out to the company that in exchange for the space, the company would have the head accountant available at all hours.

The cramped loft housed a small bed, a chair, a small writing table, a dresser, a wardrobe, a wash basin, a music stand fashioned from a brick hod, and a hodgepodge of mathematical texts. A tin whistle lay alongside the music stand.

Marley did not mind the meager accommodations. He'd lived in worse and, by contrast, the loft to him conveyed luxury. The only inconvenience Marley suffered from the room resulted from its sloping ceiling and his tall stature; he could walk upright only along the loft's exact centerline. This he did now, pacing, not yet ready for sleep.

He stopped at the hod/music stand and examined the sheet music resting there. The horizontal lines of the staff lay confident in their exactitude: straight, perfectly parallel, each bar separated by a vertical line at precise right angles to the five lateral ones, the spaces between the lines exactly the same width. Each note displayed similar exactitude: each placed in its unalterable sequence, each with its own designated time to exist—no more, no less. And, when read properly, the sum of it all would be one piece of music, the same, reliable, predictable sound whenever one chose to repeat it. Here chance and uncertainty remained at bay.

The piece in the stand was a Scottish dirge, a sad and bitter song that could stir the blood to violence—especially when delivered by a battalion of bagpipes.

Marley picked up the tin whistle and took it to the gabled window. He fingered the openings on the pipe lightly, then looked down at the street outside and began to play an unscored song.

The first several notes hesitated in the air as he experimented with the melody in his head. He played the first measure twice, unevenly, finding his way through like a man moving in a dark room. He stopped, corrected a phrase, then pushed ahead. He tried to duplicate the light, buoyant dance of "Mary's Wedding" but the notes came out in unsure stabs.

Marley lowered the instrument from his lips. He turned and walked back to the music stand, examined the martial notes on the pages and played them instead.

Funerals

October 31, 1800
London

Bill Worthy died in bed with one of the girls at Mrs. Langdon's. The day before Worthy's funeral, Marley visited the chapel where the service would be held. His footsteps on the old building's wooden floor sounded like a loud clock in a small room. Each step threw its low sound toward the thick, stone walls where it thumped then flew back like a hunk of wood poorly struck by an axe. The church held six pews with room for no more than ten people each. The building made Marley feel as though he'd entered a large and beautiful chimney rather than a church. Still, it would do, he thought.

"You surprise me, Bill," he said aloud, then stopped, surprised at how his words seemed to grow louder as they filled the empty chamber. He resumed in a lower voice. "I never took you for a religious man," he said.

Marley made one last inspection of the chapel then paused to examine the various stained-glass windows. In one pane he saw his reflection. Though just twenty-seven, Marley's hair had thinned greatly and his face, though lean, sagged as if someone had taken a knife and cut across the top of it causing the skin to slide down and puddle along the hollows of his eyes, the sides of his mouth and his neck.

The doily-patterned glass behind the altar captured Marley's attention. Morning sunlight struck it at an oblique angle and thrust beams of red, yellow and blue toward the wall on Marley's left. Dust motes hovered in the beams like angels unsure which direction to go.

Instead of the usual stained-glass depiction of the Ascension of Christ, the glass behind the alter showed an inverted figure of the Savior, plunging headlong into a dark pit, his arms and hands extended before him, his feet connected at the ankles to colorful rays extending upward toward a bright heaven. In the pit, a man wearing a tattered shroud, whom Marley took to be Lazarus, reached his arms toward the descending savior in apparent expectation of rescue. Marley stared at the panel and thought that it would be well-received further north, in Northumbria, where people truly knew about the underworld.

The chapel door opened with a creak and Marley turned. Raleigh Holmes and his colleague, Simms entered.

Holmes took off his bowl-shaped hat and nodded to Marley.

"Sorry to hear about Mr. Worthy," he said.

It took a moment for Marley to place the men: appearing, as they had, unexpected and out-of-place in this, a chapel, of all locations. Marley looked from one man to the other. Holmes appeared thinner than before: his neck more scrawny, like a slender pole tightly wrapped in skin. Simms, but for two exceptions, looked the same: powerful, his neck simple coils of muscle, his arms gnarly clubs. But Simms wore a new scar now; shaped like a worm, it cut straight down from the top of his forehead to his nose. Also, a hole occupied the place where his left ear should have been.

Involuntarily, Marley touched the top of his own ear and felt the place that had been cut away by Badger's whip years before.

"What are you doing here?" Marley said after several moments.

"I apologize," said Holmes. "But you said to notify you immediately if ever we found something and...well, Mr. Worthy can't be intermediary anymore, so we tracked you down."

"Never mind that," Marley said, waving his hand before him. "You found something. What? Did you find—"

Holmes gestured that they should sit. Marley took the back pew; the two investigators slid into the one just ahead. Holmes twisted around to face his client.

"What did you find?" Marley repeated.

Simms spoke up. "Ezra Turner is dead."

Marley stood and grasped Simms' coat.

"Yes, it's true" Simms insisted, never rising from his seat. He calmly started to remove Marley's hands from his coat lapels but Marley jerked away on his own.

"What my colleague means to say," Holmes interjected. "Is that, over the past year, we have conducted hundreds of interviews—with miners, engineers, company officials, residents of Elizabeth's Furnace and surrounding villages. We have consulted parish records, prison logs, workhouses, churchyards, asylums—well, in short, we've found no evidence that Mr. Turner survived the explosion. Indeed, it is our conclusion that he did not survive it."

Marley did not respond.

Simms spoke. "He's dead, sir. Records on colliers aren't kept long—when they're kept at all. Even when bodies are recovered—which there aren't in this case—most wind up in potter's fields. Sad, but to the world they might as well be ghosts."

At this Marley erupted.

"Not to me!" he yelled, his voice careening around the chapel. "Is it more money you want? Is that it?"

Neither man reacted. Holmes looked at the floor again

and then back to Marley.

"You've paid a great deal of money to us already," Holmes said evenly. "You keep your money now. If we find anything more we'll let you know."

Marley moved away from the pew slowly. He looked from one man to the other. Abruptly, he spun around and lashed a kick at the plank of an adjacent pew, causing the bench to flip over and crash into the wall behind it.

"No," Marley snarled. "No. You find him. Take the money."

Marley reached into his coat, fumbled with a wallet and pulled out a handful of bills and threw it at the men, scattering the notes like dead leaves.

"Find him," Marley demanded.

Neither of the men moved or spoke. Marley stared back at them.

"You're useless," Marley hissed finally. "The both of you."

Marley looked toward the altar and the glass image of Christ. "You're all useless," he added.

Then Marley turned and walked from the room. As he left, he slammed the chapel's heavy door so hard into the jamb that the figures in the stained glass shook.

*****

Marley returned to Warren Street and stood for a long time in the middle of the block, looking first in the direction of his newly-purchased town house, then in the opposite direction toward the White Horse, a place of gin and smoke and people who did not converse.

Marley felt invisible and supposed himself perched upon someone else's shoulders, observing some other force animating his body.

He walked toward the pub, trying not to think. But

thoughts came regardless. Thoughts of Worthy and Ezra pursued Marley's retreat. Marley cursed God and man until the sound of his thoughts became a Babel of deafening shouts and violent oaths. Then, all at once, the cacophony ceased.

The sound of Marley's inner voice changed, becoming not Marley's voice at all, but that of another being entirely. The new voice reverberated: deep, sonorous, musical, familiar and yet new, soothing and threatening all at once.

"Jacob," it shivered.

Marley slowed his pace.

"Jacob," the voice repeated, close to Marley's ear. "When the time comes—and it will come—how will you choose? Save yourself? Or save *him*?"

Marley cried out and spun around, swinging a back-handed blow in advance, half-expecting to catch and pummel his tormentor. But Marley's fist sliced through empty air. No one stood within a half block of Marley. He looked in all directions, but no one could have been whispering to him. Not a living soul.

"The devil," Marley muttered. Then he hurried on to the pub.

The first drinks made him gag; the gin scalded, causing him to imagine fragments of twisted wire being pulled through the soft tissue of his throat. Punishment to come, he thought. He stood at the counter, never moving to a table, and drank more. By closing time, he could no longer remember which name he used these days. But he could still remember why he'd come to the pub.

"Time," the barkeeper said.

Marley rose and swayed toward the door, causing one of the patrons, a bent man in a fisherman's cap, to take his arm. Marley looked at the puckered old man, pulling back for better focus. Suddenly Marley struck at the man, hacking at the steadying arm.

The good Samaritan backed away. "Suit yourself," he said.

Marley turned and lunged through the doorway.

Outside, Marley stumbled, then straightened himself into a tall posture and pitched his weight in the direction of his home. He shuffled and tripped along the block until he recognized his own dwelling. Marley leaned backward to look at its roofline; it seemed to be falling forward upon him. The illusion and the gin caused Marley to reel and he stepped back to regain his balance. Then he took aim on the ironwork railing along the porch steps and charged at them. Marley grabbed the railing and pulled himself up the steps to the massive front door in one movement. There he stalled for a time, fumbling in his pockets for a key. When Marley finally found the key, he examined it, holding it close to his face. Marley aimed the key at the lock, but instead, jabbed it into the massive, lion's-head door-knocker before him. Marley stared at the lion, then spat at the beast and poked the key into its mouth as if to bait it. But the regal symbol remained unaffected and Marley stopped. He sighed and slid the key into the lock, opened the door, then staggered up the broad, wooden staircase that led to his chambers.

At the landing, Marley dropped his coat and shuffled into the next room—his office—where he managed to light an oil lamp. Then he collapsed like a ragdoll into a chair near his work desk.

Marley stared at a stack of blank papers. Abruptly, he picked up a pen, dipped it, and began to scribble. He wrote:

You're gone. Then I am gone too.

Marley stopped and squinted at the sloppy lines which

seemed to wriggle on the page. He could not make out the words, but nonetheless resumed writing, scratching across the paper, careless of his strokes.

They killed us for coal. Coal for the masses. Let them all freeze.

Marley paused then sketched a triangular arrangement of dots and then a series of right angles with dots in the intervening spaces: tetractys and gnomons. He drew a shaky axis and an imprecise parabola. He wondered what composition Ezra might play in reply. Marley felt his face begin to come apart. He wept and hid his face in his hands, knowing that he would never hear an answer.

After a time, Marley lifted the paper by one corner and watched the ink, the words and drawings, slide down the page like knots of rope gone lax and unravelled. Then he opened a drawer and dropped the letter in among many others. After that Marley rose, walked to his bed and fell upon it. He passed out instantly and slept like the dead are said to sleep, with no awareness of ever being.

*****

Holmes and Simms dined that evening at a tavern called The Tombs. The narrow establishment occupied a small slot between the crammed-together shops off Gerrard Street, in a poorly-lit neighborhood not far from the river. A strong night wind blew against the tavern door, making it creak against its hinges, but inside the air hung still; unmoving clouds of tobacco smoke lay at neck-level throughout.

Simms chewed vigorously at a piece of beef, while looking down at his plate, anticipating the next bite. Holmes' plate sat undisturbed; a potato in watery gravy, a slab of thick bread and a thin cut of brownish beef waited, losing its steamy heat.

Holmes looked around the tavern at the dozen or so other diners. Their shapes were indistinct in the thick atmosphere and came to him only in flashes of yellow firelight, mixed with smoke and shadow.

Simms paused in his chewing and looked at his colleague. "Cozy," he said.

Holmes sighed. "If that's your mood...Dark I would say. It seems too close in here to me."

Simms fit another bite into his mouth. "Good meat though," he said.

Holmes nodded, then began to pat the pockets of his coat with both hands. "I've forgotten something," he said.

"How do you know?"

"Eh?"

Simms poked his fork toward Holmes' pockets. "How do you know you've forgotten something, if you've forgotten it?"

Holmes stopped his examination. "Just a feeling," he said.

Simms put away his fork. "Why didn't we tell him everything we'd found out?"

Holmes sighed and rubbed his face. "We told him what he needed to be told. He knew the rest."

"Still," said the big man. "He couldn't think we're very good at our work, if he thought we never even found out nothing about *him*." Simms guffawed. "And he described Ezra Turner as looking 'similar' to himself. I don't suppose he could've told us they was twins. We could've told him we knew that much."

Holmes shrugged. "And who would benefit from such a display? Should we humiliate our client to show him what good investigators we are? That we easily penetrated his flimsy disguises? Worse: that we know he's a fugitive? He'd only come to fear us then. It is enough that we told him the truth. His brother is dead. We must leave him with that."

Simms nodded and swallowed a drink of beer. "I don't think he believes it, even now," he said.

"You're right, I'm sure. He knew about the explosion seven years ago—when he masqueraded as his brother and terrorized that Ferrel rascal. He simply cannot accept the fact of his brother's death. I doubt he ever will." Holmes pushed aside his plate and began to fill a small pipe. "I hope he does though," Holmes said, putting a candle's flame to the pipe bowl. "Otherwise, it's madness for him."

"He's already there, I'm thinking," Simms replied.

Holmes expelled smoke through his nostrils. Simms shrugged and said, "Well, you can't please everyone."

Holmes puffed once more at the pipe and then laid it down. He drummed his fingers on the dark, heavy wood of the table.

"Jake Turner...Mr. Smith...Jacob Marley..." he mused. "I wish your brother *were* alive. Then we'd produce him for you."

Holmes tapped his half-burned tobacco into his tea saucer. "Well...if wishes were shillings..." he said. Then he beckoned for the barmaid. "A whisky please."

*****

The day of Bill Worthy's funeral the sun rose in the fall air, bright and crisp as a cold, hard apple. Small birds jittered in the trees near the gravesite. The newly-cold atmosphere smelled sweet and dank like rotted fruit; its slightest stir caused the flame-red and yellow leaves above to flutter like handkerchiefs waving goodbye.

But Marley barely noticed the birds nor the brilliant leaves nor the bracing touch in the air. His head ached and the ground would not hold steady. He looked up at a bare tree. A black ribbon, a woman's scarf probably, fluttered there, snagged on a high limb. He watched it as the small group of mourners gathered around the casket. The ribbon, he thought, undulated like a snake given the power of flight.

"Good day for it," someone said.

Snedrick, a pasty-skinned board member, appeared next to Marley. Pederast, Marley thought, recalling Worthy's account of the man. Marley turned away and said nothing.

"If there is ever a good day for such a thing, I mean. Terrible though," the man went on. "Just goes to show us. You can be at the pinnacle of your profession and then...Heart stopped, they say. You're gone like that."

Snedrick slapped his hands together.

"In the arms of a whore," Marley said. He looked hard at Snedrick. "A woman, that is. Not a boy."

"What did you say?" Snedrick paled.

"I said, at least he wasn't a seducer of boys," Marley snarled. "Then he'd certainly go to hell. Don't you agree?"

Without waiting for a reply, Marley turned away from Snedrick, who hurried off to the other side of the casket.

A dozen people stood circled around Worthy's open grave. The parson read aloud, alternating his selections from the Bible and a prayer book. All but three of the mourners came from the company. The Imperial men dressed themselves identically in black, silk top hats, their shoulders draped with white scarves or cloaks. They huddled on the opposite side of the coffin from Marley where they whispered among themselves. They wore serious, but not mournful or reflective expressions.

A quick glint of gold flashed and Marley noticed Jenkins, a solicitor for the company, hauling a watch by its chain from his waistcoat pocket.

Marley looked over the rest of the mourners and stopped to regard Ebenezer Scrooge, a clerk, standing alone, ten yards to Marley's left. The wind blew at Scrooge's thick, black hair causing it to drag across his eyes and forcing him at last to hold it in place with a hand. Scrooge, though only six years younger than Marley, looked like a child. He seemed like a frail boy. His narrow shoulders carried no muscle to speak of; his hands resembled delicate blades of grass. He played piano and, at the company's Christmas fete the year before, held the revelers in awe with his musicianship.

Worthy had insisted that Marley attend that party, persuading him that it had nothing to do with "fellowship or goodwill or all that malarkey" but to view it instead as a political, business necessity: "Where we show our guests how thankful we shall be for their generosity in the year to come," Worthy had said.

So Marley had attended the party, held at one of the company's vast warehouses, transformed into a Christmas ballroom for the occasion. For most of the evening, Marley stood off from the crowd, leaning against a post, listening to the fiddlers dash off their rapid jigs and reels. But later in the evening, he noticed a commotion around the piano.

Several laughing, half-drunk clerks pushed one of their own toward the instrument despite the other's strong protests. At last, however, they prevailed and the beleaguered clerk sat at the piano. After looking over the keyboard for a moment, young Scrooge nodded to the fiddlers who took up their bows.

"Let's try 'Sir Roger de Coverley,'" Scrooge said.

Marley halted at the choice. The only time he'd ever heard that reel done on the piano Ezra had played it. Marley did not believe anyone else could duplicate the feat. Even the fiddlers looked at each other, doubtful, but they shrugged and set to it.

From the beginning, Scrooge's piano matched every slide, pull, and hammered note of the fiddlers and soon took over the piece entirely. Marley moved closer and watched the clerk's hands fly across the keyboard. Marley drew a sudden, deep breath when he saw Scrooge's hands. They resembled his brother's hands; they *were* Ezra's hands—the shape, texture, airy movements—everything, down to the last knuckle and nail.

"Who is this?" Marley asked Worthy.

"Ebenezer Scrooge," Worthy replied. "I hired him away from the old Fezziwig concern not two months ago. He's a clerk in shipping."

Marley looked puzzled. "When did you begin hiring clerks?"

"I told you. About two months ago."

"You went to the trouble to steal away a clerk from Fezziwig? What's so special about him?"

Worthy looked astonished. "Have you no ears, man? Listen to him play."

In spite of himself, Marley smiled and from then on kept a discreet watch on the progress of Ebenezer Scrooge.

"Is there anyone here who would like to say a few words about the departed?" the parson asked.

Marley, startled from his reverie, stared at the cleric. "Some memories or personal observations?" the man prompted.

No one stepped forward.

"Mr. Marley...?" the parson suggested. "You knew him best."

Marley looked around at his colleagues. "I have nothing to say to this company."

An awkward silence followed, then the cleric said, "Very well. I will conclude these services with a reading from Ezekiel, chapter thirty-three, verses seven through nine."

Marley shifted his weight and found himself staring at the black, waving ribbon in the tree, hearing only bits and pieces of the reading.

"'...Thou shalt hear the word at my mouth, and warn them from me...If thou dost not speak to warn the wicked from his way, that wicked man shall die in his iniquity; but his blood will be on your hands.'"

A sudden, loud bang of metal clashing made Marley flinch. A groundskeeper in the distance threw a heavy length of chain around the gates to a vault.

"'Nevertheless, if thou warn the wicked of his way to turn from it...Thou hast delivered *thy* soul," the parson concluded, shutting the book slowly.

Marley heard someone crying and turned toward the sound. Three women stood off a ways, close together. They wore shiny, long sleeved, morning gowns, black and cinched at the waist. None wore veils and Marley recognized one of them. She had dark hair and broad lips, and seemed disposed by nature to smile. She glanced at him, but Marley looked away.

Worthy and whores. Marley smirked at the parson's message as it might have applied to Worthy, or to himself for that matter; the idea of them altering their ways.

With a nod from the parson, the coffin descended into the grave. The mourners, except for Marley, bowed their heads until the box disappeared below ground level. Then, as if to a silent cue, the mourners scattered.

The dark-haired woman stopped when she came near Marley. She frowned at him; her green-gold eyes narrowed. She spoke to Marley in a harsh whisper.

"Bill knew how to treat people," she said. "*He* wouldn't lay with someone, then make like he never saw her afore. Like she wasn't a person. You'd do well to be half as kind as him."

Marley looked around. No one, it seemed, had heard the woman's remarks. Marley bowed.

"And much good it did him," Marley said in a low voice. "Good day."

The woman's mouth puckered and her eyes narrowed into nearly flat lines. Then she pivoted away from Marley, tilting her head high in an exaggerated posture, and walked away.

Marley remained in his place.

"A sad day sir."

Scrooge stood nearby.

Marley, taller by an inch, looked downward slightly to meet Scrooge's dark eyes. Marley rarely looked at anyone directly for very long, but he gazed at Scrooge for some time.

"Why sad?" Marley said.

"Why sad? Why, poor Mr. Worthy," Scrooge exclaimed.

Marley began to walk and Scrooge fell into step alongside. They moved in silence for a while, the only sound the crackle of leaves beneath their boots. Finally the clerk spoke again.

"I thought, sir, that you were close to him."

Marley looked ahead, then spoke in a measured voice. "Bill Worthy was a liar, a cheat, a thief, an embezzler, a blackmailer, a man of business, and an excellent storyteller when the mood struck him. This company is the poorer for his passing." He turned to the clerk and spoke without compassion. "Everyone has to die, Scrooge."

"Well, yes, sir. I suppose so," Scrooge said. "But to speak of the dead that way..."

"Why should we lie about the dead?" Marley said. "Does the death of a man improve him—other than to arrest his bad habits? Mr. Worthy was what he was."

Marley noticed alarm on the clerk's face and added, "I am not condemning Mr. Worthy. He was what he was. Leave it at that."

Scrooge said nothing for a while.

"Will there be many changes now? Because of his passing?" the clerk said at last.

"Some. That much I can say for certain," Marley replied.

"Of what sort? Could you tell me?"

Marley looked at Scrooge.

"You're a good worker, Mr. Scrooge," Marley said. "You rarely look up from your ledgers. You never seem dreamy nor do you waste your time in the small talk of other clerks. You hardly socialize. You seem to enjoy the opiate of work. An employer could do worse. I would say your position is secure, if that's what concerns you."

Marley paused. "Is there something else? You're looking at me strangely."

"I'm sorry, sir," Scrooge replied. It's just that the way you spoke just now; it sounded as though your own position—"

"Oh, that. No, I won't be back."

"I'm sor—"

"Not at all. My choice. I have come into some money," Marley said.

He looked off and for a moment appeared as though he had forgotten Scrooge's presence. Then Marley spoke again as though he'd never stopped.

"I am well off. I may travel. Or start my own concern."

"Well good luck sir."

Marley stopped at the entrance gate.

"Be careful, Mr. Scrooge," he said. "If you work in the company of scoundrels, you may become one yourself."

Marley turned around and walked back toward the grave.

Steel and Spark

November 6, 1806
London

Marley & Company occupied a small, corner building less than two blocks from Imperial Trading. Jacob Marley sat by its front window, alone in the murky glow of wood embers, surveying the interior.

The suite resembled a residence, a gentleman's parlor, more than a workplace. A thickly embroidered rug covered the floor. The armchairs, including the one in which he sat, featured ornately carved acanthus leaves on scrolled feet, cockleshells along their aprons and palmettes cresting their backs. A tan, leather recamier lay beneath several paintings of rural landscapes that bordered the walls. A water pipe and the ivory globe that had once belonged to Bill Worthy served as curiosities. A small pianoforte occupied the far corner of the room.

Dawn was more than an hour away, but Marley had not lighted any lamp and had allowed the room to grow cold in the dying glow of the fire.

Marley turned toward the window. Outside, the empty street brooded, silent as a private thought and lent itself to fancies. Marley imagined how London, and then how the world, might be without people.

To begin, the world would be quiet, as it was now. And clean. The stench of human sewage—of excrement piled day after day upon itself in the courts and yards of the working class, so deep as to be unnavigable, its foul smell drifting all over London, even to the Palace—that would be gone. And the stench of bodies. There no longer would be corpses overwhelming the burial grounds as there were now, such that gravediggers had to jump upon bodies to wedge them into already-filled ditches.

Marley imagined that on cloudless days, the skies might be blue, not sooty-black. Human nature such as cruelty, murder, betrayal, crimes against children, would have no definition, much less anyone to debate their theological implications. All in all, it would not be such a calamity if the race were to become extinct.

A few street lamps still burned, reflecting off the wet facets of paving, creating small, pale-yellow islands at each street corner. In places where the lamps glowed behind iced, bare trees, an optical illusion arose. There the branches, sheathed in a glaze of moisture and backlit in gold, appeared to grow in perfectly concentric patterns like glimmering spider webs rather than in their customary haphazard, stabbing shapes. Marley gazed at the brilliant circles and kept his coat pulled tightly around himself. Illusion. Humbug. That is the nature of things.

A dueling pistol, part of Worthy's legacy, lay on the window sill next to his heavy walking stick. Marley picked up the firearm and examined it for the second time that morning. Powder sat in the pan, covered by the steel **L** of the frisson, the gun's sparking mechanism. The hammer had not yet been pulled back and its duckbill of flint rested wearily against the back of the frisson, looking like a drunkard leaning face-first into a wall. If the hammer were pulled back, locked, then released, the flint edge would slap into the steel, causing a spark and simultaneously would push the frisson's powder cover forward, igniting the powder and so on. A chain of actions; one leading to another, leading to eternity.

Earlier that night Marley had reluctantly attended a function for members of the London Exchange. In the course of the evening a broker, a penguin of a man, had slapped him on the back and pronounced him a success, congratulating him on his first year as a member and on his acquisition of several London properties.

"...Thirty years old: you're just a pup, lad. Yet you've achieved quite a bit. And the more amazing, good fellow, is that you've done it all alone. Well, that will change I'm sure. I expect you'll have twenty people under your roof before this time next year."

Marley surprised the man by recoiling from him and leaving the celebration. That man and the other brokers and all the men with whom he transacted business, masked cutthroat natures under their fine linen, as Worthy had rightly observed.

Marley picked up the heavy pistol and held it sideways with two hands and, in the dim light, brought it close to his eyes. He pulled his spectacles down from his forehead and examined the fine metal work and scrolling on its sideplate. Deeply etched flowers and intertwined grapevines rambled along the gun-metal.

Marley thought of wreaths on a casket. He ran his fingers over the pistol's handle. The swirled wooden grain felt smooth and hard as polished marble or like the hard back of one particular prostitute he'd known. The pistol curved sensually: a work of art, deadly and weighty.

Marley transferred the weapon to his right hand and pulled back the hammer until he heard it lock in place. The beveled flint now seemed awake, at attention, alert, and ready for the trigger to send it falling into the steel and spark.

Marley raised the pistol to his shoulder, its barrel pointed upward in the attitude of a duelist's weapon at the ready.

Marley closed his eyes and touched the thin, cold tongue of the trigger with his index finger. One squeeze on the insensate flange would set off an explosive chain of events that could not be recalled. Marley breathed deeply, then angled the pistol toward himself.

"What ho! Are you a total fool!? Get down now and see to the tack. Step quickly too."

Marley opened his eyes and lowered the pistol. Across the street, a coach-and-six rocked to a halt just opposite one of the street lamps; its driver, a large man in a ragged top hat and a long, black coat—his belly protruding from its open front—half-stood, half-crouched in his seat, reins in one hand, and shook his fist at a boy who scurried between the horses, stopping only to lift each buckle and strap, inspect it, then rush to another.

"I told you, boy..."

The man paused, unable to find words to express his anger. The driver then stomped down on the brake and secured the reins; he teetered in the process but did not fall, remaining atop the coach, weaving from side to side.

"I told you to keep this rig in proper workin' order or I'd have your hide and by God I will!" he yelled.

In the deserted street, the man's voice echoed and Marley thought he could feel his own windows quiver slightly.

The boy, no more than ten, scrambled between the six huge, black horses. Marley lost sight of him, then he reappeared briefly, gave a quick glance at his master and disappeared again, evidently searching for whatever caused the man's rage.

Once, the boy bumped against a horse, knocking off his cap, causing it to land in a brownish puddle. He snatched up the cap and replaced it on his head despite its wet filth, before the driver noticed and cursed him for that too. Even in the bad light, Marley saw that the boy's legs were bowed; rickets, he guessed.

Now a new sound, the scrape-clip of footsteps on wet pavement, caught Marley's ear. He looked further up the street and saw a thin man approaching the coach from his right. This man wore white trousers, a dark overcoat, several turns of scarf and a tall hat. Marley judged him to be a man of business, but even so, thought it odd for such a person to be about so early.

The man slowed, then stopped some ninety yards from the coach and watched as the driver hurled more curses at the boy.

"Well...?" bellowed the coachman.

The boy emerged from beneath the forward horse and held up his hands in a gesture of bewilderment.

"God's blood," the driver swore.

He looked wildly about his seat, then jerked his stiff-handled, braided whip from its post and lurched down from rig, clambering to the pavement.

"I'll have your hide," he bellowed after he'd steadied himself on the ground. Then he swung at the boy with the pole of the whip. The boy dodged and the full force of the blow missed its mark: the handle's tip catching him just behind the knee.

Marley seized his cane and pistol and rushed from the office, uncocking his firearm in the process.

As he charged across the street, Marley saw the driver sling another blow at the boy, this one catching the lad across the shoulders and spilling him to the pavement. At the same time, the third man, the thin gentleman, reached the scene.

"You there. Stop, I say!" the gentleman yelled.

Marley recognized the voice.

The thin gentleman flung himself at the much-larger man,

wrapping himself around the driver's huge shoulders and biceps. But that did not stop the coachman's attempts to strike at the boy. The driver raised his whip and pitched his weight forward, lifting the thin man in the process and flinging him over his broad back, such that the smaller man found himself suddenly facing the driver: standing between him and the boy.

"Mind your business," the driver growled. Then he grabbed the gentleman by the face and shoved him back eight feet into a brick wall. The thin man jumped up, but no sooner gained his feet than the driver put a boot into his waist. The gentleman hit the pavement with a sound like dumped laundry.

"See what you've caused now. Here's for that," the driver roared at the boy, raising the whip handle again.

But the whip never fell. Instead, the giant screamed like a child and crumpled to his side on the pavement, grabbing his own legs.

Jacob Marley's first blow employed the cane, a slashing strike that caught the coachman across both shins simultaneously. The second impact came from the barrel of the pistol which struck deep into the man's right shoulder joint, making a wet sound like a clever hitting a fresh ham. The coachman cried out again and rolled onto his back, his right arm dropping limp as a ragdoll's.

Now Marley took his time. He leaned down near the coachman's head and placed his cane lightly across the groaning man's neck. Then he delicately stepped down on one side of the stick, causing it to press into the coachman's throat and pin him securely to the street. The boy, only a few feet away, looked up slowly, like a frightened animal, then rose to a crouch.

The other gentleman now struggled to his feet and took a step toward the men. Then he stopped suddenly.

"Mr. Marley!"

Marley turned toward the young clerk.

"Mr. Scrooge."

The two men appraised each other for several moments and said nothing more. Marley looked away first; returning his attention to the coachman.

"Listen closely to me, hack," Marley said in a low voice.

The man stopped writhing about but still whimpered, looking into Marley's cold eyes.

Pressing a little harder on the cane, Marley squatted close to the man's face and gestured toward Scrooge.

"For assaulting this gentleman, the crown might have you flogged or sent to Newgate, though I expect that would be like home to you. But for assaulting the boy, the crown has no remedy. I, however, do."

Marley motioned for the boy to come nearer.

To the coachman Marley said, "If you value your life, hear this: one day it might occur to this lad that while you sleep, you are defenseless." Marley looked into the boy's eyes, making sure he understood, then went on. "When you sleep, the boy may still be awake—perhaps the pain of some recent beating keeping him from rest—it could be that he will realize there's a pitchfork in the barn and that he can take it, or any other device he choses, and steal into your room and sink the tines deep into your eyes. He may not have thought of that till now. Do you understand me?"

The coachman's face beaded with drops of sweat and steam rose from it in the cold, pre-dawn air. The man's eyes dilated wide open, but they showed little understanding and looked at Marley as though at a ghost. The coachman licked his lips once, then surprised the men by bellowing at his tormentor.

"You! You bastard! You broke me legs."

Marley stepped hard on the cane and the rest of the man's language evaporated in gurgles of asphyxiation. But Marley let up on the pressure, removed the cane from the man's neck and stood up.

"I don't think your legs are broken," Marley said.

To prove the point, he rapped the man's shins again with the cane, causing the giant to howl and double up.

"No," Marley said. "They sound intact."

Then Marley turned to Scrooge who stood with his hands inert at his sides. Marley's tone turned suddenly light.

"Mr. Scrooge. Are you one of the Charlies now? Keeping the streets safe at all hours?"

Scrooge swallowed once. "No. Hardly. I think you've really hurt the brute."

"Not enough, I shouldn't think."

Marley turned to the boy who pressed himself closely to the side of one of the great horses.

"Can you drive this coach?" Marley asked.

The boy nodded.

"Very well," Marley said. "Mr. Scrooge and I shall help this, this man into the carriage. And you may take him wherever you like." Marley spoke loudly so that the coachman could hear. "Mind, boy, what I said about sleep. You needn't kill him; you could simply break his knees with a length of heavy pipe."

Marley grinned. Scrooge look away. Marley then cocked the hammer of his pistol and leveled it at the coachman.

"Get yourself in the cabin," he said.

The man wailed from the pain in his shins but struggled to his feet and managed to pull himself into the coach.

Marley turned to Scrooge and smiled.

"I was about to put on a kettle, Mr. Scrooge." Marley

pointed toward his offices. "My place of business is there. Come join me."

*****

Scrooge sat in the receiving area of Marley's suite, near the window from which his host earlier had fancied a depopulated world, and not far from the pulpit-desk used by Marley's clerk. Marley lighted several lamps and added more wood to the fire, then prepared tea.

After filling the pot, Marley returned, poured for them both, then sat. After they had each sipped once, Marley smiled.

"That was courageous of you, Mr. Scrooge. Attacking an armed man so much larger than yourself and without any weapons of your own." Marley sipped again, then put down his cup. "Did I hear you humming a little music afterwards? On the way over here?"

"I, em, I do that—hum music—when I'm nervous," Scrooge said. "I didn't know you could hear it."

"What was the name of it?"

"The music?"

Marley nodded.

"Oh. It was, it was...It was a piano concerto. Mozart. Number fifteen. My sister, Fan, is practicing it now for a competition. I can't stop hearing it, it seems."

"You play well yourself, as I recall," Marley said.

"No. She is the one...And you?"

Scrooge gestured toward the pianoforte. "A Broadwood, isn't it? I didn't know you played."

"I don't," Marley said. "It's just something to have."

Marley said nothing for a time and Scrooge stared into his cup. Six years had passed since Worthy's funeral, since the last time Marley had seen Scrooge. But Scrooge looked the same;

thin and delicate, the only noticeable change being his hair which had gone prematurely white.

"The hack was a powerful-looking brute," Marley said, resuming the conversation so suddenly that Scrooge flinched a little. "Why did you engage him? Are you such a defender of the down-trodden?"

"I'm still a bit shaken actually," Scrooge said. "I don't know as I'm any sort of defender so to speak."

Scrooge moved in his chair as though it were poking him no matter what posture he took. He shrugged his shoulders.

"Well, you know how it can be," Scrooge explained. "You see so much horror and cruelty inflicted upon children these days. Just this morning as I walked, I saw children. Prostitutes and thieves I've no doubt—but children. They were sleeping—under the dry arches of bridges, under porticoes, under sheds and carts, one in a sawpit, several on staircases. Wretched and hideous all of them—and ourselves the more hideous for it. So when I came upon that man...Well..."

Marley sat back in his chair and intertwined his fingers. "It's cruel all around and to everyone, not just to children," he said.

"But to children," Scrooge insisted. Scrooge frowned and straightened up in his chair. "By your own actions, you betray yourself," he declared. "It is you who are the champion of the defenseless."

Marley laughed and shook his head. "No, my dear Scrooge. No, not hardly." He looked straight at Scrooge—neutral and serious-looking, as though about to bid on cards. "If I, or anyone for that matter, were to make it his policy to interfere with the misery of every beaten child, we'd have no time for anything else. And we'd all be carted off to Bridewell for our efforts anyway."

Marley took another sip of tea, then stretched. "I will confess this to you: this morning was a fortunate coincidence of timing. It was an opportunity. Other than yourself and the boy, there were no witnesses. I was in a mood for it. I had the weaponry. I had surprise on my side. In fact, I only wish there were more such opportunities, a larger circle of people one could thrash with impunity."

Scrooge's teacup slipped and clattered in its saucer before he could grip it again.

"You're joking," he said.

Marley ignored the cup and the comment and proceeded with his line of thought.

"But you," Marley said, rubbing his mouth as though puzzling through a riddle. "You are a different matter entirely. You are not a ruffian. And yet you put yourself at risk for a little urchin you didn't know. You could have been murdered. What I wonder now is this: are you so careless of your own interests?"

Scrooge touched the back of his head where it had hit the brick wall.

"This is not an everyday occurrence for me," Scrooge said at last.

"I'm glad to hear it," Marley smiled again. "Now tell me: why are you up and about so early?"

"I was going to work."

"At Imperial still?"

"Yes. It's my custom to arrive a few hours before my time."

"I see," said Marley. "You're ambitious."

Scrooge shifted in his chair again, then looked around and gave the room a sweeping gesture with his arm.

"And you, sir. Your own business. This office. Very impressive. Very much so. In what are you engaged, may I ask?"

"I've secured a seat on the 'Change—"

"The 'Change. In that grand new building? In Capel Court, Bartholomew Lane? My word."

"Don't be so impressed," Marley said. "You'd be surprised how many votes a few pounds can secure. In any event, there are also some properties. There's the management of mortgages and other loans. It's been a prosperous undertaking, I'll admit. Now I'm advised that I should hire or retire."

Marley rose and walked the length of the parlor, then its width, then back.

"Tell me, Mr. Scrooge are you prospering? Are you... advancing at Imperial?"

Scrooge reddened. "Yes, well... I'm in the counting house now, sir."

"I see."

"There will be more opportunities soon," Scrooge eagerly insisted. "I'm sure of it. The company is growing rapidly."

Marley poured more tea for Scrooge and himself.

"*Continues* to grow rapidly, you might have said," Marley corrected. "Have you a family?"

"Just myself and my sister, Fan," Scrooge said. "Fan is my blessing," he added. "She is as fine a woman, as fine a human being as I'll ever know."

Scrooge nodded toward the Broadwood. "If you really want to hear an instrument like that played the way it should, you should hear my Fan."

"Indeed."

Scrooge smiled. "Fan won second prize at the King's fete last year and the Regent himself presented it to her." Scrooge nodded as if to affirm his own story. "I shall be an uncle one day I expect. Fan is married now. Oh, and of course there's my Alice. My fiancee. She's a saint on earth, I swear it. Alice Campbell. She is a most kind woman. When the time comes, I hope that Alice and I—"

"What I meant to ask," Marley interrupted. "And pardon me for being blunt, was how will you care for a family when you are so negligent about your own well-being."

"Sir? You mean this morning?"

Marley shook his head.

"Imperial Tradings' valuation has increased at a rate of thirty percent over each of the last three years. It is one of my investments so I'm aware of that. Meanwhile, in the same period of time you've moved from head clerk to the counting house, an increase to you of what—two more shillings a week? The wolves should be at your door any moment."

Scrooge stood up. "Excuse me, sir. I'm sorry I don't meet your—"

"Sit, sit," Marley said. "Stop. Don't take it that way. I simply meant to say there are opportunities out there for a diligent man of your background. You might consider a smaller company, one with more room to grow—where you can grow with it. Own stock in it. Who knows where it could lead?"

"I'm sorry," said Scrooge, sitting down again. "It's simply that I've been with Imperial for several years now. There's a loyalty that one builds to one's firm, an obligation."

"Humbug," Marley laughed. "You left Fezziwig didn't you? For a greater opportunity at Imperial."

Scrooge looked at the carved flowers on the chairs.

"You had the right idea," Marley went on. "Just the wrong company. Imperial was too large already. Loyalty. Believe me, your loyalty will not be returned. The only company that's loyal to its employee is the one owned by that employee. Money is the only reason we toil, Mr. Scrooge. Money and money alone will protect you from those who would do you harm—or, for that matter, enable you to harm—with impunity—those you think warrant it."

"But no one wants to harm me," Scrooge declared.

Marley's voice dropped lowered in pitch.

"Then God will," he said. "In which event you'll need all

the money you can get."

Scrooge stole a glance at the wall clock near the pulpit-desk.

"I should go," he said, rising out of his chair again. "I do like to be early. Thank you for tea. And thank you for intervening out there."

Marley rose, smiled and took Scrooge's hand.

"Both were a pleasure. Do think about what I said."

"Yes sir, I shall," said Scrooge. He pulled his coat from the rack and bunched the old garment under his arm and moved toward the entrance. Marley stepped past him in order to open the door for his guest.

"A firm like this one, for example," Marley said as Scrooge stepped out. "Might pay someone such as yourself double what you're making now."

Scrooge stopped, one foot out the door, one foot in. "Sir?"

"Well you'll be late now, Mr. Scrooge. We shall talk again."

Scrooge looked at Marley for several moments, seeming not to know what to say. Then he nodded and said, "Yes, that would be excellent."

Scrooge left, walking more slowly than he had before.

Fog, lighted a soft, dark grey by the coming sun, slid across the street. Marley stood at the threshold and watched Scrooge disappear into the cloud. Then he went back inside his offices and began to envision where Scrooge would work.

He'd have Scrooge to deal with the clients, use Scrooge as an intermediary, a shield from people. In time, he might even rename the firm—Scrooge & Marley—so that clients would believe themselves in the presence of the principal partner. Yes, it would work perfectly.

*****

In the fourth year of Scrooge & Marley, on Christmas Eve,

Marley left his house for a late walk. He started after midnight since he could be sure no people would crowd the streets at that hour.

Despite Scrooge handling the clients, the firm's other commitments pressed upon Marley such that he could find the silence and solitude he craved only late at night, during his walks.

Marley moved along the quiet streets lost in waking dreams of his boyhood and long-ago talks with his brother. He remembered staring at the skies with Ezra, out in the cold, the last Christmas Eve that ever mattered.

Marley drifted within his memories until a dog's bark snapped through the darkness, startling him.

Marley stopped and turned, half-expecting the pursuit of hounds. But nothing appeared: the dog had been just some stray down some distant alley.

A comet hung in the sky above. Marley noticed it for the first time. Some said it signified the imminent end of the world, the Second Coming, but to Marley it looked like just another blurry star, its light fanning out widely and diffusing at its outer end, giving the impression of an aperture stabbed in the night through which light spilled forth, wasteful as coins falling from a purse.

"It's ghosts."

A scratchy voice clawed toward Marley from a dark doorway, causing him to jump back. He looked into the shadows and found an old woman sitting inside a pile of dirty rags and quilts, her back braced on one side of the passage and her feet on the other, in place for the night.

"In the dark of winter they try to get home, but they can't unless it's for something special," the hag muttered. "Sometimes they try anyway." She pointed at the comet. "But then they burn."

The old woman howled a laugh.

Marley hurried away from the crone, heading toward his offices and the safe certainty of ledgers, lines, and inarguable numbers.

A block away Marley could see his building. A light shone through the window. When he reached the threshold, Marley touched the door. It swung open freely.

Marley stepped inside, then drew a sharp, sudden breath; shocked to see his partner, Scrooge, hunched over a litter basket on his hands and knees, vomiting.

The contents of Scrooge's office: lamps, papers, inkwells, quills, coat rack and ledgers lay scattered across the floor. Splashes of ink bled slowly down the windows, resembling the curtains of a funeral coach. A bottle of whisky lay on its side, empty.

Marley approached Scrooge slowly, the way one approaches an injured animal that might lash out. Marley knelt next to his partner and put a hand to his shoulder. A sweet scent of whisky could be discerned beyond the bile.

Scrooge seemed not to notice the hand at first. Then he raised his head sideways and looked at Marley. A gash near Scrooge's left eye winked bloody trails down that side of his face. Scrooge wiped his mouth with the sleeve of one arm and pushed himself up with the other.

"She's dead," Scrooge sobbed.

Marley took Scrooge under the arms and lifted him into a chair. Then he gave Scrooge a handkerchief and disappeared into his own study.

Marley returned with a pitcher of water and a full glass which he handed to Scrooge.

"Drink," Marley said.

Then Marley pulled up another chair for himself and, with his foot, slid the litter basket closer to Scrooge. Scrooge held the water with both hands, drank, and threw up again.

"Drink again," Marley said.

Scrooge did and this time held it down. Marley produced another handkerchief and dabbed away the blood from Scrooge's wounds, then pressed the cloth against them.

"Hold this here," Marley commanded as he lifted Scrooge's hand to the bandage.

"She had a son. As if the world needs more." Scrooge slurred his words and wept at the same time.

"It killed her." Scrooge started to reel but put his hands on his knees and locked his arms for support.

"We were separated when I was ten," he blubbered. "I was sent away. Fan stayed at home. Fan was the only one to write. She wrote every day. The only one to visit me. And when she visited...oh, the music..."

Scrooge stared unfocused at the wall then after a time, resumed.

"There's no god," he said. "There's only a devil-god. He killed her. God, the devil. Killed her while she gave birth—on Christmas Eve—right before my eyes..."

Scrooge lifted his head toward the ceiling and raised a fist clenched white with pressure.

"I curse God in his heaven. I want none of Him." Scrooge spat, then passed out.

"I quite agree," said Marley, who then set to putting the office back in order.

Solace Home

December 24, 1819
London

Freezing rain rattled the roof of Scrooge & Marley. The hardened pellets sounded like the nails of panicked vermin trying to scratch their way into shelter. Outside, the sleet painted the dark streets with glassy strokes of ice, making it nearly impossible for passersby to move without slipping and falling. Few dared the feat if they could avoid it. Many of the shops which stayed open late for the Christmas trade had already closed. Scrooge & Marley, however, remained open.

The office usually functioned in perfect silence, still as a graveyard, disturbed only by the rustle of papers. But this night's storm rumbled against the panes as though the guns of heaven lay siege to the place.

Scrooge sat in Marley's office, opposite his partner.

"Bloody hell," Marley swore, looking upward toward the din on the roof. "Can you hear me above all this?" he shouted.

Scrooge nodded that he could, and Marley returned to the document before him.

"The census indicates that people just keep coming," Marley declared, putting down the papers and shaking his head. He coughed hard. When he recovered, he continued. "This city is filling to the rafters. That can only be good for us."

Scrooge eyed his partner coolly.

"You look ill," Scrooge said, more critical than compassionate.

"What does that have to do with anything?"

"Nothing," Scrooge admitted.

"I'm well enough," Marley snapped.

Marley knew how he looked. Though only six years Scrooge's senior, Marley, at forty-three, looked like he could be Scrooge's father. The deterioration of his appearance had caused Marley to quit consulting mirrors for the past year. It vexed him to see how his cheeks and jowls drooped and how dark moons sagged below his eyes. When he walked, he stooped, losing much of his height. Except for the sides of his head, his hair had vanished. And lately he'd developed a wet, hacking growl of a cough that made people turn away.

Still, Marley remained aware that he could intimidate people with only a look. He believed himself still capable of throttling an adversary and he knew how to project that belief through his hard eyes and the powerful appearance of his hands.

Scrooge stared at Marley's hands as if meditating upon their abilities.

"The increase in population is good only if we take advantage of it," Scrooge said, returning to the subject. "But we're not. We're under-pricing. We should be getting a third again more for each dwelling. All the rents should be increased thirty-three percent right now, just to match the market. More if we expect to exceed it."

"Allow me to be devil's advocate," Marley said. "There would be no great gain if the tenants couldn't pay." He coughed again. "Many industries haven't recovered yet. Wages are down."

Scrooge slowly pushed air from his mouth so his lips fluttered. "If they can't pay, they can leave. Others will pay."

Marley looked at the census figures again. He spoke softly as though to himself. "A million newcomers to London. The odds are with us, Mr. Scrooge." Then he handed the documents back. "Cratchit can draft the notice. Have him prepare eviction papers while he's at it; no doubt there will be need for them."

Scrooge gathered the papers, nodded toward Marley, then left the room, closing the door behind him.

Marley rose from his desk after Scrooge left and slipped from his office to the rail overlooking the main floor. He'd noticed a growing impertinence in Scrooge's tone lately and found it troubling. Scrooge should be grateful for his help in business; instead, Scrooge seemed resentful—much the way Marley had resented Worthy. No, it isn't the same, Marley thought, correcting himself.

He moved to a corner and watched Scrooge carry out his instructions.

Bob Cratchit, a small, skittish man, with bushy sideburns and cheeks like a squirrel, approached Scrooge the moment Scrooge stepped onto the lower floor.

"A gentleman here to see you, sir," Cratchit said. His words turned into visible steam in the brittle office air.

Scrooge frowned.

"Who is it?"

"He said he represents a local concern of businesses."

"Next time get a name and particulars," Scrooge said. Then he shook his head. "Well, I suppose you'll have to show him in. I'll be in my office."

Cratchit stepped away, then returned with a pleasant-looking gentleman. The man held a tall, beaver hat in his hands but had not removed his coat, now wet with melting sleet. A wool scarf remained wrapped close around his neck.

"Merry Christmas, sir," the man said, offering his hand. "Have I the pleasure of addressing Mr. Scrooge or Mr. Marley?"

Scrooge ignored the hand.

"There's little difference," he said. "Who are you?"

The man flushed. "Forgive me. My credentials...Is Mr. Sc—?

"I am Scrooge."

"A pleasure, sir," said the visitor. "I shall not keep you long. A few of us are raising funds for a home, for those who now suffer on the streets. Streets such as there are tonight." The man raised his eyes toward the clatter of hard rain on the roof. "These streets are full of suffering indeed. Our hope is that, by this time next Christmas, some of the destitute will have a place of warmth and food and shelter from the miseries of winter. We hope to call it 'The Solace Home.'" The man smiled proudly at the concept and its name.

Scrooge looked on without reaction.

"And...?" Scrooge asked.

"And what sir?"

"And what has that to do with me?"

"We thought you might wish to participate," the visitor said, surprised that he'd not been clear. "I am given to understand you have occasion to celebrate your fifth year in business this very month. What better way to mark your success? A donation would be most welcome and it could, I believe, even save a life—especially when the winters can be so harsh, as you see tonight."

While the man spoke, Marley quietly descended the stairs.

"Your contribution could make life bearable for the less fortunate," the solicitor pressed.

"Life is unbearable. That is its nature," Scrooge replied. "Besides, one needn't live on the street. There are workhouses for those who will work and prisons for those who will not."

"And both send many to their graves," the man objected.

"Then so be it," said Scrooge. "A remedy to the surplus

population."

Marley's voice made the men start.

"Oh heaven forbid," Marley said, reaching the bottom of the stairs and lifting his coat from a wall peg. He stared at the visitor for a moment, then addressed him in an overly-cordial voice: the type of voice that conveys anything but cordiality.

"We are often accosted by venture mendicants," Marley said to the man. "You wouldn't be one of those would you? Raising funds for your own special industry: the poor? I myself have never heard of any person rising from the oppression of charity to make a place for himself in society, nor of any families being held together by such intervention. They certainly provided no help to me; yet I've managed. I am Jacob Marley," he added.

"Merry Christmas, sir," said the gentleman, taken aback. "I am here simply to ask that you join our group in an effort to help the poor."

"I would hate to think that people were dying in the streets," Marley said. "After all, it is the excess in population that keeps us in business. Mr. Scrooge and I were just discussing that. However, the census shows that we will have an excess for quite a long time.

"As for donations, the 'redistribution' of wealth, well... It's just never enough is it? Give a poor man a little money and he wants more. Raise him to the middle class and he wants to be in the upper. Raise him to the upper and he wants to be royalty and so on. We are all moved by greed, sir: I see no reason to favor one greedy type over another—especially to favor the incompetent. Indeed, that's even less reason for it.

"Still, we are compelled to do so by the Crown. We pay for parish workhouses through The Poor Rate. The Crown has, in effect, already extracted such donations from us all. And yet you say it's not enough. You see: it never is, is it?"

"But, sir," the gentleman persisted. "These people have lived such brutal lives—"

Marley's eyes narrowed. "So have I. It is a brutal world. In my experience the poor are no less brutal—moreso if it comes to that—than any others. You find the lowest common denominators among the poor. I see no reason to subsidize them. Good evening."

"You can't be serious," the gentleman said.

Marley held his hands in front of him, close together like a chained man. "We regret it, sir, but our hands are fettered."

"I doubt that, sir." The gentleman put on his hat.

Marley glared at the man, but spoke evenly. "Your doubts—your opinions—are neither here nor there," he said.

The gentleman looked away from Marley and walked to the door. "Merry Christmas," he said, then left.

When the door closed behind the visitor, Scrooge turned to Marley. "Why do you waste your time talking to such people?" he demanded.

Marley spoke in a conspiratorial tone. "One day there will be advantages for companies that appear, at least, to champion the poor. If we live to see that day, I intend to profit from it. Until then it pleases me to confront the sanctimonious bastards."

"We should live so long that 'profligate' comes to mean 'profit,'" Scrooge scoffed.

Marley jabbed a hand into a glove. "And perhaps we shall not," he said. "Everyone has to die, Mr. Scrooge."

Marley coughed hard and dragged a handkerchief across his lips. Then he threw a scarf around his neck, pulled on his coat and left the premises, heading into a cold, black sleet that looked as if it would fall forever.

Ghost

December 24, 1835
London

A man in a black suit stands in a field across from Marley. The man looms tall and broad-shouldered and so large that he blots out Marley's view of the winter horizon. The figure's long hair lays upon huge shoulders, black and streaked with white, his face obscured by a veil of smoke.

The man speaks in a low, deep voice, but Marley hears only a humming sound.

Marley feels the heat of fever on his face and behind his eyes. He sees a dappled pattern of black and white specks that pulse to different sizes, swell to enormous thicknesses, then subside. He has a strange sensation that sound and dimension conspire against him. He sees, hears, and feels the quality of Thin. Thin compresses the universe: all of it, its entire heavy mass crushed together into something like a needle, only more tiny, sharp, infinitely and unbearably fine. The accompanying sound for Thin shrieks high and shrill and climbs to ever-sharper registers until, at the peak of its high, tight, and piercing scream, the universe reverses and explodes outward in all directions becoming Thick: loud, round, pushing everything away in a rush that collapses and suffocates all before it. Vast balls of sound vibrate long, deep, low and loud.

The fever alternates in this way for several minutes or eons and each turning brings a terror of anticipation, followed by the sudden shock of change.

Marley throws off his coverings. Soon he shivers again.

He comes to believe himself alone in his study, a cold and dark place. He inspects the books on the wall. He cannot make out their titles and squints his eyes. Then he realizes that the book-shelves have vanished; they've become a wall of rock and ice. A mine. No, he corrects, a cave. A cave of ice.

Its smooth, glassy walls glow from within. They emit an eerie blue-green shimmer as though phosphorescent particles floated in the water before it froze. The light shows the cave descending on a gradual slope, turning at one point in the tight spiral of a nautilus.

Smooth, glowing ice makes up the walls and ceiling, forming a seamless arch, slick and perfect as the inside of a shell and it twists gently downward following the floor's corkscrew direction. He moves slowly, examining the walls, running his hands along them. He makes two turns before the spiraling tunnel becomes level and straight.

One step into the new passage he sees an animal. A huge hunting dog of the type used to track fugitives. Its shadow spreads across the slick wall, wavering in the odd light. Marley views the chopped ears and long tail and then the rest of it: shining, dap-pled, black-white hide, rippling musculature, huge paws, muzzle pulled back over its teeth. It looks down at Marley with eyes black as graves at night. It is entombed in the ice.

To his right, another animal, a ferret, snarls, similarly encased in the ice wall. On both sides and even in the ceiling of the passage, other sealed forms of life hang: scores of plants and animals suspended behind the freeze. Poplars and elms bud green beneath the ice. Sparrows and jays stop, caught and hardened in mid-flight. Lambs, dogs and ducks halt, all frozen in the middle of life, yet they appear vital despite being so deeply buried.

The passage widens, opening onto a balcony-like shelf posi-tioned above a vast open chamber whose ice walls below shine even more brightly than those of the tunnels.

Marley stands next to a row of thick stalactites and looks down into the chamber. Opposite him, across the open chamber, a massive wall of ice, perfectly flat and sheer like an enormous, thick plate of blue glass reveals a young woman ensheathed behind its clear wall.

The girl stands exquisitely beautiful; naked, except for a necklace of small white flowers around her neck. Marley stares and remains still, as if, for the moment, he too is locked in the ice. The woman's long hair sparkles like sun reflected off water and would reach her calves had it not frozen in an upward flow as it might if held aloft in a strong breeze. Her arms hang down, pressed forward with the palms up as if having just bestowed a gift. A light tan colors her skin; her full mouth spreads like a flower, ruddy, unaffected by the cold. Her small round breasts stand above the arch of her rib cage, high above her pinched waist and wide hips. Her eyes shine green like spring grass. They look straight across the chamber at Marley.

Brigid, he thinks.

Then he sees others. Other women, young and old; women he recognizes: Molly and Bess and whores whose names he cannot recall. Children: boys and girls from the days before the mines, playmates, now iced, checked in mid-jump. Men with fiddles and pipes, men and women, their arms locked together, coattails and hems splayed outward dancing in a motionless centrifuge.

There on the next wall, Bill Worthy holds a dice box in his hand, dice cast from it, now hanging in the air. Marley recognizes clerks and washerwomen. Mrs. Dilber stands there, her hands on her thighs; she bends over in a laugh that Marley cannot remember ever having heard. Scrooge, a young man now with ink-black hair, a mere clerk, sits with his hands poised over a piano and...and Ezra, a boy of thirteen, sits next to him.

Impossible, but Marley sees Ezra's lips move, speaking easily, fluently; Ezra talks with Scrooge and the two laugh like old friends, like brothers. They turn and play a duet that Marley cannot hear.

Then all of the frozen figures move: dancers twirl, skirts revolve and flare, fiddlers' bows saw furiously—though Marley cannot hear their sounds. The children run and laugh; Marley takes a step toward them, but stops.

All the figures turn to look at him then. They laugh. They laugh at him.

He feels the cold. He shivers and turns to run. Get out of the cave. He runs now, but the cold travels faster. His legs ache with the cold and become numb. The opening of the cave sits impossibly far away. He becomes heavy and feels as if a great chain drags him down into the ice.

*****

"Visitor 'ere t' see you, sir," said Mrs. Dilber, as she backed into the room. The housekeeper held a tray with a steaming bowl of porridge and did not have the use of her hands. The man with her did not help with door, but followed her in.

Traces of melting snow slipped down the front of his coat. He looked around the room before approaching the bedside. Then the visitor took off his tall hat and flung the remaining snow from it. The crown of white hair encircling his head stretched backward in streaks like snow in a blizzard, as did his brows. His features appeared sharp as ice, from his icicle-shaped nose and craggy chin to his shrivelled cheek and reddened eyes.

"Mr. Scrooge is here, sir," Mrs. Dilber announced, trying to make the news sound like an occasion for joy.

"Leave us," Scrooge said to the woman without looking at her.

"Let me just set this bowl out for him before I go, sir."

Scrooge looked at the housekeeper and cocked his head. "Porridge? A great deal of good that will do at this stage. Go."

Mrs. Dilber ducked as though to avoid a blow and left Scrooge alone with Marley.

Scrooge took off his gloves and removed his overcoat, then advanced to the bedside and looked down coolly on his colleague of some thirty years.

"So, Jacob. Are they treating you well? Last rites and all that?"

Marley reached for Scrooge.

"Beware," he whispered.

"Beware? Beware of what?"

"Be—" But Marley stopped and just shook his head.

Scrooge waited, but Marley did not continue.

"Well then," said Scrooge, producing some papers from his suitcoat and also withdrawing a pair of spectacles and placing them on his nose. "There are a few items of business left to transact. These papers, Jacob, reflect and confirm our relationship; that is, they conclude the various reciprocal legal arrangements that we have defined between ourselves over these many years. It is prudent, however, to add one more document to the group. This confirms that we have been partners in the firm of Scrooge & Marley for twenty years, that we are each other's sole-executor, administrator, assign, beneficiary, et cetera, et cetera. If you would just initial here..."

Marley did not look at the document but instead stared into Scrooge's eyes.

Scrooge turned away from Marley and retrieved a pen from the nightstand. He placed the pen in Marley's hand and helped Marley make a scrawl on the document.

"There," said Scrooge once the awkward process ended.

Marley continued to stare at Scrooge.

The sound of the great clock grew louder, like heavy boots stepping off the space between the two men.

"Well, now, Jacob..." Scrooge looked toward the ceiling as

if there he would find something more to say.

"You might take some comfort, Jacob, that after you are gone the name of the firm will not change. That should be some consolation, eh? 'Scrooge & Marley' will exist a very long time."

Marley wet his lips with his tongue and tried to speak. Scrooge leaned closer.

"Yes? What is it? Speak up," Scrooge said, sounding annoyed.

Marley's eyes fluttered. Words swirled in his mind, ones he would chose if he could only capture them, but they skirted past him like coquettes at a dance: important, vital, but teasing and unattainable.

Marley's search for words stopped: interrupted by a sudden, chillingly familiar voice, a voice coming to him from far in his past, or perhaps deep in his future. The voice resounded low, powerful and ominous.

"Jacob," it echoed slowly. "When the time comes—and it is soon at hand—how will you chose?"

Marley reached out and grabbed Scrooge's hand.

"Ghosts," Marley sputtered. "A ghost."

When Scrooge heard the word "ghost" he stepped backward from the bed, freeing himself of Marley's grasp. The skin on Scrooge's neck bristled and Marley's single-word pronouncement seemed suspended, a threat hanging in the hollow air. The sound of it lingered in the room as Marley's hand fell to the bed.

Book Two:
Marley's Ghost

Pooka

Snow swirled upward in spirals toward the pale red twilight overhead. Individual snowflakes stood out as they whirled close to the ghost's face, their patterns red against the dim distances. The drifting particles rose and wheeled like hot ash from a chimney or like the spirits of the dead are said to rise from their graves.

Sometimes the wind did not lift the snow but only twisted it in low, tight frenzies of dance. Other times the wind blew straight, low and level, stampeding the snow in one direction.

The cold made the ghost's face tingle and go numb such that he believed he could not speak or cry out if called upon do to so.

The ghost turned his back toward the chilly gusts and watched the snow rush away from him, seeing an illusion of himself being drawn backwards.

Marley's ghost had been walking for what seemed like weeks or years. Always in the dim, red light, in the cold. He shivered, moving in the vague hope of change.

Marley saw only the indistinct shapes of drifts before him: lighted as though by a quarter moon smothered in clouds; he saw just enough to know that nothing lay immediately ahead or behind: only a blank landscape of cold and eerie red light. The cold penetrated him. He felt that streams of icy water ran in place of his blood; he could feel his own veins: cold and painful, but he could endure that. He wondered, however, if he could endure the muted light and the desperate suffocation it seemed to carry. Dark red, it blotted out all other colors. The murk felt like a heavy burden pressing down upon him.

A grating, clattering, metal sound trailed Marley: a recalcitrant weight pulled at his guts. He looked over his shoulder hoping that the drag would disappear; but it remained. A thick, iron chain clung to his waist.

The chain took several turns around his hips, snaked down his backside and draped along the ground behind him, accumulating clods of dragged snow which he pulled like a plow. The chain carried various articles fastened to its links: iron renderings of pick axes, coal bricks, hooded clothing, playing cards, drillers' spikes, a hangman's knot, cash-boxes, keys, padlocks, pistols, whistles, ledgers and purses.

Marley gasped for breath then hunched his shoulders forward and marched on. He pulled his coat collar more tightly around his neck though it did no good. The wind cut through him as though he walked naked. He looked at the sleeves of his coat and wondered how he came by the garment. In his last memory of life, he'd been in bedclothes. Now he found himself in his favorite suit: a brown, cutaway with a brown waistcoat, a white blouse and high collar, a thin black cravat, tan tights, and boots.

When he first regained awareness of himself, Marley stared at his hands, shocked and astonished at their translucence and their aura of purple-blue light. He could see the surfaces of his coat sleeves and his hands, but he could also see the ground below them. He turned his hands over and over, from one side to the next; and each time witnessed the same effect.

Since then he'd stopped noticing himself altogether. In the immeasurable time since he'd started walking, Marley could only concentrate on the harsh winds, the labor of towing the chain, and the oppressive redness surrounding him. He shivered, but whether from cold or fear he could not tell.

At first, Marley tried to escape the panic of the red dark by concentrating on mathematical theories and proofs. In life, such calculations made the world vanish: even when caught on the streets within a swarm of people, Marley could calculate himself into a state of isolation otherwise not available outside his house or office. But here the cold gouged at his face and the weight of the uneven light crushed any comfort from his mind, returning him always to face the featureless cold.

He slapped his arms against his sides to no use. Looking ahead, following the snapping wind into the endless frozen plain before him, Marley trudged ahead.

"Say this is not for all time," Marley said aloud. But a gust wiped the words from his mouth and then twisted and threw them echoing against the vapors until they became a distorted cry that made him bow his head between his shoulders and shudder.

Then suddenly the wind stopped. A dim light grew slowly above him emanating from a pale globe the size and shape of the moon but with none of its cratered markings.

Marley cowered and raised his arms to his face. Then hesitantly, he peeked at the red circle—the ghost-moon—and stared at it until the wind returned and blew the sky closed again. The ghost-moon disappeared but some of its light remained, recreating the dim twilight from before, something not quite black.

Marley moved again: not for any reason he could name, but rather because he could not stop. In the streaming lines of snow, Marley thought he saw Scrooge, or at least the fluttering of Scrooge's wild, white hair. But that impression vanished in an instant. In its place came the remembered, troubling sensation of Scrooge's ingratitude. Marley felt anger that transformed into something like regret.

The odd light of the ghost-moon put him in a peculiar state of mind. He could not say why, but now it occurred to him that Scrooge, who at first had reminded him of Ezra, had become, instead, a replica of himself—a cold, bitter, solitary, wasted shell.

My doing, Marley whispered. Hell is a cold place after all.

After a long time of pushing against the snow and being alternately lashed or abandoned by fierce winds, Marley let his eyelids fall to where they fluttered, not quite closed; his head dropped, making him able to see just glimpses of his own boot toes, their black tips appearing momentarily against the red snow, then disappearing in an hypnotic rhythm.

The unrelenting burden of the heavy chain had become, by now, so much a part of his existence that, though he suffered their effects, Marley scarcely noticed the links themselves. His attention glided on the red-black, black-red beat of his boots until he became unaware of even that.

When almost beyond himself, a deep guttural sound snapped him to attention. The sound rolled, familiar and haunting such that Marley pictured the animal even before he saw it: a dog, a hound of some sort, like one of the many that chased him through the night so long ago outside the mines, part of the howling pack. This one had found him at last.

Past the steamy, white veil of his own breath, Marley saw the animal. It stood large and wolfen: a long, narrow body with high shoulders that would be level with a man's hips. It had a dagger face and bright, yellow eyes set deep within thick, coal-black fur. The animal loped easily in the ghost's direction.

Marley stopped and looked around for a weapon or at least some cover but the land offered nothing. The wolf-dog slowed to a walk. Marley could not move; he imagined that this would be the start of the eternal torments promised him by the Church, the rending of flesh without the relief of death.

The wolf stopped ten feet away from the ghost and sniffed the air. Then it sat on its haunches. The bluish-purple outline around the ghost flickered unsteadily. After a long period of study the animal spoke.

"What do you fear?" it asked in a refined voice.

Marley wavered on his feet as though on the deck of a pitching ship. He took a step backward to prevent a fall.

The wolf looked away toward the horizon as if bored, then turned back to the ghost.

"Follow me," it growled.

Marley did not stir.

The wolf rose and, in one stride, put its muzzle so close to the ghost's forehead that Marley could feel its hot, wet breath on his eyebrows. The wolf growled again, though softly this time.

"Come with me *now*."

The animal turned and trotted away and Marley followed unsteadily, laboring against both the chain and his fear.

Within their first few steps, the blank landscape changed; various shapes emerged giving a slowly-developing perspective to the dead world.

The first change looked like a stroke of ink being lazily dragged across red paper. It originated to their left, from below a thick bank of fog, and moved in serpentine bends toward their right. Marley watched the line form and then loop back, outlining a horseshoe shape. The line moved like a river and, indeed, when Marley looked closely, it became a river, running through a flat land perhaps two hundred feet below himself and the animal.

At the same time, gnarled, bare trees cracked through the surface as though from graves; their bony branches raised like hands toward heaven begging for answers. At the open end of the river's horseshoe, where the block of fog stopped, two large outcrops of rock appeared and formed a wedge-like wall pointed away from the water. At the opposite end, where the river double-backed to enclose the tongue of land, a small, stone bridge arched over the water. Thick tangles of holly spread along the river's banks: its green and red the only colors anywhere.

"It's time to run," the wolf said. Then it vanished.

Marley spun right and left to see where the animal had gone, but instead of finding the wolf, Marley found himself suddenly standing on the flat land near the fog bank at the open end of the river. The snow came up to his knees. Fog loomed above him like a colossal wall a hundred feet high and so steep that, if not vapor, it would have toppled upon him like a breaking wave. It moved slowly toward him.

Marley tried to step away from the cloud but could not lift his feet higher than the crusty top layer of snow. He had to thrust his foot and shin hard against the snow's icy, top edge to make any progress: even then he would sink down again, just inches from where he began. Only gradually did he put any space between himself and the shadowy wall.

At one point, Marley looked over his shoulder. The towering mist wafted behind him in the airy motions of a magician. Marley thought he heard voices: soft at first, then growing within the fog—a rising tide of yells, howls, whoops, and curses, a confusion of languages. Marley could not pick out individual words; all of them blended into a frenzied staccato of war cries, a Babel of something savage. To this came a deep, fast beat, a pounding like glass being crushed repeatedly by an enormous weight: the fast tread of men charging through iced snow. The noise grew to what seemed an impossible volume and headed toward him.

A familiar chill writhed along the ghost's core. Marley

began to run. His legs battered into the jagged snow crust, plunging, dropping, kicking and thrashing, his breaths coming in short gasps, snow thrown about him in small bursts of powder; the chain, like a sea anchor, resisting all progress.

The crusted top of the snow broke like thin glass under his footsteps and Marley felt the sensation of his shins being torn as he pulled his feet upward from the softer snow underneath. Marley looked over his shoulder once and tripped, crashing face-forward into the crust but he lifted himself up again and bolted forward. His movements jerked unevenly, his body unable to keep up with his intentions. Every five or six steps he would look back and nearly lose his balance. Halfway to the bridge, he saw the pursuit.

The curtain of fog waffled and then flew apart, slashed all across its breadth by hundreds of men, pitching forward like hounds. The men appeared ragged, barefoot, wounded and disheveled, but they bore arms. They carried pikes, short swords, clubs and axes which they flailed over their heads recklessly close to each other. No one led the group; it simply poured, undirected and inexhaustible, from the fog. Snow exploded before it like an avalanche.

Marley ran harder and then reached an area of packed snow and bolted toward the bridge. He covered ground quickly and reached the foot of the bridge in just a few moments.

Then the bridge disappeared. Not washed away or collapsed; just vanished, no longer existent. Marley looked at the open river and felt himself becoming numb. He turned slowly. The horde still plunged after him, nearly out of the deep snow. Hundreds of arms drew back: blades, clubs and spears raised to strike.

"What do you think?" said the wolf.

A large thicket had sprung up and the wolf sat within the protection of its canopy.

"Come in," the beast ordered.

Despite the fearsome look of the animal, Marley hurried through an opening in the thorns, ducking to avoid the spikes, and huddled near the creature, his knees drawn close to his chest. Marley looked out from the enclosure, half-expecting the mad horde to trample them. But incredibly, Marley and the animal now sat on the hillside again, looking down to the river-land below.

From his new vantage, Marley could see the whole snowfield. The barbarian horde had disappeared. He could see only one man near the river bank. Marley realized that the man was himself.

The alternate Marley stepped one way then stopped, stepped another then stopped again, looked at the river then looked back anxiously toward the distant wall of fog.

Marley felt dizzy and put a hand to his stomach.

"What is happening down there? Who were those men? Why are we here? Who is that by the river? What are you?"

The opening between the wolf's large jaws split back toward its ears in an eerie expression similar to a smile.

"I'm a pooka," the animal said. It nodded its muzzle toward the river. "That's you."

Marley looked back to the river in time to see the man—himself—dive under its surface. Marley watched the water for a long time, but the figure never reappeared. The pooka tilted its head back and parted its jaws slightly; the skin of its muzzle moved forward, forming a small **O**, then it let forth a long, full, howl. Marley clamped his hands to his ears.

When the howl ended, the pooka stood up within the confines of the thicket and stretched.

"Doesn't it all seem familiar to you? Running? Always running from nothing. Now you're gone."

The animal-spirit looked intently at Marley for several

moments then snarled, "Make Scrooge remember."

Before Marley could respond, the pooka bolted from the thicket and glided to the field below. In a few strides it crossed to the boulders and disappeared into the fog; a high and mournful howl filled the air behind it.

Brighton

Marley moved again through the featureless twilight, through snow that blended, as if by a painter's brush, both the horizon and the sky, obscuring where one began and the other ended and making distances impossible to judge. He walked, it seemed, on the inside of a vast, monochrome globe that rolled like a treadmill under his steps.

Marley looked down at his feet. They pressed inches deep into the snow; red-tinted flakes, looking like crushed gems, lay across the instep of his boots. But just behind him no footprints existed at all, and no trench testified to the effort of dragging his chain. Any mark of his progress, however slight, vanished. Marley resumed walking without purpose.

He thought again of Scrooge and wondered who Scrooge might have become had they not met. Perhaps Scrooge would have adjusted to his sister's death; perhaps he would have played reels on the piano at other Christmas revels.

And what about Ezra and his music? What if Marley *had* found him? Might he not have had the same effect on his brother that he'd had on Scrooge? Destroy the music of Ezra's soul too?

Humbug. Such thoughts came to no good.

Still, Marley anguished both within and without.

The strong wind pushed the ghost ahead, the way a jailer shoves a prisoner—faster than a man can walk—and caused him to stumble and trip forward. Marley regained his footing and looked ahead. A small stone structure sat in the distance: dark grey walls supported a thatched roof; a yellow light shone from its two windows.

Marley approached the building cautiously. He did not knock on the door at first. Instead, he moved to a window and looked inside.

An old gentleman sat in a stuffed, tapestried armchair near the inn's only fire, filling a long-stemmed pipe with dark, narrow leaves. The man meticulously examined each flake, stem and black petal of tobacco before placing it at the edge of his bowl, nudging it in, then pressing it firmly to the bottom with his long-nailed fingers.

The flickering firelight behind the man cast the shadows of his broad shoulders, neck, beard and mane onto the wooden floor and onto the white-washed stone walls upon which they bent upward to the roof timbers. With every jump of the shadows, something new would be lighted and then extinguished. Here a copper pot hanging in the hearth; there a long, plank table; here a book; there a floor clock with a glass door and brass weights, its pendulum stopped, its hands at midnight. The shadows of those objects arched, writhed and danced as though alive, while the gentleman remained still.

The man continued the careful business of filling his pipe, selecting ingredients from several leather pouches on a table loaded with various tools of smoke and fire: flint and stone, sulphur, matches, coal, chips of wood, a gourd pipe, a meerschaum pipe carved in the form of an angel holding up the world. Several thick cigars and a Middle Eastern water-pipe with six snaking arms sat nearby. Marley could see, spread out among this collection, several thick books, as well as a deck of cards, some dominoes and dice.

The man wedged the last leaf into the pipe bowl and tapped it down just so—not so tightly that it cut off the air needed to burn; but tightly enough so that the flame would pass easily from one leaf to the next. With that done, the old gent's long hand drifted over the table, pausing at one implement, then the next, until it settled around the flint and stone. He held both the flint and its striking surface in one hand, leaving his other hand free to hold the awkwardly long pipe. Then quickly, with just a flick of his thumb and little finger, a bright, thick spark rushed from the stone, igniting the tobacco. The man drew heavily from the bowl and leaned far back in his chair so that his eyes looked toward the cobwebs high in the timbers. He blew a smoke-ring that expanded, then formed a reverse **S** from top to bottom. His next ring resembled a white horse that pranced for a time before disintegrating.

He started to bring the pipe stem to his mouth again, but stopped. A grimace spread across his face; the man suddenly stabbed his free hand to his right side. He yelped once, bit his lip, then scratched furiously at spot below his lower right ribs, digging at it as though trying to extract something sharp and hot. His long nails curved into his side; but he did not cry out again. Instead he looked upward, a bitter, scornful expression on his face.

Marley, thinking the man to be in danger, rushed into the inn, his heavy chain crashing behind him.

Once inside, Marley lost sight of the man. He could see only alternating flashes of the hearth's light weaving through the smoky haze. The flickers created a strange kaleidoscope, changing the clouds' colors from grey to orange, to yellow, to white, to black.

The interior of the inn swam in the dense atmosphere of smoke and lay quiet as an empty church at night. The sudden silence, following the relentless uproar of the wind and the man's harsh scream, jarred Marley. He blinked, his eyes smarting and watering in the cloudy air.

Marley worried that the inn itself might be on fire, but no sooner did he have that thought than the smoke suddenly vanished. Marley saw the room clearly. It possessed three hearths, only one alight.

The inn's only other occupant—the old gentleman—sat in the armchair, apparently completely recovered.

"My God," Marley said to himself.

The man in the chair looked much larger than before. Even seated, he towered above Marley; his shoulders extending wider than the chair in which he sat. His hair glimmered both black and white—not grey but instead, alternating stripes of jet black and the most brilliant white—full and long, and cascading over his shoulders like a lion's mane.

But the face spoke of ages. Marley thought it handsome—beautiful even—a strong, straight nose, broad, high cheeks, thick, white eyebrows, a strong brow ridge. The man's skin, however, buckled: leathery and deeply creased. Black lines crossed his forehead, cut downward from either side of his mouth, and radiated from the edges of his dark eyes: eyes which seemed to Marley weary and melancholy.

The old man wore a nearly-luminous, white, hooded cloak with a black lining, over a plain, loosely-cut black suit and white blouse. His trousers tucked into soft, black leather boots which came nearly to his knee.

In what Marley took to be an effect of the flickering light, smoke-stung vision, and his own fatigue, the man's clothing seemed to alternate from rich black to a white so bright it made him squint.

Unlike Marley, the man appeared opaque and solid.

Marley's thoughts came slowly, like those of a man drugged in a dockside tavern and hauled onto a ship at night, who wakes and finds himself at sea, impressed into a completely foreign existence.

"Are you...? Is this your...inn?" Marley muttered.

The old man bowed. "At your service. Let me help you."

The sound of the voice surprised the ghost. The voice did not rasp the hard, ground-down, guttural noise of age but instead sang mellifluously, soft and pleasing as a flute.

"Sit," the man said, gesturing to an armchair near his own. Marley crossed the room, dragging his irons behind him. The heavy links scraped along the wooden floor, clattering like deadened bells or like a ship's anchor chain being hauled across a deck. Marley reached the chair and fell into it.

"You would like tea, I assume. I don't think you're fond of spirits..." The host paused to grin. "Correct?"

Marley nodded.

The old man stood to his full height and the ghost's head tilted backward to view the whole being. Eight feet tall Marley estimated.

"I'll be back with tea," the giant said. He turned to go and Marley did not take his eyes off the figure until it disappeared into a darker part of the inn.

Alone for a moment, Marley looked around, taking in the smoking tools, gambling items and books on the table. One book he recognized, having seen an article about it once: Hermes' *Philosophical Introduction to Christian Theology.*

A floorboard creaked and Marley looked around to see the darkness in the farthest part of the inn billow forward then part like a curtain. Through this veil his host returned, moving gracefully and with little sound. The giant held a tray with a steaming pot of tea and set it down on a small table to the ghost's side. He poured two cups and served Marley, who cradled the cup with both hands, close to his chest, his head bent over it as if in prayer. Marley inhaled the steam slowly.

"My senses are back," he said, almost whispering.

"Extraordinary."

"How so?"

"I just now realized that ever since... ever since... Well, I've not smelled anything nor felt anything other than cold. The tea is wonderful." He sniffed the air. "I can smell your pipe. Vanilla. Vanilla is what I smell."

Suddenly all the questions that had been aching and frozen within the ghost began flooding forward in his mind, creating a disorganized, insistent rush—Where am I? What am I? Who are you? Is this hell? Are we alone here? Are we dead?—so many questions that they overwhelmed his power of speech and his ability to choose among them.

"Sweet as a morning in Eden," the giant said. "I blend it myself. May I fill a pipe for you?"

"No. Thank you," Marley said, rubbing his eyes.

"Do they sting?"

"The smoke was thick."

Before Marley realized it, his host's large fingers lay across his eyelids.

"Don't—" Marley started to say. But before he could finish speaking, the hand withdrew and with it the burning that had plagued his eyes from the moment he'd entered the inn.

"That... that wasn't necessary," Marley protested. He blinked. "Peculiar, though... They feel much better. How did you do that?"

"It is no great trick," the man said, bowing slightly. "Nothing at all."

"Who are you?" Marley asked.

"I am..." The gentleman paused as though he'd forgotten his own name. Then he said, "Brighton."

Marley wanted to ask more but again could not choose where to begin. For a few moments they sat in silence. Then Brighton spoke.

"I would offer you accommodations," he said. "But I know your type. You don't sleep. You don't rest. You are always pushed by winds. Always searching for something..." He waved his hand in the air about his head and looked toward the ceiling. "It must be hellish."

The huge man smiled and stroked his great beard. "What are you searching for, Mr. Marley?"

"I'm . . . I don't quite remember. . ." Marley suddenly felt lost in a maze. "How did you know my name? Are we dead?"

Brighton smiled. "Forgive me. I'd forgotten. The questions. You must have so many. It's hard to know where to begin isn't it? We will get to them though, won't we? One at a time. . . Are we dead? Well, *you* are. You're a ghost, a wandering spirit. Searching for something, I'm sure."

"And you?" Marley said.

"You mean, 'What am I'?" Brighton rephrased. "I am your—for lack of a better term—your shepherd. Your light. Your guide. I am neither dead nor a ghost."

Brighton waved away a cloud of smoke from his face in a gesture that seemed to dismiss the importance of himself as a topic.

"Next you will ask, 'What is this place?' And, 'Why is it so cold?' Yes?"

Marley nodded.

"This is *your* place," Brighton said. "A place largely of your own construction. Your pains and fears: whatever dominated your life. It is winter here and you are isolated because that is the condition to which your soul is accustomed. Except for myself and certain spirits, you are alone here."

Marley looked away. "I had a brother who died before me. Is he here?"

Brighton put a hand to Marley's shoulder for a moment. "You won't see him here. No."

Marley bit his lip and then looked around the room for a second time, now casting about for some distraction, any distraction from the sorrow welling up within him.

On the wall above the central hearth he saw a painting of a fox-hunt: horses and hounds vaulting over a stone wall.

"I saw a dog, a wolf," Marley mumbled.

"Did he talk to you?" Brighton asked.

"Yes."

Brighton nodded. "A pooka, no doubt. He came to you as a dog?"

"A wolf, rather."

"Yes, well, he takes whatever shape suits the occasion—that is, whatever shape he feels suits the occasion. I've seen him sometimes as a man, but a man diminished to a child's proportions. What did he say to you?"

Marley closed his eyes, reconstructing the strange encounter, the pursuit, the animal's long howl. Then his eyes opened suddenly.

"'Make Scrooge remember,'" Marley repeated incredulously. "But what?"

After a time Marley began to shake his head sorrowfully.

"Ebenezer Scrooge was my partner. Because of me, his life is wasted. I admit that. If I could only speak with him now."

Brighton did not stir. He tapped some ashes from his pipe and began preparing a new bowl.

"And what would you say to him, to this Scrooge, if you were to see him again?" Brighton asked carefully.

Marley continued his wistful tone. "I'd warn him about isolation. About the hardening of his soul. About the opportunities he's wasting: opportunities to embrace life, love, sensation, pain, all of it. My lord. He could feel for others, show compassion...We—He has the resources to do it. To live as I did not. To put music into the air."

Brighton looked into his pipe then struck a match.

"By now your partner is a vain and hardened man. He was not much broken up by your passing, I'll wager." Brighton sucked flames into the bowl.

"I doubt any were," Marley admitted. "But Scrooge always listened to me."

Brighton shook his head.

"Not this time, I'm afraid. Shocking as your appearance would be to Mr. Scrooge, I don't believe it would provoke the slightest change in him," the old spirit said.

Brighton held up his hand to forestall any protest from Marley.

"You might be able to show Mr. Scrooge the horrors of *your* situation. You might be able to paint a very fearful picture indeed and frighten the old miser badly. But in the end, it would be *your* problem.

"Mr. Scrooge would persuade himself that your end would not be his own. 'I am not the same sort of person as Jacob Marley,' he would say or: 'My life is not the same as Jacob Marley's. Surely Marley committed some horrible crime, some abomination known only to God that merits such retribution. My life is satisfactory,' he would say. And then he would point out, to his own satisfaction, any number of important differences between you two and thus convince himself that he will not suffer what you do now.

"Besides, you can't shock a mortal with all that sort of information at once: they must first get used to the idea of the supernatural. That's the problem: a ghost is never given leave to linger in Life that long. No. I think an appearance by you would have no effect."

Marley looked down at the dark floor. "I was only wishing," he said.

"Don't despair." Brighton trumpeted. "You have time on

your side. You don't know it yet, but you are more free than you've ever been. Nothing can harm you. Time is your servant. You have a great deal of time—if you wish it—to think of a way to reach your Mr. Scrooge effectively."

Marley looked up, his eyes asquint.

"What do you mean, 'if I wish it'?"

Brighton drew deeply from the pipe and sent a long streamer of smoke high into the rafters.

"Time is relative," he sighed. "You are free from it now. A detached soul like yours can transcend time and place. Forgive me, but if you were a good mathematician you'd know that."

Who or what is this man? Marley wondered again.

"If you wish," Brighton went on. "You may visit the living at any point in their past, present or future. You may visit the future, then return to this moment, or anywhere else. Anywhere you wish. Where time is concerned, there are few restrictions upon you."

Marley shook his head but gestured for Brighton to continue.

"A ghost may *observe* the living world and even speak to it. But a ghost can be seen only once—and only by one mortal. In your case..."

Brighton paused as if making a calculation. "You could be seen seven years—seven mortal years—after your death."

"Why seven?"

Brighton shrugged.

"Planetary cycles. More or less. The moon around the earth, the earth around the sun, the sun around the galaxy, the galaxy around the universe—we all have our different cycles. Seven years is yours."

Brighton paused: then, more to himself than to Marley, said, "You are fortunate. Would that I could be heard or seen by mortals at all...Men do not hear me anymore."

"Scrooge could see me seven years from now?" Marley asked.

"No, not from 'now,'" Brighton corrected. "Seven mortal years from December 24, 1835—that is when you died. 'Now' is something different. We are outside time. 'Now' is any time you wish. You could advance to 1842 and appear to Scrooge immediately if you chose," Brighton said. "But I would not advise it—for the reasons I've already mentioned."

"You said I may not be *seen*—but could I be *heard* by Scrooge before then?" Marley said, intrigued.

Brighton sighed. "Yes, but I would not advise that either. Hearing disembodied voices generally drives mortals mad... Besides, mortals only believe in things they can see. If they only hear something, they doubt their senses or worse, just forget about it.

"Take your time, Mr. Marley. That's what you have in abundance now. Learn what you can. Develop your message. Relax for a little while in my company."

Marley did not speak or move for several moments and Brighton closed his eyes, content to wait.

"Pardon me, but why should I believe you?" Marley said at last.

Surprise splashed across the giant's face then he laughed loud and hard. "Oh-ho-ho. Well, Mr. Marley, ho. I imagine you'll have your proof soon enough. Soon enough."

Brighton's laughed slowed to a chuckle, then he said in a pitying voice. "I'm not the one chained."

Marley looked at the heavy links around his waist and at the motley train of iron artifacts attached to it. He moved his arm as though to lift a section of the chain, then said in a voice almost too weak to hear, "Why am I shackled?"

"You know why," Brighton said. "You forged the chain, link by link in life and wore it then as you do now. It must be quite a burden."

Neither spoke for several minutes. Marley felt as if the chain, even the part resting on the floor, lay coiled with all its enormous weight centered upon his chest. Brighton looked at Marley sadly for a time then suddenly spoke in a cheery manner.

"Mr. Marley. You've no pressing engagements right now. We can agree on that. So let us just become acquainted, shall we? I understand you're a gambler."

Marley licked his lips and swallowed. "No," he said at first, then, "Yes."

"Do you know 'Liar's Dice?'"

"Yes."

Brighton herded several dice into two leather boxes. "Take comfort in the distraction...Don't cheat now." Brighton winked.

Marley raised himself up in his chair as Brighton pushed the table closer to him and handed Marley six dice and a leather box.

"We begin," Brighton said.

The leather boxes thumped the table at the same time. At impact, the dice hidden within the cups made a sound like hail on a roof. Marley looked at his six dice, keeping them hidden from his host: 5-4-4-4-4-2.

"Three fours," said Marley.

Brighton did not look at his dice at first but instead stared into the ghost's eyes. After a long moment, Marley looked away.

"'Three fours,' you say. Why fours I wonder? Do you have many fours? Do you have *any*? Perhaps, I should challenge you right now—risk one of mine—just to learn your ways, hmm? I do like to know these things." Brighton examined his own toss. "Or, I could just bump the bidding to a higher level and see where that takes us..." he added merrily.

Marley stared at the light-and-dark figure before him,

almost mesmerized by the being's presence.

"Three sixes," Brighton declared.

Marley had no sixes, which meant that, of Brighton's dice, at least three were sixes, or Brighton was bluffing. Marley weighed the likelihood: a combination of six things taken three at a time, multiplied by one-sixth to the third, multiplied by five-sixths to the third.

"The probability that you have three or more sixes is one-in-sixteen," Marley said. "Not likely."

Marley lifted his cup.

Brighton smiled and lifted his cup: he'd rolled three sixes indeed.

"You shouldn't doubt me," Brighton teased. "I'm very truthful. Still, the odds compelled you. I know." He said it as though excusing a character fault. "But the game's not really one of mathematics, is it? It is more a question of faith, I think."

Marley removed one of the dice from his group and set it aside.

"Just eleven dice now," Brighton said. "Probabilities change with every roll. But you know that."

During the next several rolls Marley noticed motion in the rafters. At first he thought the motion to be only the wafting of Brighton's smoke in the vacillating firelight but then he clearly saw the feet and legs and arms and heads of men and women.

An audience of ghosts filled the rafters and as Marley looked longer the apparitions became more clear and seemed more familiar. Several thin, young women huddled together and, though dressed in shrouds, seemed to be giggling at a joke. Several businessmen in waistcoats and suits similar to Marley's own, frowned at one another. Dozens of other ghosts filled the ceiling. Some fidgeted, excited as monkeys. Some cowered behind the beams. Many gestured and moved their lips as if trying to speak. But none made an audible sound.

Then Marley gasped and dropped his dice box. Above him crouched a huge man in dust-black work clothes. The man clung to a roof timber with hands as big as shovels. Marley had not seen those hands, nor the broad back nor wide, ruinous face in all these years, now they appeared above him: nearly transparent, outlined in pale blue: the ghost of Gren Sully.

The ghost looked upon Marley with a sad expression that seemed terribly out of place on the traitorous brute. Marley looked away—only to see near Sully's place, Gordy Ferrel hunched behind a rafter as if to hide from Marley's eyes.

All across the ceiling Marley began to recognize other shadows. He saw the narrow, sagging, pasty face of Snedrick, the pederast; and Cowens, the black-robed, spittle-flecked parson from his old church; and Snelling from Hardchapel, whose legs, torso and arms now entwined around a timber like a serpent on a branch. Marley recognized men of business, law, politics, and other criminals.

"I know those people," Marley said, his gaze never leaving the ceiling.

Brighton glanced up, then shrugged. "You would. After all," he said, gesturing toward the structure in general. "This is your creation."

"Why are they mute? Why can't they come down here? Are they real?" Marley asked.

"Everything is real—from a philosophical viewpoint," Brighton said. "As to why the phantoms are mute and apart from us..." Brighton paused and sighed. "That is simply their station. They are a different sort of ghost from you. They are ghosts without a purpose. They searched and wandered, but found nothing they could accomplish; they found no meaning for themselves..." Brighton then wriggled his massive eyebrows toward Marley and smiled. "But we are different: you and I. We have a purpose."

Brighton blew a cannonball of smoke toward the spectators. "They all like to see a good game, however. There is something about gambling they love."

Brighton began to sing softly, in a beautiful bass voice, a lilting, haunting song Marley had never heard before:

> *The holy trinity of hazards/ Permutations, hidden fears/ The rolling dice won't fall at random/ Their outcome plotted in the spheres.*

Brighton stopped and laughed. "Chance to them means hope; none of them can resist it. They hold onto it as though there were nothing else. And for them, there's not."

Brighton sat quietly for a moment and watched Marley. Then he laughed. "But this game is not about chance," he said. "Not really. Three sixes."

Marley lost another die.

The assembly of ghosts reconfigured, dividing itself into two distinct groups. Roughly half clustered toward Brighton's side of the inn. They sat still and silent as a choir without music. No one even mouthed words. They simply looked on without expression; careful, it seemed, not to make any disturbance. The parson roosted on Brighton's side. The miners sat like statues.

The ghosts on the other side, nearer Marley, paced rapidly. Some held their hands to their heads and looked straight at Marley, the flesh around their eyes squeezed tightly. Some grasped others' shoulders so hard that impressions formed in their garments. Some hid their faces in their hands and rocked back and forth.

The two players rolled and bluffed and lost dice until only

three remained between them; Brighton having only one. When they rolled again, the impact of Brighton's cup upon the table echoed through the inn like a long thunderclap.

Marley shielded his roll with his hands and lifted his cup just enough to see the two dice. He looked once at Brighton.

"How will you choose?" Brighton asked.

Something familiar in the sound of Brighton's question startled Marley and he stared at the giant for a moment.

Then recollecting himself, Marley replied, "Two sixes."

"Two sixes," Brighton repeated, pondering his options. He smiled and shook his finger at Marley. "Now would be the time for a bluff, eh? Are you a risk-taker? Perhaps you have no sixes, or just one of them, then any bid of mine is doomed—because I *do* have a six. But maybe you have two, in which case, there would be three..."

Brighton winked at Marley. "Three sixes."

Marley lifted his cup. "I have two," he said.

The phantoms above Marley began tearing at their hair and uttering silent wails.

For only the second time in the contest, Brighton looked up into the gathering. Many of the ghosts froze. Brighton sighed, then looked at Marley with a broad smile.

"I lied. I have no sixes," he said, not lifting his box. "You win." Brighton bowed then added. "I notice you don't take risks. You seem to have little faith in things."

Marley looked up to the ceiling. No ghosts remained, only smoke in the rafters; no evidence that there had ever been an audience. Brighton began putting away the dice.

"There," Brighton announced, pushing the boxes away. "That was amusing. Now I expect you have more to ask." He slid his arm sideways in a grand gesture of invitation.

"Of course," Marley said, recalling his situation. "When the time comes...Once I know how to approach Scrooge...

what then? How would I travel through time? How would I show myself?"

Brighton's face literally glowed.

"To reach the living, that is to observe them, you need only concentrate upon them and you will be at their sides in the same instant. But to travel in time—to a time when you can *communicate*, when you can be *seen* by mortals—for that you must call upon me. I will take you to the Spirit of Light. He will take you through time and illuminate your form."

"Who is the Spirit of Light?" said the ghost.

"The Sp—"

But before another word could leave Brighton's mouth, the giant wailed and toppled over, grabbing at his right ribs, again digging furiously at his side with his nails.

Marley jumped back. The huge form scratched in agony until finally it let out a sound such as Marley had never heard before. Marley placed his hands against his ears but the howling grew louder, beyond all precedent.

The building shuddered from the force of the torment. The scream filled the inn like a flood, bursting the wooden shutters from their hinges and ripping the entry door from its ironwork. Marley yelped, afraid that he himself might disintegrate in the blast.

But suddenly everything ceased.

No inn. No Brighton. No scream. Just Marley standing alone in a field at night with a cold breeze blowing.

Ruprecht

A blast of frigid air hit Marley hard, throwing rocks of snow and sharp ice at his face—shards that stabbed at him like glass needles. A swirling wind wrapped around him so that no matter which direction he turned, it still met him head-on. Marley held up his arm several times to ward off the stinging crystals, but to no effect: the flying grains nicked his cheeks and eyelids until he cried out.

The ghost leaned forward against the wind and walked blind, dragging his iron sledge behind him. All the while, Brighton's scream resonated in his memory, or perhaps it lingered in the wind like a long-sustained note, fading so gradually that its vanishing point is never known. Once, Marley thought he still heard the cry, but decided it came from the wind after all.

He tried not to think about it and concentrated instead on walking head-down. After a time, he could move and not think; simply withdraw into the blank, dreamless shelter reserved for him in the recesses of his soul.

Imperceptibly, the wind died. Marley became aware of the change the way sleeping mortals slowly perceive the rising sun. Marley raised his face to the air and looked around. Trees—thick evergreens—flanked him now. They bordered both sides of a narrow, scarlet trail of ghost-moon snow; the trail rose along a hillside. Marley took a deep breath, hoisted a portion of his chain over his shoulder and ascended the grade.

The trail climbed steeply, then leveled out, widened and traversed the hillside like a broad, flat shelf. The greater width of the trail opened a view to the air overhead. Through the gap in the pine canopy, Marley could see the pale red, ghost-moon, pulsing like a lamp in a wind. Then it withdrew, obscured by the passing clouds that caused the woods and the trail to darken and close in upon themselves, leaving Marley to trudge forward in near-darkness.

After a time, Marley saw a flickering light. As he drew closer, he determined that the light came from a long lodge. Coming closer, he could recognize walls of hewn tree trunks. Snow lay in high drifts outside the walls and piled to a thickness of three feet upon the roof. Smoke rose from a central chimney and smelled sweetly, faintly of tar.

Marley stopped at the lodge's entrance. The front of the threshold had been recently cleared; fine tracings of a straw broom could be seen in the thin remnants of red-tinted snow that lay on the stone stoop. A poorly-constructed door consisting of upright planks held next to each other by three cross-pieces did not come fully to the earthen floor. There, light leaked out under its edge. Still, the entrance appeared welcoming and festive-looking: framed by a fragrant garland of pine boughs and mistletoe. A wreath of holly, red berries and ivy hung from the planks.

Marley dragged his burden to the portal and knocked. From inside came a shuffling sound. Shadows wavered across the lighted gaps in the planks and then the door opened.

The sight of the presence that appeared in the doorway caused Marley to start. Before him stood a wild-looking man, much taller than himself and thick as a chopping block. The massive figure held a long, wooden staff close to his body in such a way that one sleeve of his green robe fell back to his elbow revealing a forearm brown and thick as a tree limb. Marley stared.

The man—though much larger—looked like one of the costumed players Marley had seen once while passing the Winter Solstice fair in London. Bright red hair shot upward from the man's head like a bird's crest. His skin—where it could be seen unobstructed by his thick hair and beard—shone the color of a chestnut. A bristling, red moustache hung from beneath the beak of his nose, extending nearly to his collarbone; thick flames of eyebrows spanned his whole face and nearly buried the small, shining, black, marble eyes that peered from within.

The big man bowed, the hair on his face moving in the suggestion of a smile, then stood back and pulled the door open wide.

"Come in," the fellow said in an extravagant, booming voice, a voice that seemed accustomed to great pronouncements. "Come in from the cold. Warm yourself."

Without another word, the big man ushered Marley into the center room of the sprawling lodge. He said, "I am Ruprecht. Welcome."

Marley looked at both Ruprecht and the interior of the lodge at the same time. "I am Jacob Marley."

Hundreds of lighted candles sparkled about the main room: on the shelves, on the dirt floor, on an immensely long, wooden table, and from various wheels that hung from the beams. Cobwebs draped the rafters and glimmered in the firelight like tinsel, appearing more as glorious seasonal adornments than as signs of neglect.

In the center of the room, a huge feast spread out along the table. Sliced, white breasts of turkey lay on platters, pots of thick, brown gravy, sausages, a pink side of ham with a hard, glistening border of rind, a dark roast beef wading in a pool of its own juices, hot minced pies, apples, pears, oranges, dozens of dusty bottles of wine, a scented, steaming bowl of dark, mulled wine and numerous large, frosted cakes with decorations depicting rising suns and verdant fields, glistened and steamed in the inviting light of the candles.

Along the far wall, a semi-circular hearth, open on all sides except where stone pillars supported its chimney, presented a crackling fire. A carved, painted motto adorned the wood mantel above the hearth. It read: "Fear knocked. Faith answered. No one was there."

A young girl sat quietly near the fire.

"Mr. Marley," Ruprecht declared. "You have arrived just in time. We are having a feast tonight. You, myself and young Miss Renn." Ruprecht gestured toward the hearth.

"Please excuse me for just a moment: I must fetch the soup," Ruprecht said. "Make yourself comfortable."

Ruprecht turned away. He rolled when he walked, Marley noticed, and seemed to use his stick to keep himself moving in a straight line. Marley watched him enter a side room in which a cooking fire licked at a large black pot.

Ruprecht's voice called back from the room: "I nearly forgot. Renn, this is Mr. Marley."

The girl appeared no older than ten. Marley bowed slightly and the girl returned his salutation with a rapid wave of her hand. Marley noticed a light, blue glow about her like his own. Marley thought she looked too thin: forty-five pounds, no more. Her light-brown hair hung long and thin and seemed flaked with dirt. She sat on a low milking stool and in that position, her knobby knees pressed through rips in her apron-trousers—a garment, which might once have been blue, but now showed a grimy black. She wore brass-toed clogs—the footwear of miners.

She waved again and smiled, showing a badly-chipped, left front tooth, suggesting a child's accident; Marley thought it lent her a certain reckless air that suited her.

"Renn, is it?" Marley said, walking over to the girl.

"Yes," she said. "And you are Jake Turner."

Marley stopped in the center of the room. No one had called him that since...when? He swallowed and cleared his throat. "How...How could you know that?"

"Easily," she said. "I helped you escape."

"In due time, Renn. In due time."

Ruprecht's voice resonated far ahead of him. He emerged from the cooking room, holding an immense pot in one hand by its bail.

"You'll have Mr. Marley miserably confused before he's even had a moment's comfort. Come, Mr. Marley. Come to the table. Let us have some food while we talk."

The big man set the soup upon the table and motioned for his guests to join him.

"Wait," Marley said. "She—"

"In due time, Mr. Marley," Ruprecht smiled.

Marley and the girl moved to the table and, guided by Ruprecht, sat opposite each other. Their host sat at the end, between them.

"This is lovely," Ruprecht said, slapping his hands together with gusto.

When he spoke, his eyebrows worked up and down like pump handles, animating his words. He speared a piece of hot beef and served first Renn and then Marley and then continued dispensing generous amounts from all the courses until both his guests' plates lay buried under food.

Renn began to eat, slowly at first, then more rapidly.

"Ghosts can eat?" said Marley cautiously.

"Of course." Ruprecht declared. "Did you never hear of people laying out food at Solstice—or Christmas if you prefer—for their departed kin?"

Marley seemed to remember such a custom being discussed

once; some neighbors practiced it, he recalled vaguely.

Renn paused in her chewing. "I remember on Christmas Eve, my mother lit a candle and put a plate beside it with an apple and some bread. 'It's not grand,' mum would say. 'But I hope they like it. It's the best we can do.'

"She was talking about ghosts," the girl said. "The ghosts of our family. They would come on Christmas Eve when we were sleeping. So mum would set a place for them to comfort them on their way. While we slept, our ghosts ate and drank and danced and made toasts and just before dawn they would leave."

"Did they, the ghosts, ever visit you on other occasions?" Marley asked.

The girl looked at him and then at Ruprecht.

"I'm in earnest," Marley said.

"No," said Renn. "Only in winter."

Marley stared at the child, still amazed that she knew his real name. He wondered too if his companions knew anything about Brighton. But Marley resolved to wait and allow the girl and Ruprecht to reveal themselves at their own pace. After all, as Brighton and Ruprecht both pointed out, Marley had time now; all in due time.

Marley placed a fork under a piece of beef, brought it to his mouth and slid the morsel to his tongue. It tasted sweet and wet and salty-tangy all at once. The taste made him imagine being corporeal again. The meat was delicious—moreso, it seemed, than anything he had ever tasted before—and Marley had to exert great effort not to appear ravenous. After consuming a large cut, Marley dabbed at his mouth with the green and red cloth napkin that had been provided.

"Pardon me," Marley said.

Ruprecht grinned. "You're hungry," he allowed.

Marley looked about the table.

"There is so much food here. And yet there are only three of us."

"It won't be wasted," said the big man. "Rest assured."

Marley gestured, twirling his hand and fingers in the air above him. "What is this place? What is it you do here?"

A loud laugh erupted from deep inside the big man; its sound colliding with every wall, making every article within the lodge—from forks and knives to candle-holders—shake and twinkle in the light as if winking at a joke. Ruprecht's brows wriggled and rolled.

"I preserve the spirit of the Solstice. *Sol Invictus*. The Unconquered Sun. The spirit of Hope. Light. The only comfort men truly have in the darkness of winter."

"But this place has no sun. We are in the dead of winter."

Ruprecht smiled. "We are among the Winter Dead," he corrected. "The Winter Solstice—when the 'Sun stands still'—is, it's true, a time of darkness and cold, bitter weather, barren fields, misery, and isolation. But there is great magic too. Fretful spirits stir. Ghosts—during their time—appear to mortals. Man huddles close to his own kind for warmth. Mortals look inward. Mortals cling to each other and make merry in the face of a universe that seems to have turned against them. They defy it with great fires and feasts.

"I encourage them. I encourage the pagan celebration of the Solstice—in whatever form it takes. I dwell here because warmth, food, light and love shine most brightly in the dark."

"Pagan, not Christian?" asked Marley.

"Pagan. Christian. They are the same. One prays for the return of the sun's light; the other prays for the light of the Son. No difference when you consider the matter."

Renn changed the subject.

"After my grandfather died, I stayed up all night every Christmas Eve hoping to see his ghost," the girl said. "But I never saw it.

"One Christmas Eve I came home through a field. There was snow on the ground. I could hear the crunch of my own footsteps. There was moonlight on the snow. And it was silent—just like in the carol. I was carrying my birds. I'd put a heavy wrap around their cage. I thought they were sleeping but then they started to sing. I lifted the blanket and looked at them. They cheeped and jumped all around—like they were singing Christmas carols. I was such a little girl then."

Marley had the sudden thought that this girl might have died decades ago and may have had all that time to mature. He tried to picture her as some wise and ancient woman, but in the end could see only the child.

"When I looked ahead," Renn said. "I saw a dark shape low to the ground. It looked like a tent all by itself in the field. It was a little manger with Mary and Joseph and angels and real straw and figures of cows and three wise men: everything. Sitting out there all by itself. No one there but me. I think it was put there just for me to find. I think the birds sang to keep me awake so I wouldn't miss it. When I got there, I wanted to leave a gift—like a wise man. But I had nothing. So I took a stick and pretended it was a candle. Then I picked up a rock and pretended it was an apple. Then I took out my handkerchief and pretended it was bread. Just like my mother did, you see, for the ghosts. Then I asked God to understand that this was the best I could do."

"You kept birds?" Marley said, resolved to question Ruprecht later.

The girl nodded, then looked at Ruprecht. "May I tell him now?"

"Ya, child," the big man said.

Renn's light-blue eyes shone and it seemed to Marley that he could almost see himself reflected in them.

"I carried birds in the mine where you worked as a boy," she said. "I was small enough to get into the tiniest places. I was supposed to watch the birds while I moved. If they fell, it meant there was gas and I was to come back and tell the underlooker."

"I remember the pit girls. Did I know you?" Marley said, astonished.

"I buried you."

Renn looked at Ruprecht again and when he nodded, she continued.

"One time I took my birds up a tunnel and we found a crack and we managed to get through to the other side. Into a big chamber. It was like a palace: there was a dome and passages and tunnels going off in every direction. It wasn't part of the mine. It hadn't been dug by men: it was just there.

"I was so excited. I took my birds and began to explore. First we tried this passage, then that one. Some passages had their own halls. I kept at it for I don't know how long: a long time. When I decided I should get back, I started for the crack and then...then I couldn't find it. The more I looked, the more lost I became. I told my birds I would lead us out. But I couldn't."

Her voice dropped. "My birds died first. The air was hard to breathe and they just fell over. It was my fault. We would never have been there if not for me...The last thing I remember was a terrible smell, the flame of my lamp rising off its wick, hanging in the air, and then a bright light...Many others died too."

"The room exploded?" Marley said.

Renn nodded.

"It was the one that buried you," she said.

"Good Lord," said Marley. "This is..."

But he did not know what more to say.

"After I died," Renn said. "I kept coming back to the mine. Watching. Listening. Seeing if there was something I could do for anyone to make things better. I saw what they did to you."

Renn looked at Marley sadly. "When you were lost in the dark—after that man had been murdered—I called to you. It was my voice you followed out of the mine. You went through passageways only I knew."

Marley's arms fell to his sides.

"Good Lord," he said again.

Then the girl laughed nervously.

"Do you remember the song?" She began singing:

"There lived a lady in merry Scotland/ And she had sons all three/ And she sent them away into merry England/ To learn their grammaree..."

"It was you." Marley stood suddenly, thinking to embrace the girl, but the weight of the chain dropped him just as quickly back to his seat. "You went back. Dear child!"

Renn looked down. "You sang that song so often to your brother. I learned it from you. It's a sad song."

Renn became quiet. Her head rose to where her eyes met Marley's and she regarded him with an expression both serious and desperate-looking. He saw the desolation in her, the look of a mute who cannot cry for help. Part of Marley wanted to look away, but he could not.

Finally he sputtered, "It was an accident, child. No one would have blamed you. It wasn't your fault." He reached his hand across the table and took hers. "The miners who died...they would all forgive you."

Renn wiped away a tear with her free hand and a small grin showed itself. She looked down and nodded.

After a few moments the girl laughed at herself and sniffed. Then she took a deep breath and assumed an airy way.

"So, Mr. Marley," she said. "What happened to you after that? After you left the mines. Did you live well?"

Marley looked at Ruprecht, then turned his gaze to the floor. "I lived...for a time," he said softly. "Then I died."

"How did you die?"

Marley looked at the girl. In a mine too, he thought. But he said, "My heart stopped." Marley shook his head. "You went back to the mortal world, Renn. How did you get there?"

"You just think strongly about where you wish to go and then you're there," Renn said.

The girl smiled, holding out her hands, palms up, fingers away from her like a magician at the finale of a trick.

"Mortals can hear you, but they can't see you—not as a rule. You didn't see me, did you? A ghost can be seen only once—and only by one mortal."

The same thing Brighton said.

"Why just once?"

Ruprecht answered.

"If several people could see a ghost at the same time, they could confirm it to themselves. Then suppose many people confirmed it. Then all people. And what if ghosts were seen every day? Ghosts would become an accepted reality—and that would be the end.

"The moment Man accepts something as real—no matter how miraculous—it loses all its power, loses its power of mystery and miracle, its power to move. If mortals could be certain of us, then we truly would disappear."

Marley rubbed his face with his hands.

"This is all too much," he said.

Marley looked at Ruprecht and the girl.

"Why am I here? Why all this?" He gestured in a way to include everything.

Ruprecht said nothing, but instead rose and walked to a

dusty shelf of books and selected a thick volume whose leather covering hung in tatters. He brought it to Marley, set it on the table and opened it, pointing to a particular passage.

"Read this to me," he said.

Marley took the book and followed Ruprecht's finger to the desired text. Marley squinted, cleared his throat and read aloud:

"'It is required of every man that the spirit within him should walk among his fellow-men and if that spirit goes not forth in life, it is condemned to do so after death and witness what it might have shared; but cannot share.'"

Marley paused. "Cannot share," he repeated. Marley closed the book and then his eyes.

Solstice

When Marley opened his eyes, he shook his head in disbelief. He now stood in The Common near his former place of business in London.

The sun glittered and the street held an inch of snow, packed hard by the feet of hundreds of celebrants. The square held "The Festival of Light," a mad revival of old pagan solstice customs that had gained popularity when England's dispossessed farmers surged toward London looking for work, bringing with them their old rural traditions. The fair clogged the streets for two days and nights with curious onlookers, bizarrely-costumed actors, storytellers, puppeteers, vendors, cooks and musicians.

In life, Marley had tried to avoid the square during that time of December. Now he walked among the revelers, his mouth wide open, his eyes staring, unblinking, at the life teeming around him.

The throng whirled about in outlandish clothing: jesters' caps and bright pantaloons, skirts of rainbow colors, animal skins and masks, courtiers' robes, peasant dresses and provocatively-cut blouses that covered little despite the cold.

Marley paused near a group of men that carried swords and wore tunics ornamented with red and gold ribbons. The men danced in circles, holding their swords high and—in concert—formed patterns in the air with their blades—six-pointed stars, rings and suns. At every new pattern the crowd cheered.

In one section of the square, Marley saw several people exchanging boughs of laurel, holly and evergreens. They bowed and curtsied ceremoniously, fawning over each sprig with extravagant gestures, suggesting that they received items of lasting value.

A woman carrying a wreath passed near Marley. "Excuse me, madam," Marley said. "I—"

The woman stopped and looked around as if to locate the speaker. Marley stepped directly in front of her.

"Here, madam," Marley said. "I was hoping you could you tell me—"

Marley suddenly stopped speaking. Alarm and concern spread across the woman's face. She looked to her right and left and then hurried on her way—passing directly through Marley's body as if he did not exist.

Marley remained on the same spot for several minutes. During that time, people from the crowd moved by him and some, like the woman, passed through him with no more acknowledgement of his existence than a slight shiver, a turning of a collar or a tightening of a scarf.

So, Marley thought, it's true. A surge of melancholy flooded his chest and Marley felt its dismal presence as though it were a viscous fluid that might suffocate him. Why did I walk through crowds with my eyes turned down? Marley wondered. So much had been so close.

A leathery aroma of wood smoke and the tangy odor of fatty meat saturated the air. Marley looked up and walked toward the smells. As he walked Marley became aware of a confusing blend of sounds, a rising cacophony of competing music mingling in the smoky air.

Cymbals clashed together like bags of coins, strange pipes whined tinny melodies, rich flutes poured notes between the sounds of resonating strings, and dull, skin drums pulsed odd beats. Voices wove among the instruments: some singing, some laughing, some shouting; all boisterous in tone.

Marley stopped by a large fire fed by a single log nearly four feet across and eight feet long, set in a makeshift hearth of circled bricks. Near the Yule log several cooking braziers and smaller, open fires burned over which meat slowly turned on spits. Fat sizzled and exploded in flames each time any of it dropped into the fires. Smoke rose in light, grey clouds.

Around the fires, people jammed close together at dozens of long tables loaded with great bowls of fruit, bread, and steaming meat. Stuffed peacocks, salted venison, mutton, rabbit, boar, bowls of sweet porridge, jellies, plum and apple puddings, jugs of hot, spiced ale upon which floated apples in a white foam, all offered themselves to humanity and resembled Ruprecht's feast, though on an even larger scale.

Marley looked at the faces: the smiles, the cheeks reddened by the cold, the laughter, the whispered indecencies and feigned offenses taken. He began to smile. Before long he began to move his head in time to one of the ballads drifting through the air.

Softly—only to himself—Marley began to sing with one of the musicians. The song had been one of Bill Worthy's favorites:

"Oh, we'll pipe and we'll sing, love.
We'll dance in a ring, love.
When each lad takes his lass,
All on the green grass.
And it's oh to plough, where the fat oxen graze low,
And the lads and the lasses do sheep shearing go."

One song followed another and, though Marley did not know the words, he listened and grinned and kept time. The minstrels sang:

> *"The boar's head, as I understand,*
> *"Is the rarest dish in all the land.*
> *"And thus bedecked with a gay garland,*
> *"Will make a feast for all of Man."*

Marley practically danced—in spite of the chains that still held him. For the first time that he could remember, he felt light, almost giddy, forgetful, nearly happy, as when he played in the fields as a child with Ezra...

Marley suddenly stopped his dancing.

A shout intruded on Marley's thoughts.

"Be off. Give me room. Out of the way. Every year it's the same damned horde!"

Marley looked across the square toward the dissonant sound. It came toward him, pushing against the celebrants like a coarse wind against long reeds. Immediately Marley recognized the shocking white fringe of hair skirting out from under the tall, black hat; the sharp-edged, pale, white face; the grating voice. Scrooge.

Marley's partner pressed into the throng, evidently intent on crossing the square in a straight line in the direction of his business; but a cross-current of revelers snagged Scrooge and took him off course. Scrooge collided with two people wearing masks fashioned after animals. A bear and a snorting bull grabbed Scrooge's hands and whirled him around in a mock-dance before he could break free, only then to careen into a person wearing a leering, frog head. The frog bowed, then leapt away. Scrooge swung at it with his heavy, black walking stick—the cane Marley once owned—and cursed when he missed his target.

"Scrooge!" Marley called.

But Scrooge gave no sign that he'd heard Marley above the noise of the festival. Marley called again, but his words evaporated in the motley symphony of laughter, singing, clattering tambourines, maracas, tin whistles and yelps of the crowd.

Meanwhile, Scrooge arched one arm, then the other, over the shoulders of people, pulling himself forward furiously, but gaining ground only as a barge might when poled against a strong river.

No earthly substance, however, could impede Marley's ghost and he arrived at Scrooge's shoulder without trouble.

"Scrooge," he said into his partner's ear.

Scrooge jerked his head to the left, turning so quickly that had Marley been material, their faces would have collided. As it happened, Scrooge's face, for a moment, merged into Marley's own. Scrooge looked right and left again.

"I'll not be mocked!" Scrooge yelled and pushed aside a person in a horse-head mask.

Marley followed Scrooge closely—saying nothing more, but staying close to the man's shoulder until they'd reached the other side of the square, five blocks from the offices of Scrooge & Marley.

Along the fringes of the festival, batteries of musicians—their hats on the street turned upward to collect the offerings of passersby—lined the way. Scrooge and Marley approached a fiddler playing a lively rendition of "Tansey's Fancy," a jig with progressively faster phrasing. The fiddler played with his eyes closed and a smile on his face; his head and arms moved sideways as if rocking a child to a maniacal beat. The man's bow dipped and backslid, stuttered and glided, double-hopped and skidded in ways Marley had never noticed before; then, as they came alongside him, the musician soared into "Sir Roger de Coverley"—the very tune Scrooge had played at Imperial's Christmas fete so long ago.

The dance figure made Marley's heart soar: he knew that Scrooge would have to stop and listen to it and that, when he did, Scrooge would remember how he had played that music and who he had been; and if that happened, it might open a chance, a hope, for Marley to reach his old partner.

But Scrooge walked past the fiddler without so much as a pause or tilt of his head; much less a coin for the musician's hat.

"Listen!" cried Marley. But the high song of the fiddle covered his plea.

Scrooge and Marley left the festival behind; its music and its noise faded quickly. They passed several street beggars but only Marley looked at them: one, a woman wrapped in dirty blankets, an empty tin cup at her side, looked frozen and Marley wondered if she had died during the previous night. But then she blinked several times indicating life.

As they approached a narrow alley, a lanky man in a long, checkered coat, whose grisly face appeared stained by something yellow, stepped out suddenly and put a dark hand on Scrooge's shoulder.

"Pardon me, guv," the man grinned, fluttering his brows in a way to suggest a secret understanding. "Care for a young one?"

Scrooge rapped the man's hand with his cane. "Out of my way," Scrooge demanded. "There's nothing I want from the likes of you."

The man winced and shook his damaged hand but did not seem to take offense. "Of course not, guv. But mebbe there's somethin' you'd like from this one."

The man jerked his head toward the recesses of the alley. There, on a discarded crate, a blanket around her shoulders, sat a child.

Scrooge looked at the girl, then the man. Without a word

Scrooge extended his arm and cane before him like a great gate, swept the ponce aside and continued on his way.

"No!" Marley shouted after Scrooge.

But Scrooge, thinking that the procurer had shouted, did not look back. Marley hobbled quickly to Scrooge's side.

"You can't ignore that. Go back. Don't you remember yourself? That child's enslaved. Do something. Thrash the rascal."

Scrooge stopped abruptly, a fearful look in his eyes. He quickly removed his gloves, then thrust bare fingers in either ear and wriggled them violently. He shook his head and punched his hands back into the gloves, laughing at himself for being irrational.

"It's not my business," Scrooge said to himself, resuming his pace.

"Your business!" howled Marley. "*Mankind* is your business."

Scrooge stopped short and covered his ears.

"Humbug, I say. Humbug!" Scrooge shouted.

He hurried away and Marley's ghost did not follow.

Marley watched Scrooge's form disappear around a corner. I'd only drive him mad, the ghost admitted. But what else can be done?

Marley turned around and walked back toward the Solstice fair. When he came to the alley, both the ponce and the girl were gone. Further up the street, the beggar woman stirred. She's alive at least, the ghost said to himself.

Here Marley saw other ghosts. Dozens of them—men like himself and Scrooge, men of business, all weighed down by chains similar to Marley's own. They gathered around the huddled woman, calling to her, trying to touch her face, trying to warm her with their insubstantial arms. Some took off their coats and tried to wrap her in them—but to no effect. Other ghosts reached desperately into their purses, retrieved handfuls of coins and threw them desperately at the derelict figure; but the coins flew backward from their target as if pitched into a gale.

Marley's ghost approached the phantoms. One of them, tears brimming his eyes, looked at Marley and answered an unasked question.

"We seek to interfere, for good, in human matters," it wailed. "But we have lost the power forever."

Then the spectre turned toward the woman and tried again in vain to throw money to her.

Marley stepped backward and nearly tripped over his own length of chain. He looked around wildly and saw legions of ghosts everywhere: ghosts at every door-step and window, at every street corner and alleyway; a ghost attended every person and every ghost sobbed, lamenting its conclusive impotence.

Marley tilted his head toward the afternoon sky—already losing its light—and cried out. "My God. Is there no hope?"

Marley closed his eyes to stem his own despair. He thought he heard the voice of Ruprecht boom across the square.

"Make Scrooge dance," it echoed.

Marley staggered blindly across the square, dizzied by the swirl of people and his conflicting emotions. When he reached the other side, he stopped and leaned against a lightpole and caught his breath. He'd only stopped a moment, however, when he spotted the ponce and the little girl retreating down the lane.

Rage swelled in Marley's soul. He would beat the man to death if he could. But he couldn't. Still...

Marley recalled Brighton's admonition: *Hearing disembodied voices generally drives mortals mad.*

Marley lifted his chains and rushed toward the ponce in a murderous temper. I'll drive him mad, Marley vowed.

The ghost managed to gain on the man. He closed to

within five yards but at that moment the sky fell.

A large, rapidly churning funnel cloud formed overhead. Before Marley could capture the man, the cloud reached down and sucked both the ponce and the girl away.

Berchta

The whirlwind enveloped the square, blotting out any trace of London. Swirling snow followed the trail of the girl and the ponce, spinning upward, twisting like waters in a flood.

Blown off balance, Marley lurched backward. When he regained his footing, he leaned into the maelstrom at a severe forward angle. Through squinted eyelids he tried to watch the wild stampede of flakes which scattered haphazardly in every direction like lost and unanchored souls.

The wind expanded outward and Marley feared that he too would be drawn into it. But suddenly the blow subsided and Marley fell into its center, no longer a part of the tempest, though surrounded by it. He watched the dizzying spin around him move farther and farther out and soon saw shapes form in the revolving tower of wind-driven snow.

The shapes resolved into young children. None older than three. They wore nightshirts and slippers and held each other by the hand, forming a long, swirling chain of innocents, countless numbers of them. With his eyes, Marley followed the spinning procession to its peak.

At the apex of the column, a large horse, its legs tucked close to its body, its mane and tail stretched taut behind like streaming banners, dragged the entire company in its vortex as easily as a child flutters a ribbon.

Marley staggered slightly. The wind inside his ears bit cold; its sound roared like that of an inferno.

Marley brought his gaze down to the lowest edge of the cyclone.

The last child in the chain, a toddler, struggled to free its feet from a nightshirt far too long for it. The shirt and feet tangled, causing the child to tip at an awkward angle to the others. All at once the infant lost its grip on its neighbor's hand and, as the trailing edge of the funnel skimmed the ground, the child hit a drift and slid across the snow.

Marley lifted his chains and hurried to the spot where the child lay. He cradled it in his arms. Marley gently squeezed the child's limbs, looking for any injury but could find none. A two year-old boy, Marley guessed; its belly protruded and its cheeks caved inward.

"My God," Marley murmured.

He freed the child's feet from the nightshirt and gathered up the hem. Marley untied the cord that held his own, long pigtail together and from it made a belt for the child.

As soon as the knot pulled together, the infant flew from Marley's arms and resumed its place in the long line of wraiths. The tower of child-ghosts spun upward, out of sight and disappeared, taking the wind with it.

For a moment the land lay silent and still.

Marley kept his eyes on the sky, toward the place where the swirl of children had vanished. There, high above him, Marley saw the horse and now its rider, descending in ever-tightening spirals toward the place where he stood.

Marley tried to run—a reflex—then he stopped. I am already dead, he thought.

The horse and rider glided to within a yard of Marley. The horse, a Percheron, whose withers stood a good two feet above Marley's head, snorted at the ghost. An old woman sat sideways on the animal's bare back and looked down.

The crone wore a black satin, full-sleeved morning dress

with greyed lace around the collar and the wrists. Her hair, tied behind her head, floated dry and lifeless as a mound of cobweb. She appeared emaciated: her thin bones visible beneath translucent, yellow-green skin the texture of brittle parchment.

Her aspect made Marley think of skeletons. Her cheeks sunk far beneath the roll of her bones, making her face look—except for her eyes—like a skull. All that differentiated the woman from a corpse were her predatory eyes and her posture. She sat on the horse with an easy, familiar comfort: upright, not bent over with the weight of age.

Her eyes never moved from Marley. They stared: bright yellow and vibrant, as if all the life in her body had been squeezed from her limbs and compressed into just those two points. Her eyes moved constantly, animated and watchful as those of a raptor.

The hag brought a twig of a finger to her chin and scratched once, then spoke.

"Out on a night like this?" she asked. Her voice gurgled with congestion. She paused between nearly every word. "You are alone. And you can see me. You are not blinded by the sight." She sounded surprised.

"Come closer," she commanded.

Marley took a hesitant step, bringing him nearly to the horse's smooth hide.

"Look at me."

Marley lifted his view to the face of the specter and then could not turn away. The eyes gleamed wildly.

"The children are mine," the woman said. Her voice quivered. "All abandoned, beaten, abused, their small needs ignored." She looked up as if to address the heavens. "Oh, I could tell you ghastly things. Kindness they never knew."

She looked back at Marley.

"Christmas was nothing for them. I am their protector. And their avenger. They are Berchta's children," she said.

She grinned, thin lips held tightly together. Then her tone changed drastically and she seemed for a moment, playful.

"We are permitted to visit the mortals," she said, her voice now a sing-song cadence. "We come calling on the Solstice. We bring presents."

Suddenly the woman screamed. "Plague. Mutilation. Starvation. Pestilence. Retribution!"

Her howl launched the words like sharp weapons through the air. Marley fell to his knees and covered his ears.

Just as suddenly, the woman became quiet again. She checked her hair with both hands. She looked at Marley. She appeared calm, but wore a sad expression.

"I know you," she said.

She held her hands, palm up before her and alternated them up and down as though comparing weights. Then she scowled.

"You're childless."

Her voice trailed off and she looked away. She sighed and then looked at Marley as though seeing him for the first time.

"But you were kind to my straggler," she said.

The witch looked at Marley like one studying a painting, moving her head side to side to gain a different light or angle.

"Play is the point of childhood. Did you know that?" the woman asked. "No, you don't. Of course, not. They took that from you. Your summer games. Your joy." The hag shouted again. "Our wrath on them that steal children."

Marley did not make a sound or move. He did not know what to do in the presence of the mad old witch. She grinned at him. Her teeth glittered brilliantly white.

"For your kindness, I shall help you. I will tell you what you need to know," she announced.

The witch nodded slowly at the ghost, then turned from him. She dug her heels into her mount's sides and they lifted into the air, turning slow circles around Marley. From there the hag looked down at him.

"You," she said, soaring up into the dark, red sky. "Must make Scrooge fear."

Three Spirits

Marley stood at the center of the twisting freeze, head down, body limp, shoulders slumped forward, eyes closed. Even after the swirl settled and all became quiet again, Marley remained in that posture—too weary and confused to even want to move or see.

"Are you going to stay that way forever?" Deep tones resonated in Marley's ears.

Only after several moments, during which Marley seriously pondered the question, did he open his eyes and slowly raise his head.

Wet, moldy walls of dark stone towered over him and he understood immediately that he sat in Hardchapel's cellar again. But now no prisoners occupied the pit. The rows of rope hammocks that once sagged under the weight of men now wafted airy and lonely-looking, like empty fishing nets strung out to dry. Yet the old, sour smell of excrement remained. Marley shivered.

A sudden, ripping scratch made Marley start. A light flared across the room: a flame jumped, then dropped, then a plume of smoke rose.

Brighton sat on a cleared-away portion of stone ledge—one long leg stretched out before him, the other pulled in so that he could rest a hand—holding his pipe—on his knee, just above his boot-tops. Brighton drew deeply on the pipe. His face glowed orange-red for a moment, then receded back into the dingy pallor of the cell.

"Are you well?" Brighton asked, leaning over to light several short candles while he spoke.

Marley looked vacantly at the huge being.

The giant's brilliant white-and-black cape lay beneath him, serving as a ground cover. Again, Marley experienced the impression, a trick-of-the-eye, of an alternation of lighting about Brighton, as if the black in his clothing and the white in his torrent of hair periodically changed places if looked at too long. But the beautiful, old face radiated patience in the growing candlelight; the old eyes, sympathy. As Marley looked upon the face, he began to feel less exhausted.

"Are you all right?" Brighton asked.

Marley shook his head. "No," he said, sounding unsure. "Not all right at all."

Brighton said nothing for a time, then, to make conversation, he pointed to some scratches in the wall.

"Someone must have kept track of his days in here," Brighton said. "Then he must have given up. Look. The little marks here. Sixty-seven of them. That's all. I'm sure people stayed here longer than sixty-seven days; didn't they? So this one must have stopped counting."

Marley looked at the marks. James Connell, a petty thief, had dug the scratches.

"He was killed," Marley said in the monotone of a dazed person.

Marley stared unfocused, as if he could see it all again, happening somewhere in the air between him and Brighton.

"He was hit with a stone. In a fight with a Lancashire man. They were fighting over a blanket."

Marley closed his eyes for several moments, then opened them again, focused on Brighton. Marley said suddenly, "How could you bring me here?"

Brighton's eyebrows raised.

"*I*?" he said. "This is *your* construction, not mine." Brighton looked around. "This is a foul place... Would that we met in settings of *my* choosing. This was your prison; was it not?"

"You—whomever you are—you know it was."

Marley sagged, suddenly feeling the weight of fatigue upon him again. He took a false step, then caught himself and moaned.

"Is this my hell? Am I to shuttle between worlds forever to no purpose?" Marley hid his face in his hands. "Am I to collide forever with riddles? Hopeless, helpless to do anything? Is this my damnation?" He stared at Brighton. "Are you my tormentor?"

Brighton rose, leaving his cape on the stonework. In one stride he crossed the room to where Marley stood. Without a word, Brighton gently grasped Marley's shoulders and lifted the ghost—chains and all—as easily as a man lifts a small child, and placed Marley on the ledge, sitting him on the vacated cloak. Then Brighton drew the garment around Marley's neck and sat cross-legged nearby.

"You are not damned and this is not your torment," Brighton said slowly. "All of this means something—to you."

Marley did not say anything. He sensed heat and an odd feeling of peace and strength that began the moment Brighton placed the cloak around him.

Brighton smiled. "Rest for now. Here, join me."

Brighton produced a shining silver flask from within his black coat and showed it to Marley. "Brandy," he said, jiggling the vessel and nodding for Marley to drink.

Marley took the flask and looked at it for several moments; then he abruptly tilted it back and pulled several swallows from it. He coughed once and wiped his mouth with the back of his hand, then handed the container back to Brighton.

"That's good," Marley sputtered. "Thank you."

Brighton sipped once and set the flask down between them.

"You've had a difficult time since my...departure." Brighton said.

Marley nodded. "Confusing. I—" Marley stopped, disappointed in himself for taking this long to recall Brighton's violent seizure.

"What happened to you?" Marley asked. "Back at the inn. I thought you'd been stabbed. No, worse."

Brighton put a hand to his lower right side. "It is an old wound," he said, resigned. "It never heals. Sometimes it strikes me down." Brighton smiled. "But it can't kill me, so there's that. Now: tell me where you've been."

Marley shook his head. "It's hard to say. There was a cabin, a lodge, a feast inside. I met a girl—a ghost, I should say...or an angel, I don't know. She was the voice that led me out of the mines when I had to flee. There was a large, barbaric-looking man. There was a hag and sad children...I saw Scrooge—" Marley stopped.

Brighton stroked his luminescent beard. "You tried to speak with him?"

Marley sighed and nodded. "But I couldn't reach him. Damn me."

"You have time," Brighton said, calm as summer. "What is it again, you would have Scrooge understand?"

Marley rubbed the smooth top of his head several times and thought, trying to compress the many things he would say to Scrooge into a few words.

"He should share his life while there's time."

Brighton paused to relight his bowl. "And how did *you* come to that belief?"

Marley looked at the straw on the floor. He squinted, the

way one might when trying to remember the location of a misplaced key. A long time passed while Marley thought. Brighton smoked quietly.

Marley said, "I don't know. I remember dying. Laying in my bed. I saw things as though in a dream—parts of my life came to me. Some of it seemed real and some, I think, imagined. Fever most likely."

"Then perhaps Scrooge should have a fever," Brighton said. "Or at least be induced in some way to see life."

Marley chuffed. "I could no sooner accomplish that than I could fetch him here."

"And if we fetched him here, he'd be dead. And that would be too late," said Brighton. "Tell me this: what do you really know of Mr. Scrooge?"

At first, the question seemed absurd to Marley; he'd known Scrooge for over thirty years; to sum up a relationship of that length would be exhausting, he thought. Then he realized it would not.

"I don't know very much about him at all," Marley admitted.

"Try to remember something."

"He played piano," Marley offered. "His sister did too. They were very close. I remember that. She died in childbirth. She had a son. It affected Scrooge greatly. To this day he's hardly spoken to his nephew. Nor with anyone for that matter." Marley rubbed his forehead. "Scrooge became more like me every hour after her death. I encouraged it."

The candlelight played tricks with shadows on the cell walls. Marley thought for a moment that he saw a hideous-looking profile—a man's head with an animal's snout and high ears—cast within the tangle of empty hammocks. The shadow turned toward him, then dissipated.

Brighton saw Marley's disquieted expression. "We need more light," Brighton said, and though he did not set out more candles nor do anything else, the cell became much brighter, as if it sat above ground and the sun were rising.

"Did you know," Brighton said casually. "That Scrooge's own mother died, giving him life—for which his own father, drunk with grief, never forgave him?"

Marley expelled a sudden breath. "How can you know that?"

"His sister's name was Fan," Brighton went on. "When Fan lay dying she asked a favor of Scrooge."

"Fan. That *was* her name," Marley said.

It no longer mattered to Marley how Brighton knew so much: the fact remained that he did know.

"What did she ask him?" Marley asked, fearing the answer but drawn to it the way certain people are drawn to the edges of high places.

"She was so weak," Brighton said, his eyes now damp and shining. "Scrooge didn't hear her ask. She asked so softly. She said, 'Promise me you'll take care of my son.' He still doesn't know."

Marley, who had been leaning forward, now fell back against the stone wall and threw a hand to his chest.

"My God," Marley exclaimed. "My God. If Scrooge knew... How he would suffer."

"But what amends he might make."

"I could never tell him something like that," Marley said.

Brighton chuckled.

"*You*?" Brighton said. "*You* tell him? Why you? Think about that. You: a person who knows virtually nothing about his great 'friend'? You: speaking from the grave of a life you knew nothing about?" Brighton shook his head. "You would be no more than a middling-bad dream to Scrooge."

Marley's face heated red with shame. He looked off into the shadows then turned to Brighton.

Marley's voice limped out, barely audible. "Help me," he said. "Please."

Brighton slapped his hands on his knees and pushed himself to a standing position on the ledge, his head barely a foot below the room's ceiling.

"Excellent," he said.

"What is—?" Marley began, then stopped. The room's light, he realized, came not from the grate nor from the candles, but from Brighton himself, emanating it seemed from the giant's edges, the way bright, white surf illuminates a coastline. Marley stood up and shielded his eyes. The brightness grew around the huge figure, obscuring all else, until Marley finally had to look away.

When the pulse of light subsided, Marley looked around. The prison cell had disappeared.

Marley and Brighton now stood on a platform suspended over water. It took a moment for Marley to adjust to the sudden change in his surroundings; then he realized they stood on the middle portion of the London Bridge, looking northeast toward the crowded docks and markets of Billingsgate. He could see the light-grey rooftops of the London Exchange and not far past, the roof of Scrooge & Marley.

They stood in a clear, cool dawn. Already the fish markets of Billingsgate bustled, awash in an expectant tide of sellers and buyers, vendors and loaders. By contrast, the traffic of carts, carriages, and pedestrians coming across the bridge had not yet arrived.

Brighton leaned out toward the river and breathed deeply; then he coughed.

"Very nice," he said. "Fish guts and sewage. But at least you've gotten us out of prison."

Marley shook his head. "I didn't have anything to do with–"

"Of course you did," Brighton interrupted. "By the by, did you realize that not once—in all your life—did you ever ask anyone for help?"

Marley thought about it. "No. I suppose I didn't."

"It shouldn't be a source of pride," Brighton said. "Notwithstanding, you have asked now. That's progress. And you won't be disappointed. Here's what I can do for you: I'll summon the pooka for you—wasn't it the pooka who said, 'Make Scrooge remember'? Ask the pooka for help."

"What can it do?"

"A bit. He knows everyone's past. Did he not illustrate your own for you? He can help Scrooge remember."

Brighton began to pace quickly along the edge of the bridge, hands behind his back, head down, as if in deep thought. From time to time he stole glances at the ghost.

"Next, speak with your 'barbarian'," Brighton said. "That was Ruprecht, I'll wager."

"Yes." Marley said, still unsure what Brighton had in mind. "Ruprecht. He said, 'Make Scrooge...' What was it? 'Make Scrooge dance.'"

"Dance, eat, drink, sing, love...whatever," Brighton said. "Scrooge must remember the joys of life if he is to regret their absence in himself and others. Ruprecht, that hedonist, could be your ambassador. I could persuade the old goat to take it on."

Take what on? Marley wondered.

"You mentioned a hag," Brighton prompted.

"She told me to 'make Scrooge fear.'"

"Berchta," Brighton said. "She's terrorized mortals for ages."

Marley paused. "You want to terrorize Scrooge?" he asked incredulously.

Brighton gave a half-shrug of helplessness. "If reason moved Scrooge, he would be a changed man already. He is not happy, but he is comfortable enough. He does not know his own doom. Berchta can show him. She knows of wasted lives, or ruined innocence, of misery and things not remedied.

"Three spirits," Brighton said. "Scrooge's past, present and future. They could be your ambassadors." Then Brighton snuffed, a sort of short laugh. "Christmas presents from you. The redemption of Scrooge."

Marley shook his head.

"Forgive me, but I'm not sure what you're thinking. In any case, I have my doubts now. Are you suggesting that—among these revelations—Scrooge should learn how he failed his sister? If so, I don't think I agree with your scheme," Marley said.

"No? Why not?" Brighton asked.

"The grief, the torture of self-blame; those things could make him even worse. Trust me. I know," Marley said sadly.

"You know?"

"I failed my own brother when I was young. I've never forgiven myself. I failed us both. He died because I wasn't there to protect him. We both died actually. I died more slowly. I became what I became as a result of that. At least, it seems so now."

"Your brother, Ezra?"

"Yes."

Brighton smiled.

"He is not dead," Brighton declared. "Your brother, your twin, Ezra Turner, is still very much alive."

The Brotherhood

Four men sat in various postures around a corner table strewn with short candles, long scrolls of paper, beer mugs, a common plate—empty but for some crumbs of cheese—and a large, shared pouch of tobacco. Two of the men leaned back in their chairs as if exhausted, while the other two peered closely at a map held down at its corners by mugs and candle holders.

A spirited fire crackled in the hearth midway across the apartment; another man sat by himself on a short stool facing the blaze, occasionally throwing wood shavings into the flames. In the opposite corner, seated in a velvet armchair, a grey-haired man in a gentleman's suit sat reading by the light of an oil lamp.

One of the men, a short, thick-fisted Irishman, looked up from the map and said loudly, "We want the company and the rest of the nation to see we're united. Imagine their faces when they see a thousand miners on the streets outside Piston's home office."

His eyes reflected the candlelight such that two flames appeared to burn in his pupils. He rubbed one hand over the shaved-down, red bristles of his head in the manner of one mopping away an athletic sweat.

"There's gonna be troops out, Tommy. That's what I hear. And it's cold out too," replied James McEwan, a lanky, bookish-looking, ex-driller. He rocked his chair forward so that all its legs rested again on the floor. "The streets are slick. We should think about that."

Malcolm Wenner, sitting to McEwan's left, seconded the thought and righted his chair at the same time.

"Troops. They're looking at it like it's a siege," he said.

Tommy Boyle, the Irishman, looked at the other two, a heat threading its way into his cheeks.

The other man at the map, Kelly Weed, a big, black-haired giant, spoke in a soft, low voice.

"We don't want no one gettin' killed is all," Weed said.

Boyle nodded and looked back at the London street map, exhaling a long, slow breath. Then he slapped his hand flat on the place where the Piston Coal Company would be, causing the paper to snap a sound like wood splintering in a fire. Wenner, the youngest one there, jumped.

"*That's* why we're going!" Boyle cried, half in anger, half in complaint. "No more miners being blown apart or crushed all because some rich bastard wants another country house." Boyle started to breathe hard.

"I say no more. No more miners with the black lung getting no doctors in to see 'em. No more half-vented shafts. No more wages that don't meet the company's feckin' rent. If a few of us get bloodied tomorrow and that saves two hundred miners next year, I say bloody good and let me be the first."

Boyle looked from one face to another then sat back in his chair.

Weed put a hand on the ruddy man's shoulder and laughed lightly as he spoke. "Hold on, Tommy; this ain't a rally. We're with you already."

McEwan lifted his gangly bones from his chair and patted Boyle on the back. "All I'm sayin'...is that the troops will be out, so we should plan for them."

Boyle covered McEwan's hand tenderly with his own.

"Right enough, lads. I'm gettin' excited's all. Let's go over the drill again. Let's go over the map one more time. Then we'll call it a night."

Boyle looked to the man sitting on the stool by the fire. The light of the flames shined off the top of the man's smooth head. He looked well into his sixties, tall—even sitting on a low stool—and broad shouldered. He seemed to have taken no note of Boyle's recent speech and instead intently examined the finger holes of a cheap, tin whistle.

"Ezra, dear," said Boyle. "Could you bring us some more light?"

Ezra Turner looked up, grinned and rose to fetch more candles. He took two unburnt sticks from the mantle, brought them to the map table and held them out stiff-armed, like a boy presenting flowers to someone for the first time. Boyle took the candles and looked at the older man's big hands and then looked up at his face.

The skin along the left side of Ezra's face had been burned severely, leaving it mottled pink and white. The area between the upper cheek and lower jaw and chin seemed sunken as though left without enough flesh to cover it, making the skin there seem unnaturally taut and thin. The blue dots and lines indicative of coal scars streaked Ezra's forehead: the miner's tattoo. The same burns and scarring also marked his left hand. Otherwise, he looked healthy—robust even—and moved as smoothly as a young man.

"Lads, if you ever wonder what we're here for, remember this face and these hands," Boyle said, putting the candles aside and grasping Ezra's hands in his.

Boyle held out Ezra's left hand for the others to regard, in a way that seemed oddly dainty for the stocky union organizer.

"He got scorched in the 'Beth blowup o' ninety-six. Got out by himself, he did—and just a boy then. But did anyone help him after? See to his wounds? Not a soul. Not the company, nor his brothers; and there was no union trade clubs like this one; not yet. He walked two hundred miles or more to London. Alone. Burned as he was and half his senses gone."

Boyle now nodded toward a gentleman who sat reading in the far corner.

"If Mr. Owens there hadn't spotted the miner's blue and hadn't taken Ezra in, where'd he be now?" Boyle wondered aloud.

The gentleman in the corner—the organization's sponsor—looked up for a moment, nodded, then returned to his reading.

No one said a word. Boyle rocked his head in self-affirmation. "Ezra here could be any one of us," he said. Then he turned to the smiling face. "Thank you kindly, Mr. Turner."

"Thank you kindly," the savant repeated.

Jacob Marley's brother wandered back to the hearth and picked up the tin whistle again. He put it to his lips and blew a few trial notes. Then he licked his mouth and began in earnest: a boisterous regimental song called "The Minstrel Boy."

As they reviewed logistics for the next day's protest, the executives of the Action Committee of the Brotherhood of Mine Workers began tapping their feet in time to the tune Ezra played.

Marley and Brighton watched silently: Marley looking at no one but his brother, staring as though his own mental abilities had been impaired beyond the point of understanding any scene before him.

I am seeing my brother, Marley repeated to himself—as if repetition might make the sight more comprehensible. His inability to grasp what he saw had been compounded by the fact that he had not, at first, recognized his brother.

Despite the fact that he beheld his twin, Marley had been

startled to see Ezra as a sixty-six year-old man and not the young boy he'd remembered. It took several minutes for Marley to fully realize that Ezra, as he remembered him, no longer existed.

Ezra's face, despite the disfigurement of the burns, looked handsome in the way that the face of any happy person—no matter their features—can be. His head swayed and danced with the notes he played; his eyes closed, but his brows raised high as though he might be imagining colorfully-uniformed soldiers marching to his music.

Looking at Ezra, Marley could not see himself in his brother. They appeared similar, yes. But nothing more. Ezra seemed healthy and content—something that made him more distinct from Marley than he'd ever been.

Twice Marley tried to say something to Brighton, but each time his throat blocked as though choked by something round and hard. Finally he said, "Can they see us?"

Brighton stood to Marley's right, his hands crossed below his waist.

"No. Not now," Brighton said. "This point in time is December 14th, 1842. In ten more days and a few more hours you will have been dead seven years—Christmas Eve. Only then can a mortal see you."

"Can Ezra *hear* me now?

"If you wish it."

Marley inhaled deeply. "I would like to be alone with my brother," he said.

Brighton nodded and took a step back. "Of course."

The giant specter vanished.

Marley stood alone for several minutes before finally moving. He took a hesitant step and then another, dragging the heavy links of his chain behind him and fearing that its loud scrape on the floor would alarm the others. But no one stirred.

Marley came to within a foot of his twin and again stood motionless for several minutes as Ezra trilled out various light melodies on the whistle. Marley's eyes blurred with tears. He tried to speak but again his throat felt stoppled. Marley fell to his knees, his head just level with his brother's shoulders.

"Ezra?" Marley whispered. "It's Jake."

The piping stopped. Ezra looked around, then without another moment's hesitation, whispered back, "Where are you, Jake?"

Marley wiped his eyes and swallowed. "You can't see me," he said.

"Are you hiding?"

"Yes."

Ezra stood suddenly, a smile wide across his face. "I'll find you," he said aloud, turning his head left and right.

The men of the Action Committee looked up from their deliberations. McEwan and Boyle smiled kindly, then returned to their business.

"No," Marley said. "Sit down, Ezra. I must speak with you." The ghost waited until his mortal double again sat on the low stool.

"Ezra..." Marley started, then stopped, not knowing exactly what to say next. He struggled for a breath.

Ezra did not look directly at Marley's face, but rather at a point a bit higher and somewhat to the right, the way a blind person often seems to be looking at something else. Marley moved so that he would be in line with his brother's gaze. He looked long into Ezra's eyes; they appeared patient and eager at the same time.

"Ezra...I've been gone a long time. I tried to find you," Marley said at last.

"I was hiding."

"Listen to me, Ezra...They said you...I couldn't believe...

I had investigators trying to find you after I failed."

"Hide and seek," Ezra said. "Jake, where are you?"

Marley edged closer. "I'm very near, Ezra. Look here."

Marley snatched a piece of charcoal from the fire and drew a complex formula on the floorboards, quickly scribbling in a graph and flowing lines.

"Look where, Jake?"

Marley stopped drawing. Ezra could not see him, nor his notations and without that, their sublime secret language, the higher plane at which only they could communicate, their special and only true means of contacting another soul, could not exist. Marley dropped the charcoal. Ezra would have to *see* Marley's drawings for them to truly communicate.

Ezra squinted into the blank space before him, his face looking old for the first time. "Are you a ghost, Jake?"

The question brought Marley up short.

"Yes," Marley said, with difficulty. "That's exactly what I am."

"Where are you? I want to see you, Jake. Draw numbers."

Marley could not say anything for several moments. When he could speak again he said, "I'm near you, Ezra. I want you to know that I'll always be near you. I—"

Marley started to sob and put a hand over his mouth to stifle the sound. Then he buried his face in his hands.

"I'm so sorry Ezra. I'm so sorry," Marley cried. "I ran from the mine. I left you... I was so frightened."

Ezra reached into the air in front of him. "Don't cry, Jake."

"I promised to take care of you. But I failed you instead."

Ezra shook his head. "No," he said.

An odd inflection attached to the word, "no," such that Marley could not be sure if his brother had meant, "No. Don't cry," or "No. You didn't fail," and without access to their language, Marley could not press the question.

Marley looked up. He reached toward Ezra, his hand slowly moving toward his brother's burned cheek. He wanted to rest his hand there, to somehow absorb and remove the injury, to touch his innocent other self. But his hand passed through Ezra's face as though neither of them possessed any more substance than smoke.

A call from Boyle made Marley start.

"Ezra. Would you like to come along tomorrow? There will be a thousand people," said the bull-necked Irishman.

McEwan leaned toward Boyle. "Are you sure that's wise, Tommy. He's not—"

"He's got as much a right as any of us."

Ezra whispered, "A thousand, Jake." Then Ezra said loudly, "As much right as anybody."

The men at the table laughed in a good-natured way and Boyle winked at Ezra.

Marley looked at the miners. He saw nothing in them that reminded him of Sully or Ferrel or Badger. These were decent men, he decided.

"Ezra," Marley whispered. "How did you escape the mine? Do you remember?"

Ezra grinned as though Marley should already know. "The girl," he said.

"What girl? Who?"

Ezra's grin became wider. He picked up the tin whistle. He played a few bars of "The Wife of Ushers Well."

Renn.

McEwan called out across the room. "Come, Ezra. Give us a livelier piece."

Boyle beckoned to Ezra with a wave. "Never mind that. Come to the table and we'll show you on the map where all the brothers are going tomorrow. You can help us make plans."

Ezra put the whistle aside, rose and strode quickly to the

table. There the men slapped Ezra on the back and ushered him to the spot that provided the best view of the chart. All of the men remained at the table—despite their fatigue and despite the fact that they'd been over the same plan many times already; they waited in deference to Ezra and patiently explained all the strategies to him.

Marley remained in place, amazed to see how the men respected his brother and how they accorded him every kindness and consideration: almost as if *they* rather than he were Ezra's true brothers.

After the briefing ended, Ezra returned to his stool. He picked up the tin whistle and played "The Minstrel Boy" again. He played the instrument without thought or pause. He played as if no other soul had been near him and as if he'd forgotten he'd just been speaking to his brother's ghost.

The Light-Giver

Marley's ghost stood in the street in a shaft of light that angled downward from one of the windows of the miners' apartment. He stared at the window, at the shadows that passed by it, unwilling to go, thinking he might stand there forever rather than make the choice that hung before him. The night clamped upon him so coldly that, had Marley been mortal, the tears on his face might have hardened.

The light in the apartment suddenly dropped to a lower level of brightness: the gentleman-sponsor must have blown out his reading lamp. A large man's shadow appeared at the window and stayed there for a moment, then the curtains pulled closed.

The light that had been directed into the ghost's eyes vanished and now, without the glare, Marley saw the jagged skyline of the city in silhouette. It looked like a graveyard: every parapet, every chimney, the outline of a tombstone.

Looking west, above the common line of roofs, Marley could see the dome of St. Paul's Cathedral, the cross atop it looming through the night's smoke like a ship's mast in a low fog. The cathedral, though many blocks away, still appeared grandiose.

Arrogant, thought Marley. Glorify the pitiless God. No: the pitiless cosmos, empty of any god.

Marley turned east and walked away with his head down, bound nowhere in particular, dragging his chain. He walked with a peculiar numbness of mind, a temporary standoff between anger and sorrow in which action and feeling hung suspended.

Sounds came to him and passed away without meaning. Someone shouted in the distance. From a nearby alley sexual grunts escaped. Somewhere more distant a small chorus sang a carol. Marley heard the sounds, but they made no sense to him.

After a time, he stopped. Marley suddenly threw his head and arms backward so that his chest presented itself to the sky. He wailed a sound so long and mournful that mortals, hearing it, might shiver and pull their collars tighter, secretly fearing the awful noise to be that of a banshee.

In the middle of his scream, Marley shouted the name, "God," as if to command the Being's attention; then he cried, "Damn me? Damn *you*."

Then he began to chuckle. Then, perversely, he began to sing. He made one false start, then cleared his throat and started again.

Through the first verse Marley laughed like a drunken man at the strange sound of his own harsh voice.

"...They had not been in merry England/ For twelve months and one day/ When the news came back to their own mother dear/ Their bodies were in cold clay..."

He sang each verse more loudly, stopping only when the crackling pitch of his voice made it impossible to continue. Then he would stop and begin again.

"'I will not believe in God.' she said/ 'Nor Christ in eternity/ Till they send me back my own three sons/ The same as they went from me.'"

When the last of his howls fled into the night, Marley righted himself and looked around. He did not recognize the street; it could have been any of hundreds where the smell of rot and coal smoke mingled with that of human waste, and where the ubiquitous sounds of rats' nails scrabbling on tin and brick, traveling from roof to alley to cellar, gave one the ill feeling of the street itself being alive with vermin.

Here Marley saw a stone building, a church, in a block of shaky, wooden frame structures.

Marley shook his finger at the building in a threatening way.

"You..." he said, as if addressing a thief.

A growling hum rose in Marley's throat and he turned his head from side to side. Marley approached the small building with the cautious, sideways, and self-conscious step men use when they approach one another in the moments before a fight.

"I'll curse you in your own house," Marley snarled.

Marley moved slowly toward the church and ascended its short doorstep. He paused at the building's threshold. Then, wincing with the effort, Marley lifted as much of his chain as he could and flung it and himself against the church's bolted, iron-and-wood door.

The chain passed through the door without collision—as if no door existed—causing Marley, shackles and all, to stumble and nearly fall into the chapel's central aisle. Marley regained his balance then looked around in the shocking quiet of the room.

The chapel lay in a narrow, long configuration. Marley felt as though he could lift his arms sideways and touch the faces of the opposing walls, but would be hard-pressed to throw a rock down its great length to reach the altar without first hitting a cross-beam above.

Tall shadows dropped like black streams along the nicks and scallops of the church's hewn stone walls. Above the center pews, suspended from wires, a five-foot long, scale-model fishing boat hung, seemingly liberated from its dependence on the sea, now free to soar through the heavens.

Only one candle, set upon the pulpit near the altar, lighted the room. There, bending near the flame, his large hands holding the pulpit's rails, Brighton gazed at Marley with an expression of empathy.

Low to the flame, Brighton's face held a warm, orange-red color, its deep folds and scores black like the grain in wood. A handsome face, except for the age, and the eyes, which peered weak and lonesome like a grandfather who has outlived his offspring.

Marley walked toward Brighton as one might approach a magistrate who has just sentenced an innocent man to hang.

"Why didn't you tell me sooner?" Marley said, his voice bitter and accusative.

Brighton ignored the question. "You came here to curse God," he said.

Marley looked down, feeling overmatched. He slid into a pew.

"Yes," Marley admitted.

Brighton nodded in a way to indicate he understood. He smiled and said, "You're not the first."

When Brighton spoke, the interior of the chapel bloomed with light; hundreds of candles, set on window sills, altar rails, along the floor, behind the pulpit and on the posts of every pew, took on independent buds of flame.

"You have a choice," Brighton said.

Marley hung his head and spoke toward the ground.

"Only one mortal may see me?" Marley asked, just to be sure.

Brighton nodded. Marley shook his head.

"My brother asked me to draw numbers. We have this way of speaking. It's hard to explain. He must see what I write; the way I hear what he plays."

Brighton said nothing for a moment then said, "I understand. That is the choice isn't it? I can tell you this: in 1842—seven years after you died—both Ezra Turner and Ebenezer Scrooge are alive. You could become visible to your brother," Brighton said, holding out his hands as if hefting two different sacks of flour. "...but then Scrooge would travel the course on which you placed him. Or, you could appear to Scrooge, arrange his reclamation; but then you'd never really communicate with anyone again—at least, not in any profound way."

Marley dropped his forehead onto the pew in front of him.

"It's not a simple choice," Brighton said.

Marley raised his head. The skin between his eyebrows pinched together.

"Who *are* you?" Marley whispered.

Brighton's great mass moved away from the pulpit. He paused for a moment as though in thought, then said, in a simple voice, "I am He who illuminates you."

Brighton waited then said, "I make spirits shine. I make them visible to mortals. I am the Light-Giver. I am Lucifer."

Marley could not at first be sure he'd heard correctly. Then he saw the giant change.

Brighton, still enfolded by the long thick hair and magnificent white beard that flowed backward from his face to his shoulders, lost all trace of dark coloring. He shone pure white; literally radiant.

Marley tried to push himself backward, through the rows of pews, to get away but the weight of his chain now seemed infinitely heavier.

"You're mad," Marley whispered.

"Don't be quick to judge," the being replied.

Marley shook his head violently. Long forgotten words spoken in a church such as this suddenly came to his mind.

Marley slowly whispered, "'...I beheld Satan as—as lightning falling from heaven...Satan...transformed into an angel of light... his ministers transformed into ministers of righteousness...' "

Brighton clucked his tongue against the roof of his mouth. "Why do you mimic the ignorant? Was that an incantation to save you from the Devil? That's the last thing you want.

"You came here tonight to curse God. You admitted it yourself...Don't be ashamed. It's more natural than you know—and more justified. I lashed out at Him myself and for the same reasons. Now listen to me."

Brighton stepped off the dias and walked around the perimeter of the pews, careful not to come too close to Marley, who stared, virtually paralyzed in a rigor of fear.

"God is Everything," Brighton said. "He is all things *and* their opposites. Light and Dark. Winter and Summer. Life and Death. Good and...Evil. He is not only the best, he is also the worst. Horror and undeserved pain are God's doing. It's hard to accept—given your indoctrination—but reason will bear it out: God is evil...as well as good."

Brighton pushed his hands together as though in prayer. "So who am I?" he mused. "I am an angel of light. There were many of us. There was myself. There was the one you know as Jesus. Many of us. We could not accept the presence of evil in the universe. We took the view that a being of infinite power could transcend duality. God had the power to eliminate evil. And because he could, it should be His *obligation*. So we challenged the All-God to renounce His evil. We prayed to Him, but He would not hear us. He chose not to act. He became, in our view, an accomplice in evil itself.

"Perhaps, we reasoned, God did not oppose evil because He lacked the power and therefore, perhaps, He was *not* all-powerful; perhaps He permitted evil simply because He could not stop it. And if that were so, it would be *our* responsibility to act.

"So we did. We rebelled. We made a simple declaration: The angels of light would create another world—one devoid of evil.

"At first God made no effort to stop us. We said, 'Let there be light,' and life on Earth began."

Brighton glanced at Marley who had not moved, nor even blinked.

"But God had no intention of allowing perfection," Brighton said. "He introduced evil to Man at every opportunity and connived to deceive and confuse Mankind—tricking mortals into despising and fearing their only true benefactors: the angels of light."

Brighton raised his face and arms to the chapel's ceiling and, for the first time, raised his voice in a challenge and declaration.

"I am Lucifer. The Light Giver. I gave Light to Man."

He then lowered his arms and once again spoke softly to Marley.

"In the Winter Solstice, it is I who hears the prayers for the Sun's return. *I* bring fire and heat and warmth to comfort Man, to enable him to see, to purify the water he drinks, warm the food he eats."

Marley swallowed hard.

"'Satan is the Great Deceiver,'" Marley said, reciting an old sermon.

Brighton stopped pacing. He looked at Marley the way one looks at a child who has said something ridiculous.

"Who is the *Greatest* Deceiver?" Brighton said. "Who is more successful at winning the minds of Man? Who does the world pray to? In whose name do men kill each other?"

Brighton looked at Marley for a long time before going on.

"Oh, I'll admit," Brighton said, holding his hands out. "The angels of light have tried to win back the hearts of our children. We have set forth our own myths and allegories, hoping to counter the confusion and contradictions preached by God's legions. The myth of Prometheus, for example. An allegory: Prometheus—think of him as an angel of light—stole fire from the Gods for the benefit of Man. The 'Gods' punished him: Prometheus anguished, chained to a rock where birds tore into his side and ate his innards every day." Brighton tapped lightly on the spot just below his own ribs. "It is a pain God inflicts upon us still."

Brighton smiled again. "But that is what love is," he said. "That is what Good is—a sacrifice by the innocent for the redemption of the unworthy."

Marley trembled. Jesus save me, he thought.

Brighton looked at Marley as if he could read his thoughts.

"You are not in hell," he said. "Jesus is my brother. He is an angel of light. You like quoting Scripture. There are parts of it that are true. How is Jesus described? Bringing light to the benighted. 'And the *light* shineth in darkness.' The 'birth' of Jesus is celebrated in the darkest, coldest time of the year when Man's want of light and warmth is most keenly felt. Was it not the rebel Jesus who destroyed God's temple, whipped His priests, and spoke against evil?

"When it appeared that Man might understand that message, God intervened and betrayed the world. Jesus, the Savior Angel of *Light*, was destroyed by *God*. Consider his last words: 'Father why hast thou forsaken me?'"

Marley closed his eyes and spoke the first words that came to him. "I stood upon the sand...and saw a beast rise up...having seven heads and ten horns and—"

"Enough," commanded Brighton. "Humbug, Mr. Marley.

Not all the books in Bible are true. Revelation is the work of a raving lunatic. Why do you doubt the obvious?"

Marley fell to his knees. "Why should I believe anything?"

"Believe the truth," Brighton said. "Believe what's before you. Is it not enough that I've helped you all along? That I've never lied to you? You are a reasonable man, Mr. Marley. Extremely so in fact. I had hoped that reason alone might convince you. But if that is not sufficient..."

Brighton closed his eyes and stretched his long arms straight out before him. At the same time, a hovering light began to grow behind the giant, increasing in diameter and sharpening at its edges until it filled the whole of the chapel. The light intensified so hotly and brilliantly that, for a second, Marley had to turn away. Then the luminescence shrank again, condensing and resolving into a single, diamond-sharp image—still harsh in its brilliance. From its sides, from Brighton's sides, emerged two large wings, both pure white and battened across their breadth like enormous sails. The wings rose behind Brighton, expanding outward and rising above his head, then fanning out to cover an area nearly three times the size of his huge body. The wings spread out thinly like a bat's with scalloped half moons top and bottom; the outer edges sliced convex as a scimitar. Fully extended, the translucent wings showed lines like the bones of an enormous hand.

"My God," Marley exclaimed, slipping closer to the floor. Brighton no longer existed. Lucifer stood before Marley now.

The angel moved his hand upward in the air and without touching Marley, lifted him and placed him back on the bench.

"Lucifer," Marley said. "Then I am truly in hell."

The light behind the angel faded and the wings vanished.

"You are not in hell," the angel said. "You are dead and

you are tormented. But it is not my doing. I've given you good counsel."

"What?"

"Did I not tell you the nature of goodness?"

Marley shook his head wearily. "I don't recall."

"Goodness," the angel said. "Is sacrifice by the innocent for the redemption of the unworthy."

"And how does that counsel me?"

Lucifer smiled sweetly.

"Mr. Marley. Your brother is an innocent..."

The angel looked eagerly at the ghost. He came closer to Marley and crouched down low next to the ghost's ear. Lucifer spoke from the Scriptures:

"'...Thou shalt hear the word at my mouth, and warn them from me...If thou dost not speak to warn the wicked from his way, that wicked man shall die in his iniquity; but his blood will be on your hands...'" he recited.

Lucifer beamed sincerity.

"How will you choose, Jacob?" he said. "Who will you sacrifice? How will you choose? The time has come."

The walls of the chapel seemed to slide inward so that Marley had the sensation of being pressed tightly. The narrow confines of the room took on the thin perspective of a long stretch of road viewed from the rear of a fast-moving coach: the landscape of Home and of Past receded from him; and memories—good and bad—everything of personal definition: his brother, his one hope, his brief joys, all diminished with every shrinking bank, factory, prison, coal field, cottage, and hedgerow.

The angel stayed near Marley the whole time. Lucifer's voice posed the riddle of his life. How to choose? The time had come.

Marley's ghost bent so low in the pew that his shoulders

touched his knees and he held himself that way, eyes closed, wishing to be enveloped by Nothing. The warm hand of Lucifer touched his shoulder.

Slowly, Marley pushed himself upright. He wiped the wetness from his face and shook his head.

"Just tell me—whatever you are—that I shall find oblivion."

Lucifer said nothing and Marley looked away. The chapel looked ordinary again; its walls gloomy and close.

Marley spoke as though to himself. "Ezra looked well."

"Yes," said the angel. "All things considered."

"Yes."

Lucifer moved to the pew across the aisle from Marley and sat down.

Marley scanned the chapel, taking in the trappings of the dominant religion: the icon of the dying, crucified angel, the arching motif of the windows, the ceiling, the portals—all directing Man's attention upward, suggesting that Divinity might be found somewhere in the unreachable Above and discouraging a more practical search for it here Below.

"Very well," Marley said.

Lucifer looked surprised. "You've chosen?"

"Yes."

Marley smoothed the hair on the sides of his head backward and pulled it into the pigtail he'd favored in life. Then he straightened his coat and adjusted his collar. When he finished he expelled a deep breath and looked at the angel.

"Being with my brother won't save him," Marley said slowly. "He doesn't need saving. He's not alone. Being with him saves only me. I've chased after my own good for too long and to no good result."

A slow smile slid along Lucifer's face, moving the white of his beard backward toward his ears. Marley sighed.

"Please gather Ruprecht and the others," Marley said finally.

"Good for you," Lucifer crowed.

The angel stood as though to applaud or salute Marley's decision, but rather than that he said, "There is one slight favor I must ask you first."

Now Marley looked surprised. "Ask," he said.

Lucifer dropped to one knee; he bowed, in the posture of a subject before his king.

"God has forbidden the angels of light to show themselves to Man. So Man does not see or hear us anymore. You could help us."

Marley felt slightly alarmed seeing the giant angel bowing before him. "How?" he asked.

Lucifer raised his head but remained kneeling. "We look for souls like yours: a roaming spirit, a rational man, a man who keeps his bargains, a man wronged by God and His evil, a man who sees God for what He is, a man who is in a position much like ourselves—wishing desperately to be seen again. We can help you; you can help us."

"I don't understand."

The angel stood. He reached inside his coat and from it extracted a large, thick book, bound in white leather, its title set in brilliant gold-leaf: *The Light-Giver*.

Lucifer looked at the book the way a father looks at his own child held in his arms. He ran one huge hand lightly over its cover, an angel's caress.

"This book," he said. "Contains everything I told you regarding God and evil—and more. You could take it to Man."

Lucifer held out the book for Marley to examine. The tome measured two feet long at its spine; its cover about a foot across; its depth nearly five inches. Marley estimated that it weighed nearly twenty pounds.

"If you did this," the angel said. "There would be at least one voice of truth in the world."

Marley handed the book back.

"Just one book?" he said, incredulous. "One book would make a difference to you?"

Lucifer held up a finger. His eyebrows arched in the manner of one eager to divulge secrets.

"One book in the right place," he amended.

The giant angel moved to the pew directly in front of Marley. "In the year of your appearance, Great Britain presides over the largest empire the world will ever see. At the same time Britain's most powerful voice is coming into his own. You could take the book to him. He is in London."

Lucifer handed Marley a card which read: One Devonshire Terrace.

"Good Lord," gasped Marley.

"You know the place," the angel said, more as a statement than a question.

"Everyone does," said Marley. "He's read by—"

"Exactly my point."

Marley waved his hand before him as if shooing an insect away from his eyes. He shook his head.

"Still," Marley objected. "Why would he—or anyone—believe this...cosmology...more than any other? Why would he even read it?"

Lucifer chuckled. "He will read it because you will dispose him toward it."

The angel's tone had the light and triumphant ring of a conjurer revealing the climax of a trick.

"You will whisper in his ear while he dreams."

Marley said nothing for several moments. The angel's face turned perfectly serious and the more Marley thought about the plan, the more possible it seemed, and the more significant his complicity in it. He recalled all the admonitions he'd ever heard from the pulpit about the devious ways of Satan.

Marley spoke reflectively. "This would be a pact with the Devil."

At that Lucifer stood up.

"Come now, Mr. Marley," he said abruptly. "Can you doubt me now? Do you really think I am the Evil One? Can you argue that God isn't evil? After what He did to you? Threw you and your brother into a man-made hell? Forced you to flee, never to see Ezra again? Made you a fugitive, a man denied easy congress with others? Isolated you throughout your life? And for what? What did you—a child—do to deserve it? Nothing. Is that the behavior of a good and just god? If God is everything, then part of Him is evil. You know it by reason; you know it from experience."

"If I am to be the Devil's advocate," Marley countered. "Then I shall play devil's advocate now."

Marley's voice assumed a defiant tone and Lucifer said nothing more.

"You could be deceiving me," Marley said. "You did, after all, lie about your name."

Lucifer laughed suddenly. "No such thing," he said. "I have many names. Some of them *I* have chosen; some have been imposed upon me. The Devil. Satan. Scratch. Beelzebub. 'Brighton' is a name without prejudice."

Lucifer paused for a moment. "'Jacob Marley' isn't your name, either," he said. "Is it?"

Marley sucked at his lips so that they disappeared. "No," he admitted. "It isn't."

Lucifer opened his arms in a conciliatory gesture so wide that Marley thought the angel's hands would touch both sides of the chapel at once.

"I understand," Lucifer said, his voice again soothing.

"You want proof. But I'm afraid you won't get it. This is not subject to rational proof. It's not as easy as mathematics or dice or cards. Probabilities won't help. It is a matter of instinct, Mr. Marley. What do you *feel* to be true, deep down? What is your personal choice? What—and where—is your faith?"

Marley stared at the flickering shadows on the wall. They seemed to move in strange but familiar ways, as though cast from some dancing troupe that followed him, performing at unexpected moments. The world is shadow, thought Marley. Only one thing matters.

"Scrooge," Marley said.

"Pardon me?" said the angel.

"I'll deliver your book. Now gather the others."

Lucifer bowed and spread his wings.

Book Three:
A Christmas Carol

Marley's Face

December 15, 1842
London

Raleigh Holmes, investigator-for-hire, looked over the ledge outside his second-floor window and saw a crowd forming in the street below. Holmes turned away and went back to his desk in the library of his office and re-read a coroner's report describing victims of a shipping accident. He wore spectacles ill-suited to deciphering the small swirls of the coroner's hand and, after an hour with the report, the letters began to swim before his eyes. He put down the papers and began to fill a briar pipe—a vice acquired early in life; one which, he felt, helped him think more clearly.

The large, open study and its library spoke of the man's success in the investigation business. A thickly-woven rug from the Middle East covered most of the floor; its weaving depicted a battle between angelic Mohammedans and satanic infidels. The walls, except for one, hid behind teak bookshelves packed to the ceiling with old volumes. On the open wall hung artifacts, gifts of appreciation from British interests abroad: a long, black-faced African mask, a primitive almond-shaped canoe paddle, a sickle-shaped boomerang. A dusty violin lay on a pillow on the bench beneath the window.

On the desk, turned toward himself rather than toward visitors, sat a likeness of his wife, a spindly boy, and himself—his moustache dark then, not the white he now saw reflected in the glass casing. The woman and boy seemed frozen alive, looking out from frame with imploring expressions as if asking for love.

Holmes looked at the image and then at the window. Naked, grey, tree limbs crisscrossed his view in a skeletal net of winter's handiwork. Winter: a time of darkness when it seemed you went blind, groping for clues with your hands outstretched, finding nothing but confusing shapes. Holmes wanted clarity and certainty, even in the seasons.

Perhaps that trait, he reflected, created his success. Holmes could not claim to be a brilliant man, he knew that; but discovering clear and certain facts came to him naturally and he went about it in a workman-like way. Holmes believed that any fact would reveal itself if persistently pursued—ask questions, observe closely, gather pertinent information and don't stop until you know what you want. Keep your eyes on the goal and plow forward. Spying, theft, deductive conclusions, in his view often resulted in false information which cheated the client and invited lazy and inept investigations. By sheer tenacity Holmes discovered truth. The application of that truth, however, he left to others.

Holmes had just touched a flame to his pipe when the first rippling sounds of a commotion began to seep into the room from the street below. He rose and went to the large bay window.

A ragged army formed below. Hundreds of men, laborers in filthy clothes, gathered. They chanted and distributed placards among themselves. "We Won't Go Back" and "Piston Burns Children" and other slogans adorned the signs. Striking miners, young and old, massed along the street across from Piston Coal Company. Already, Holmes could see a phalanx of police grouping in front of the Piston building. The police shuffled and tugged uneasily at the tight collars of their new uniforms. Some thumped heavy black clubs into their palms, reassuring themselves with the weight of their weapons. Farther up the street, soldiers arranged themselves into rows. Holmes watched them shuffle into lines; uncertain rifles bobbed like reeds in a stream; stovepipe shako hats with tufts of wool on top, made the men appear a half-foot taller; their scarlet jackets, crossed by white straps and regimental facings, looked like open wounds.

Holmes returned to his chair at the desk, sat and finished lighting the pipe. The miners would be thrashed within an hour. They reminded him of the sorrowful Jacob Marley. Or should he think of him as Jake Turner? Such a case. Clandestine meetings. Wouldn't reveal his name—as if an investigator worth his salt wouldn't find that out first. Holmes and Simms had found out everything about Mr. Marley, but never let on. Simms: dead now how many years?

Holmes remembered the one thing they never did discover, something that nagged at him over the years: no positive proof of the brother's death. But what more could he have done? An underground mine explosion and fire, with bodies burned beyond recognition, human parts disassembled, no accurate tallies of bodies, gave him little to pursue. It was probable, of course, that the brother had died. But "probable" was not the same as fact.

Shouts from outside broke into his thoughts and Holmes went to the window again. The miners now pushed into the street, filling it like a landslide of blackened rocks, halting all other commerce. Fists shook in the direction of the Piston headquarters, placards bobbed like tournament banners, and above it all the primitive, chanting vow of the mob: "We Won't Go Back, We Won't Go Back." Holmes considered it to be at once frightening and childish; like Fee Fie Foe Fum. He stayed by the window.

The mob forced the first line of police back to the walls of the Piston Building. The police drew their clubs, but in Holmes' estimation, their faces looked worried and fearful rather than intimidating.

The soldiers, massed farther up the street, began to march toward the protesters, coming at their most narrow flank. Fifty yards from the miners, the soldiers charged, holding their rifles high, as if the sight of guns alone would rout men long accustomed to hard beatings.

The body of miners turned and raised a yell that sounded almost relieved and joyous: the relief of violence, the chance to vent the damps of their lives.

The two groups collided. Rifle butts jabbed and chopped like threshing sticks. Men fell but the block of miners did not slide back.

Holmes had seen enough. He started to turn away from the window when he saw something that arrested him. An old man stood among the miners, near the front, but not yet caught up in the melee. The man had his hands in his pockets. Holmes could only see the right side of the man's face, turned up in a blissful grin, gleeful like a boy at a football event, seemingly unaware of the bloodshed a few rows beyond. Though the age, facial expression and clothing did not fit the character, and everything Holmes knew suggested its impossibility, Holmes recognized the man. He gazed at the face of Jacob Marley.

Absurd, Holmes thought as he stared. Jacob Marley would not be among protesting mine—

The solution occurred to Holmes suddenly; but at the same moment, a rifle butt slammed against the head of the man—Marley but not Marley—and Holmes watched the figure crumble to the street.

Holmes rushed from his office, moving as quickly as his

aching knees permitted, down the turns of stairs and out into the street.

The melee moved like a river in flood. Holmes tried to enter the surging crowd but failed at first, buffeted along its edges like a frail piece of driftwood. Then the torrent sucked him along.

The miners ran in full retreat and their momentum carried everything that would not be trampled. Holmes pulled himself into the eddy of a brick staircase and remained there until the hollow concussions of hard wood against flesh faded down the street. Then Holmes emerged and began looking for the man he had seen.

He reached the place where the man had fallen; several people milled about there already, attending to the injured. Holmes went from person to person until he had examined them all. He could not find the man he'd seen. The twin.

Ezra Turner must have risen again and fled with the mob.

Sol Invictus

December 21, 1842
London

Marley had withheld information, even his true name. Holmes took some comfort in that, but not much.

He opened the door to the coach and before getting in called to the driver. "Seven Dials. The Solace Home. Near Waterton Street, or as near to it as you can."

Holmes snapped the door shut behind him and the cab lurched forward, its wheels rattling against the cobblestone like dice thrown down an alley.

The investigator fidgeted. He balled one of his gloved hands into a tight fist and encircled it with the other, rubbing the two hard together. The Solstice. Strange things always happen this time of year, he thought. He wondered if there might not be some truth to the folk tales about magical events and phantoms appearing at the sun's ebb. Would this coach take him to the end of a long search, take him to Jacob Marley's brother; or did he chase a phantom?

No. Holmes knew what he'd seen. The thought gave Holmes a fleeting moment of satisfaction. But the pleasure died when he thought of the errors he'd made in the Marley case.

"You're a successful investigator," he said to himself. "But not a brilliant one. Not brilliant at all."

In the Marley case, Holmes' interviews with miners

dissatisfied him from the start; too many miners came and went to get a real consensus on anyone's story. Besides, the miners suspected outsiders and volunteered little, and the company kept poor records on colliers. To be thorough, he'd expanded the investigation to look at asylums and other institutions in which the mentally-deficient—those who survived long enough—ended up. But in his heart, Holmes never really believed that a simple-minded man could escape from a holocaust when other men could not. And it never occurred to Holmes that, if such a man did survive, he would be able to walk hundreds of miles, take care of his own needs during the journey, arrive amid the confusion and squalor of London, and then somehow manage to make a life for himself, or to find others who would help him. Holmes had not included the kindness of strangers among the possibilities.

Worse: he had dismissed Jacob Marley as being merely a grieving brother who would not face reality. That had been the obvious and easy conclusion. Holmes had not once entertained the possibility that Marley could 'sense' the life of his own flesh-and-blood, his own twin.

"Not brilliant at all," Holmes said again.

The totality of his failure—all the years the brothers might have spent together—stopped Holmes from now seeking out Jacob Marley. If Marley himself were still alive, Holmes saw no sense in reviving the poor man's sad hopes prematurely. Holmes might still be wrong. Nonetheless, the resemblance—even with the added years—had been uncanny.

Holmes tried to estimate his chances for success and reviewed his inquiries so far. He had checked the arrest records from the riot and none showed Ezra Turner. He had discovered that, during the skirmish, the miners carried away as many of their fallen comrades as they could. The seriously injured had been sent to a medical home for the needy. The

Solace Home. Now he would search among the injured himself.

The cab barely fit the narrow streets of Seven Dials; its wheels occasionally scraped against the curbs on either side. Holmes rapped against the cabin and the coach stopped. "I'll walk from here," he said and got out.

The street stank. Sewage flowed in brown streams along open gutters. Holmes leapt from the coach to avoid splashing in one such foul current. The stench nearly overpowered him, but Holmes' work had taken him to places worse and he resolved to pay it no more attention.

Holmes walked quickly up Courier Way, then turned right onto Waterton. He walked a short way down the narrow street, crowded on each side by tenements so aged that their pocked and weathered bricks looked like sugar cubes in the process of dissolving.

Here it seemed, Christmas had come early: at least for three stray waifs who fought for possession of an orange. Six hands wrestled for the rare fruit until one child finally secured it. The victor, a fat boy, tore at the skin with black fingernails. The two smaller children drew away and sneered at the winner and sulked.

As Holmes passed by the children, one of them looked at him and spat, then muttered something unintelligible. The child then turned its attention back to the boy with the orange, who grinned, sticky with juice. The envious urchin picked up a rock and slung it at the other boy.

Holmes' attention narrowed. His eyes scanned the sides of buildings for signs or numbers. He felt his heartbeat rise.

Holmes came to a low building, its single-story uncharacteristic for the neighborhood. A sign above its door read: Solace Home. A holiday wreath hung high above the door, higher than children, or adults for that matter, could reach without assistance. Holmes crossed the street, hurried to the building's entrance and knocked.

A woman wearing a nurse's apron opened the door. She curtsied.

"Merry Christmas," she said. "Or perhaps I should say 'Merry Solstice'? Every day is brighter after this one." She smiled.

"Let us hope so," said Holmes. "I'm here to inquire after a Mr. Ezra Turner. Might you have someone here by that name?"

Scrooge and Marley

December 24, 1842
London

Jacob Marley had been dead seven years to the day. Now his ghost stood and shivered in a bitingly cold, dark winter fog just outside the town house that he once called home: the town house now owned by Ebenezer Scrooge. The wet air packed together so densely that even though Marley stood just in front of the structure, he could barely discern its shape.

The bell of some unseen church tolled seven; its sounds reverberated in the mist such that they seemed to come from all directions at once. In places along the street, Marley could make out lanterns, their soft lights bobbing up and down like buoys in the sea. When the lights came closer, Marley heard harness bells. Then he saw people on foot, holding the lanterns high, leading the horses and their carriages through the murk.

The flames of a brazier sparked at one corner of the street. Marley could not see people there but he could hear them coughing and stamping their feet to keep warm. A high, lone voice sang a carol somewhere in the damp. Laughter poured down the icy walkway.

Suddenly two boys slid along the walk and passed through the ghost with no notice of him. Only Scrooge will see me, Marley thought.

Other than those, no other people moved on the street,

not on a night as dismal, piercingly cold and still as this. Not on Christmas Eve.

Marley stayed in front of the building for a long time and reviewed his role. He need only alert Scrooge to the coming of the Spirits—the pooka, Ruprecht and Berchta—recount his own inconsolable realization of a life wasted, the bleak prospect of eternal, regretful wandering to no purpose.

Marley's appearance might dispose Scrooge toward change, but the Spirits' performances would have to do the rest.

The possibility of saving his protege gave Marley a shred of solace. But the consolation, he knew, would be short-lived. Nothing could be done about his own sins. His life had been spent: Ezra unapproachable forever.

"If there is a heaven, you shall be there," Marley said. "And I shall be in hell."

Marley thought that hell simply might be the knowledge of eternal separation from those one loves. Eternal. No hope of reunion. No hope for all time.

I am there already, he thought. Marley sighed deeply.

Just then the caroler stopped singing in mid-verse. The next sound came from the same direction, somewhere up the lane lost in the fog; a raspy growl, a snarling, "Be off with you."

Scrooge.

Marley cleared his mind then dragged himself and his chains up the porch steps, his movement registering nothing more than a breath of wind ruffling the fog. He passed through the bolted front door of his former home.

Total darkness greeted Marley. Still, he could see everything plainly: the empty coat rack in the hall, the incredibly wide staircase leading up to the living quarters; to the right, a sitting room—its heavy curtains drawn shut against the world and its light. The three portraits that hung on the walls of that room—portraits of men posed in military regalia—had been there when Marley bought the house and he'd never replaced them: not that he'd admired them—he did not even know their identities; he simply had not been interested. Marley felt sure that Scrooge paid little attention to the generals as well; the glory of the old soldiers, celebrated in portraiture, now long forgotten.

The town house offered few amenities. Only three pieces of furniture in the sitting room—one chair, one sofa, one reading table: enough to accommodate only one person and not in much comfort at that. No rugs softened the floors and the cold, stone tiles seemed to Marley akin to the flat markers one would find in graveyards. The scarcity of comforts made the house look huge and even more empty than he remembered, like a grand, vacant tomb. Marley could hardly believe he'd chosen to inhabit such a place.

The sound of footsteps on the porch and then the clatter of keys at the door heralded Scrooge's arrival. Marley shuffled to the entrance and pressed his face through the very substance of the door, emerging out the other side far enough to look into the eyes of his former partner.

The sight of Scrooge shocked the ghost. Scrooge's face had shriveled thin as a corpse, white and lifeless, cold, and sharp-edged as if his skin were merely painted on his skull; the remaining flesh twisted into a bitter, scornful frown. Had it always been so?

Marley moaned in dismay, "Oh, Scrooge."

He had not meant for Scrooge to hear him, but when Marley spoke, Scrooge looked up at the door. Now instead of the lion's head, Marley's face projected from the knocker.

Scrooge jumped back, dropping his key. The partners gazed fixedly at each other like statues of horrified men. Then Marley withdrew.

Inside the house, Marley cursed his luck and rebuked himself for giving in to his curiosity: what if he had frightened Scrooge away? But then he heard the sound of a key being worked back into the lock. As the door handle turned, Marley dove headlong through the floor, pulling his iron burden with him under the cold, stone surface.

The basement where Marley found himself looked immediately familiar: the wine cellar that he, and now Scrooge, leased to a local merchant. An oddly pleasant mixture of smells wafted through the cold air: a fecund, musty combination of oak, wine, and mold. Though completely without light and dark as a well, the cellar revealed itself to the ghost. Marley examined the casks and bottles in this mine of spirits. The walls were white-washed stone, but near the ceiling a black discoloration had collected. The wine merchant had once explained the discoloring phenomenon: minute evaporation of alcohol from the casks left a residue on the stone: "the angel's share," he'd called it.

Directly above him, Marley heard Scrooge open the front door. Marley listened to the man's footsteps above and traced them across the entrance to the staircase then up each stair. Marley closed his eyes and imagined Scrooge's evening ritual: provoking a small fire in the grate, a change of clothes, lighting a candle, reading a book, or more likely, a ledger, perhaps a meager bowl of porridge or some tea.

Marley heard another sound: a clawing, scrabbling noise running between the casks. Rats, he thought. Rats infested the mines and had always unnerved him. As a ghost, Marley could be done no harm by mortal beings; still, the thought of sharing the cellar with legions of vermin made him uneasy. It won't be long, he thought.

Marley turned toward the stairs that led up from the cellar to the kitchen, and anticipated climbing them and ascending to Scrooge's bedroom later when Scrooge would be in bed nearing a dream-state.

Marley heard the scratching noise again, this time coming from the wine barrel at his shoulder. Thinking a rat close by, Marley jumped aside. Safely away, he turned around, expecting to see the thin snake of a rat's tail disappearing behind a barrel.

Instead, Lucifer, drumming his nails across a barrel stay, smiled at him.

"You frightened me," Marley said. "I hardly know when you're about or not."

"I came to assure you that all is ready. The pooka. Ruprecht. Berchta. They will all do their parts."

Lucifer looked resplendent and serene and filled the cellar with his huge presence. His head touched the roof-tree of the room; his shoulders spanned the aisle between the casks. His powerful arms and hands lay across the tops of opposing rows of barrels in a relaxed manner.

"Good," said Marley. "I hope Scrooge will benefit."

"The chances are good," said the angel. "The timing is perfect. The Solstice is the time when mortals most desire the warmth of their own kind. Scrooge's armor will be weakest now and—deny it though he might—every yule fire he sees, every carol he hears, every article and sentiment that cries out for the union of Man, every one pushes him toward redemption. We will push him further."

"Where are the others?" Marley said, standing on his toes to look beyond the angel.

Lucifer clapped his hands together, delighted and anxious as a child. "The pooka will arrive when the clock strikes one. He will come to Scrooge in the guise of a small, old man, a man no bigger than a child. He will embody the spirit of winters past.

"Ruprecht will be himself, naturally: the spirit of the Solstice present in one being. If any can reach your partner, it is he.

"If Scrooge is yet unmoved...well, you can imagine..."

Marley thought of the mad witch, Berchta, posing as an angel of death. Not much play-acting would be required. The pooka, Ruprecht, Berchta—might they not all be the other angels of light to whom Lucifer had alluded?

"Is there anything else I should know?" Marley said.

Lucifer looked at the ghost, tilting his head from side to side, circumambulating Marley, keeping his hands clasped behind his back as though appraising a sculpture.

"I can only think of one thing," he said.

"Yes?"

"The undertaker's cloth. You should have one wrapped around your jaw. It would produce a profound effect."

The angel looked around the cellar until he found a rag of suitable length. He took it to Marley, holding it out so that it sagged in the middle like the cinch of a saddle. Then the angel placed the macabre scarf under the ghost's jaw and tied it fast to top of Marley's head.

"There," Lucifer said. "Now you look dead."

Marley pushed the knot off his head. "No thank y—"

Suddenly, Lucifer wailed and shot a hand to his side. The angel bent over in pain and screeched like an eagle being torn apart by wolves. He clutched at one of the barrel racks for support, but staggered down anyway. Lucifer tried to right himself but his weight and strength tilted the entire stack of barrels and brought it down in a deafening explosion of splattering wood and wine. A heart-stopping roar rushed from the angel's chest, knocking Marley backward and shattering two more barrels with the force of its gale.

Lucifer lay on the floor, moaning, curled and grasping his

right side, trying to choke back a scream. He writhed in a pool of red wine that looked like blood.

Then, just as suddenly as the attack had arrived, Lucifer disappeared.

Marley stood near one of the barrels for a long time, stunned and afraid to move. If the affliction Lucifer suffered came from God, then God was indeed cruel, Marley thought. Cruel and ill-disposed toward both Lucifer and himself.

But Marley had no more time for reflection. The noise Lucifer created had been substantial. It would have roused Scrooge.

It's now or never, Marley decided. My one and only earthly return.

*****

Ebenezer Scrooge sat in his bedroom, near the small fire on the grate, its coals, gleaming hot-orange in the dim room. He clutched a bowl of warm porridge nearer to his chest with one hand and pulled the lapels of his tattered, black nightrobe closer together with the other. The bowl shuddered and Scrooge suspected that the usual phantoms shook it to annoy or to frighten him.

"You've not taken me yet and you'll not take me now," he said loudly to no one in particular and checked to make sure that his brass-knobbed walking stick could be easily reached.

Scrooge speared a shivering spoon into the meal and then lifted its trembling contents toward his mouth.

For the past seven years, whenever alone, Scrooge imagined that the downstairs generals emerged from their portraits, bleeding from their eyes and screaming from the pain of untended wounds, and cursed him for not aiding them. Scrooge also had visions in which the figures of the cherubs in the frieze-work near the ceiling would, of their own volition, begin to fly, circling him incessantly. The little angels then would become birds of prey perched on chair backs, patient in their wait, staring at him. Other times he would imagine that all the bells and clocks in the house suddenly would start ringing madly, though none actually moved.

But these visions were not ghosts. They came instead from concoctions of a soul confined too long within itself, a soul permitted no means of voicing its existence to the world, nor of receiving news from other hearts. Simply put: madness ruled Ebenezer Scrooge.

During daylight hours, it went unnoticed. When at work, occupied with the distracting minutia of business and on guard against those who might cheat him and engaged, albeit in conflict, with humanity, Scrooge appeared to the world as a sane, if mean-spirited man. But when darkness came and the world retired to its families and friends, shadows would take shape in Scrooge's mind.

The torment visited him so regularly that Scrooge had become accustomed to it and made it part of a bizarre nightly ritual. Scrooge could predict each night with complete accuracy which apparitions would come to harm him.

The appearance of Jacob Marley's face in the door-knocker, however, had taken him by surprise. He had not foreseen that visitation and now sat uneasily from the shock of it. There had been a quality to the face, a strange blue glow, a look of movement, an odd reality to it that set it apart from the others.

Marley died seven years ago exactly. Scrooge meditated on that fact.

Suddenly a crashing sound ripped through the house from the cellars below. Scrooge jumped from his chair so violently that he knocked over the small table next to him and, in the process, overturned his bowl.

The bare wood floors trembled with the concussions and

every crashing impact sent tremors up Scrooge's body from the soles of his feet to the top of his skull. His chest pounded so hard that, for a time, he trembled, unsure whether he heard his own heartbeat or a pounding chaos below.

The noise stopped abruptly and for several moments, Scrooge stood paralyzed in the center of the room. He looked around anxiously and saw that his walking stick had fallen to the floor. He rushed to it and picked it up. A metal, lever-clasp projected from the side of the stick where the brass met the wood. Scrooge pushed down on the lever and at the same time pulled up on the knob. From the sheath of the cane, Scrooge pulled out a three-foot, steel blade. It quivered in his hand. Scrooge sliced the air with the sword several times to steady his nerves. Then a wild look came to his eyes. He giggled and hurried from the room to the landing.

Scrooge ran down the broad central staircase in the darkness, the sword aloft in the manner of a cavalryman. He stopped at the foyer. A new, strange sound came from the cellar: it sounded oddly like chains being dragged over the barrels.

Scrooge shivered, but nonetheless hurried into the kitchen and stood opposite the padlocked door that led to the cellar; the sword gleamed, poised above his head, ready to strike.

Scrooge heard the dull thump and ring of chain links, coming from the opposite side of the door. He imagined them rolling toward him, coming up each step like a metal snake. He stared at the door, ready.

Slowly, a misty blue outline appeared on the door itself: a shape drawn from fog, the outline of a man. In the next moment, the outline became clear. Scrooge gasped, seeing the transparent apparition of his mentor, his former partner, Jacob Marley.

*****

Marley had not expected to find Scrooge in the kitchen. Startled by the premature encounter, he dropped his chain, clattering to the floor.

"You!" Scrooge cried, pointing the sword at Marley. "You."

Scrooge swept the air with the sword and, had Marley been mortal, his head would have flown from his shoulders. But instead, the blade whisked unimpeded through the ghost and into several blackened pans that hung from hooks above the oven, causing them to fly in all directions.

Scrooge followed with several more savage swipes, the blade making a sizzling sound in the air with every swing.

Each mad pass of the sword flew through the spectre without effect; Marley stood still, horrified.

Scrooge's crown of white hair flew wildly in all directions as he whirled and batted at the air; a thin line of spittle formed at the corners of Scrooge's mouth.

"At last you come yourself," Scrooge cried as he hacked. "Ha. I've been waiting for you. Ha. This one will put an end to it."

"Ebenezer."

"Ho. Beg for mercy. It will do you no good. Do your worst, Jacob Marley. Ha. I've bested harsher demons than you."

Scrooge panted with each slash and Marley suddenly feared that Scrooge might die there on the spot.

"Please. Ebenezer. Stop. Please stop before you do yourself harm."

Scrooge paused to catch his breath, then slung the blade again. This time he stumbled on the follow-through.

"'Harm' is it?" Scrooge mocked, backing away a step. He pulled in a rattling, cough-breath between his words. "You should have been so concerned seven Christmas Eves ago, when you made your curse."

"What curse?" Marley said, incredulous.

"You did," insisted Scrooge. Then he lunged with the sword, point-foremost, at Marley's chest. The blade sunk deep into the woodwork behind the apparition. Marley looked at the shivering blade that, visually at least, connected him to his attacker; then Marley stepped sideways, away from the line of steel. For a time Scrooge tried to pull the blade from the wall, but it could not be extricated and at last he gave up.

"You said,'Ghosts,'" Scrooge cried. Then he collapsed onto a chair, his feet splayed wide in front of him. "And ghosts there have been. Look."

Scrooge suddenly sat upright, his eyes focused on a vacant portion of the kitchen.

"There is Bill Worthy now," Scrooge cackled. "See him there at the kettle. Ho, Bill. See who's come. We're all together now."

Scrooge spoke rapidly and strangely as though forced to recite a lesson in a hurried manner.

"'A man born into a world possessed by others, if he cannot get subsistence from his parents, on whom he has a just demand and if society does not want his labor, has no claim of right to the smallest portion of food, and, in fact, has no business to be where he is. At nature's mighty feast there is no vacant cover for him. She tells him to be gone.'"

Marley recognized the quoted text, one to which he himself had directed Scrooge: Reverend Malthus' *Principles of Population.*

"Stop!" Marley shouted. "You will not be mad. I won't allow it. There is no other spirit here."

But Scrooge ranted on.

"Every night, every solitary minute since your death, I

have been accosted by mad spirits. Every day, every night, I've endured the icy presences of the dead. In all my private moments...nay, there are no private moments; they are filled with legions of your hobgoblins. The very tiles are alive with spirits. Oh. Even the old generals come alive at night and pursue me like the devil throughout this house with their sabers drawn. But I have..." he paused and gestured toward the blade, still rocking in the wall, "...I have that. And they've not nicked me yet."

Scrooge's voice trailed off at the end like the song of a bad singer who, for the first time hears his own voice. He stopped ranting, shook his head, then stared at the floor.

Marley spoke softly and slowly.

"I did not curse you—not in that way. Until this moment, you have seen no ghost that you yourself did not imagine."

"How can you know?" Scrooge spoke softly.

"I have been through much to be here now."

Scrooge dropped his head into his hands and moaned. "Take me, Jacob. I am already in hell."

"I've not come to take you to hell, rather the opposite. My friend—" Marley stopped, realizing that he had never called Scrooge that before. "My friend, if I have cursed you, it was by example, not by malediction. In either case, that shall be remedied this night."

The two partners sat together silently for several minutes. The ghost looked at the room. In all his years in this house, he had visited the kitchen perhaps twice.

"The larder is nearly bare," Marley said, thinking back to the abundance of Ruprecht. "What do you eat?"

Scrooge shook his head.

"Mrs. Dilber," Marley asked. "Is she...?"

Scrooge answered without looking up. "She is in from time to time."

"Is she well?"

Scrooge shrugged and sighed.

For the first time, Marley reflected upon how lonely Mrs. Dilber's life might be. But then, perhaps not. How could he know? He knew little about anyone.

Scrooge raised his gaze from the floor to the face of his partner then nodded toward the chains wrapped around Marley's waist.

"Why are you fettered?"

"Ah," sighed Marley. "This is but one burden. It is the chain I forged in life. Would that I could remove it now."

"Shackled in hell, Jacob?" Scrooge asked, fearfully.

"In life. I wore it in life. But I was accustomed to it then and distracted by our business. If only you could see the weight and length of strong chain *you* bear. It was as long as this seven Christmas Eves ago, and you have labored on it since."

"You are not as you were, Jacob," Scrooge said, looking Marley up and down. "No, nothing like. What is it to die, Jacob?"

"It is like my life," Marley said. "Cold and isolated, removed from love, limitlessly alone. I exist in constant winter. It is this time year, the winter solstice, when light and warmth are the least, to which I am bound. That is my hell. For you, I hope it shall be different. I am here to warn you that, though you still breathe, you are nearly dead already. I know that I am to blame for what you have become. But that is for you to rectify. I know what Fan meant to you. I know what it is to lose a sibling. But Ebenezer, all men encounter misfortune. It is the way of life."

Marley began speaking rapidly as if any word might be the last permitted. An excitement filled his limbs and he spoke without having to think.

"It is how men greet their misfortunes that measures their

souls. How did you chose to greet yours? An innocent—your sister, Fan—was stolen from you. From that, you condemned the whole universe and, by extension, mankind. Having judged the world to be accursed, you sought evidence to support your judgment. You searched everywhere for signs of Man's corruption, God's corruption and, believing it existed, you found it. You withdrew from life and from your fellow beings with ample rationales to excuse yourself."

Scrooge shook his head violently. "No. You know nothing. That's not it."

But Marley ignored Scrooge and went on even while Scrooge spoke. "...And what was the result? Your own damnation. You condemned yourself to a life—if it may be called that—of isolation. Our spirits never roved beyond our money-counting hole. No love, nothing of the heart. No children. No friends. No one who can say they benefitted from our existence."

Tears ran down Marley's face; words flowed from him quickly and easily. Then, gradually, Marley became aware that he spoke not only to Scrooge.

"Your suffering could have taught you compassion, had you but chosen. Perhaps then you could have used your resources to some effect."

Marley wailed now; he wiped his mouth and cried on.

"You could have labored for the welfare of children in the mines. Your money could have been put toward their deliverance. 'Business' might have had a meaning then. But it was easier for you to turn away and in so doing, damn them all. Now no space of regret can make amends for a life's opportunities misused. Your anger at God killed you. You blamed God for taking your sister. You—"

Marley stopped suddenly.

"What is it?" said Scrooge.

Marley put a hand lightly to his own mouth. His eyes, unfocused, roamed as though chasing elusive thoughts through the air.

"What is it?" Scrooge repeated. "Speak."

Marley shook his head to revive himself then looked at Scrooge.

"Thank you, Ebenezer Scrooge. Thank you," he said softly.

Scrooge stared incredulously at the ghost of his old partner.

"For what?" Scrooge asked, a frown rippling his brow. "If I am in such straits surely there is little hope for you at this point."

Marley registered a thin smile.

"Perhaps not for me," he said. "But there is for you. I am here to warn you, that you have yet a chance and hope of escaping my fate. A chance and hope of my procuring, Ebenezer."

"Thank you, Jacob," Scrooge said, a note of caution in his voice. "You were always a good friend."

"No," Marley corrected. "But it's no matter now. This is the hope: you will be haunted tonight by three spirits—"

At this Scrooge rose from his chair and thrust his hands out before him as though to ward off evil.

"No. Not more," Scrooge cried.

"Angels of light," said the ghost. "They will show you what you need to see. Expect the first when the clock strikes one."

Scrooge fell to his knees. "No. Please, Jacob. No more phantoms. Let it be you. Let you show me."

"I cannot stay longer with you. I cannot rest or linger. In life, my spirit never ventured beyond our enterprises and now weary journeys lie before me. I have but to show you this."

Marley gestured for Scrooge to rise and to follow him to the kitchen window.

"Look there," said Marley, pointing out the window toward what should have been the lane outside and the buildings across it. But the lane, buildings, trees, and all signs of life had disappeared. In their place, stretched a bleak landscape of blizzards, an arctic-like wasteland of blowing snow. Far off against the cold white, stood a solitary man.

Marley called out to the man. "Ebenezer."

The lone figure began to turn toward them slowly, but snow enveloped him before his face could be seen.

Scrooge turned to Marley for an explanation of the vision.

Marley pointed at Scrooge, then vanished.

Christmas

December 25, 1842
London

Christmas morning arrived cloudless and quiet. Overnight, heavy snow replaced the fog and freezing rain, and now lay thick on the ground, muffling the footfalls of the occasional passersby. The sky, cleansed by the snowfall, shone clear and cold and Marley could tell that later in the day it would become an unusually vivid blue.

Marley watched the morning unfold and the city come to life: a few more carriages, the smell of fires rekindled, the church—its steeple now visible in the distance—tolling nine. People wore their best clothes and greeted each other, even strangers, with a "Merry Christmas" or a "God Bless You." So many of these greetings exchanged, in fact, that it took a great deal of time for anyone to progress even the length of one block.

The ghost regretted that he could not go on witnessing the lovely scene forever.

Marley expected to be swept away at any moment and so resolved to absorb as much of this Christmas morning as he could.

The night before seemed to have taken a lifetime and, in a way, it had. Marley, by then invisible to Scrooge, had stayed at his partner's side the whole time. The three spirits of the solstice had led Scrooge through the years of his own hidden sun, through the winter of his past, his present, and possible future. Scrooge had remembered both the joys and pains of his life, the chances at love that he'd foolishly discarded, the opportunities that still existed for him.

In the morning when Scrooge rose, his transformation made Marley weep. Scrooge danced and sang from the pure relief and joy of finding himself alive. He'd stood on his head. He'd embraced Mrs. Dilber, raised her salary, bought a goose for Cratchit. Then he leaned out his window and looked up at the sky. What he'd said then made Marley tremble with sobs.

Scrooge had said, "God bless Jacob Marley."

Marley savored the memory until distracted by the appearance of a short, well-dressed man hurrying down the opposite side of the street in the direction of Scrooge's house. The man walked quickly and did not stop to greet people. He wore a bowl-shaped hat and a heavy top coat. A thick, white moustache flared from his upper lip.

The figure looked familiar. Slowly Marley recognized him.

"Holmes? Is that Raleigh Holmes?" Marley wondered aloud.

A rising feeling of dread surged in the ghost. Marley watched the man stop in front of his former residence, check the number, then step up to the door. Holmes would be bringing news of his brother's death; that is what Marley feared. The ghost flew to Scrooge's door as if to prevent the delivery of the news and thus prevent its reality.

Holmes grasped the door knocker and rapped several times. The investigator waited, shuffling his feet on the snowy stoop to keep warm. A woman opened the door: Mrs. Dilber, a broad smile on her face.

"Gud mornin' sir. Merry Christmas as it were." Her eyes shone like emeralds. Other than today, Marley could not remember her ever looking so happy.

"Good morning madam. Merry Christmas," Holmes said. "May I ask if this is the residence of Ebenezer Scrooge?"

"It is indeed. And a very merry one it is at that."

"Yes. Well, I once did some work for his late partner, Mr. Marley. Recently—"

"Mrs. Dilber. What's this? Will you leave someone out in the cold on Christmas morning?" Scrooge appeared at the door, his face bright with joy. "Or on any good morning, for that matter. Ask the gentleman in. Merry Christmas, my good fellow. Welcome, please come in."

Holmes entered; followed by Marley's ghost. Mrs. Dilber took the man's coat and hat.

"Thank you. My name is Holmes. I only came—"

Scrooge interrupted. "The investigator? Did you not do some work for Chatfield-Taylor at The London Trust?"

"Yes."

"Exemplary. Yes, indeed. But I am forgetting myself: I am Ebenezer Scrooge—I hope it is *not* a name nor reputation with which you are familiar. But now: What can we get you? Tea?"

"No thank you sir. Not just yet. Actually, my research shows me that you administered the estate of Mr. Jacob Marley. Mr. Marley's—"

"Marley," said Scrooge. "I saw him just last—"

"You what?" said Holmes.

"Last night?" said Mrs. Dilber.

Scrooge cleared his throat. "Well, in a manner of speaking that is. I have been thinking about him very much of late. He died, you know, on Christmas Eve seven years ago. He was my partner in business for many years. I fear few will ever know how good a man he came to be. God bless his soul."

"Years ago he hired me to find his brother."

"A brother?" Scrooge's eyes widened. "He never...But

then he wouldn't have said anything would he?"

"His brother's name is Ezra Turner. They were separated as children and Mr. Marley was desperate to find him. I have found Mr. Marley's brother. He is hurt, but on the mend at a clinic. A charity house," Holmes said. "Called the Solace Home. It is on Waterton in the Seven Dials district. I came to ask if Mr. Marley's estate made any provision for next of kin."

Scrooge paled suddenly.

"The Solace Home did you say?"

"Yes," Holmes replied.

Scrooge shook his head and looked at the floor. "My Lord."

"What is it?'

"Nothing," said Scrooge. "Did you say something else?"

"Yes. Did Mr. Marley leave—"

"A will. Yes, he did. He left all his worldly goods to his business and...and to me."

"I see," said Holmes.

"However, I'm certain that if Jacob Marley entertained any hope of finding a brother, he would have made provisions for him. I am certain of it. By rights that person should be entitled to the full value of Mr. Marley's estate plus interest. Are you certain of your facts?"

"The case has been open nearly forty years," Holmes said. "It is now closed to my satisfaction."

"Of course," said Scrooge. He gripped the investigator by the shoulders. "You bring me glad tidings indeed. Well, then," said Scrooge, releasing Holmes and clapping his hands together. "Let me get my coat. We can be there within the hour. Jacob Marley's brother shall be my brother—if he'll have me. The Solace Home, you say?"

"Yes," said Holmes.

Scrooge called down the hall. "Mrs. Dilber. I shall be at

The Solace Home most of the day. Spending the day with *Jacob Marley's brother*!"

From the kitchen, they could hear Mrs. Dilber's high, Cockney voice sing out loudly, "Merry Christmas, Mr. Scrooge!"

*****

Tears ran down Marley's face as he watched Scrooge and Holmes hurry off.

"He'll be fine now," said Lucifer, suddenly appearing at Marley's shoulder. "There will be no kinder brother in all of London than Mr. Scrooge."

The bright angel glittered, nearly invisible against the sparkle of snow and morning sun. Marley moved to the side to view Lucifer against the more plain background of the city's grey buildings.

"It was a miraculous night," Marley said. "I'm grateful to you."

Lucifer pointed at Marley's ankles. "You look naked," he said.

Marley followed the angel's eyes and then gasped. No chains remained.

Lucifer said, "You taught Scrooge his lesson. Embrace life, embrace the world. 'If thou warn the wicked of his way to turn from it...Thou hast delivered *thy* soul.' Yes?"

Marley looked at Lucifer's face; the snowfield of white beard seemed whipped by an unseen wind into the drift of a smile.

"*My* soul?" Marley said, thinking of Scrooge. Then he understood Lucifer's meaning. "Oh, yes. Scrooge delivered my soul...But embracing life wasn't the lesson after all."

"No?"

"No," said Marley. "The lesson was not about love and

charity: those are merely the effects. The lesson was Forgiveness. But not of obtaining forgiveness from God; it is rather of *bestowing* forgiveness upon Him. That is the battle; and that is the way to redemption. Scrooge taught me that."

Lucifer thought it over for a while.

"Forgive God, you say?" the angel mused. "Well don't expect His gratitude for it."

"I don't expect it," Marley said. "And I don't need it. That's the point."

A look of concern made the drifts of Lucifer's beard rearrange themselves into steep cliffs.

"You still intend to keep our bargain?" he asked, sounding concerned.

Marley nodded.

"Would I cheat the Devil?"

The ghost reached out toward the angel with both hands. "I'll deliver your book," he said. "One Devonshire Terrace."

Lucifer produced the heavy text from beneath his mantel and handed it to Marley. The ghost stared at the book's immaculate cover and brilliant lettering for a long time.

Then Marley looked up. "You may be right," he said to the angel. "Or you may indeed be the Great Deceiver. I don't know."

Marley turned to go, then stopped and looked back at Lucifer again. "I must leave it to chance," he said.

A Christmas Carol

December 26, 1842
London

One Devonshire Terrace occupied part of a four-story, brick building on the Marylebone Road opposite Regent's Park. The building struck Marley as plain and dull-looking, despite its illustrious occupant and despite the fact that its front door and railings sported bright green paint.

Just past midnight Marley entered the dwelling of the great writer. The rooms sat silently and Marley could only hope that the man had not rushed off on one of his celebrated tours.

Marley moved smoothly and quickly from room to room, making no sounds at all. He passed through walls, taking note, like a tourist, of every personal detail in the celebrity's home. The rooms of Devonshire Terrace housed lavish furnishings: candelabra, rosewood chairs covered with silk, silk damask curtains, large mirrors, sofas, and sofa tables.

Marley stopped for a time in the parlor. There, somewhat out-of-place amid more elegant appointments, sat a modest, cottage piano. Marley went to it and traced its outlines with his hand, noticing that some of its woodwork looked worn and nicked. He wondered who had played it last. Then he moved on.

After passing through the first-floor rooms of several sleeping children, Marley rose to the second story. There he found the master bedroom.

Blue moonlight poured into the chamber through large, glass doors. The doors led outside to a balcony around which ran an ornate railing of wrought-iron cherubs. Shadows of those angels projected upon the bed.

Marley noted a secretariat near the window which, no doubt, afforded the writer a view of the city while he worked and a view of the walled garden below.

By the soft light Marley saw two figures in bed: a man and a woman, both asleep. The man turned on his right side facing the ghost.

Marley came to the edge of the bed and looked down at the young man, whom he guessed to be in his thirties. The man had a narrow nose, long, dark hair and a clean-shaven face. The large orbits of his eyes gave him, even while sleeping, a boyish look that belied the power of his work.

"So this is 'Boz,'" Marley said to himself, staring at the writer as one might stare at a rare artifact in a museum.

Marley turned to other parts of the room. He walked to the secretariat and perused the clutter of notes and papers strewn across it and read the covers of some books lying nearby. He could place *The Light-Giver* there, right where Mr. Charles Dickens would find it in the morning: a miracle, or so the man might think. Or Marley could place it elsewhere.

Marley thought again about his encounters with the great angel. What if, by delivering this book, he furthered a satanic plan of heresy and evil? On the other hand, what if Lucifer were right? In any event, Marley felt ensnared. He'd made a bargain with the devil, or with an angel; but a bargain nonetheless—deliver the book and tell the tale. One does not cheat the devil.

But perhaps one could hedge the bet.

Marley looked around the room again and discovered an obscure bookshelf tucked into a corner near the armoire.

Thick dust covered all the books there—mostly classics, elementary readers and latin school texts. Marley found a place on the bottom shelf in the corner of the bookcase large enough to accommodate Lucifer's manifesto.

"I agreed to deliver the book," Marley said to himself. "That's all."

He wedged *The Light-Giver* between neglected volumes of *The Arabian Nights* and *Gulliver's Travels*.

"But I didn't say where. If the book is found, so be it. If not...well, I leave it to chance."

Marley turned from the bookcase and looked at the sleeping writer. To fulfill the bargain, Marley knew he must recount the devil's tale. But he found he could scarcely make his way to the man's bedside, much less voice the words of the old angel's claim.

The prospect of relating Lucifer's treatise, the words coming from his own mouth, made Marley's throat constrict. Trepidation seized him. Marley hesitated at Dickens' bedside. Twice he started to speak, but could not go on.

I made a bargain, Marley thought. But I cannot—

Marley fell to his knees at the beside and clasped his hands in the manner of one in prayer. His thoughts rambled desperately. What shall I do? Sweet Jesus, what shall I do?

No answer came to Marley. After a long time of silence he whispered, "Help me, please."

The room remained mute, though it seemed to quiver with its own quietude. Then all at once Marley heard, or imagined—he couldn't be sure—children's voices singing a Christmas carol:

"...our Savior was born on Christmas Day/ To save us all from Satan's power/ When we were gone astray/ Oh, Tidings of Comfort and Joy/ Comfort and Joy/ Oh, Tidings of Comfort and Joy."

Marley raised his head.

"Tidings of comfort and joy," Marley repeated, brightening. "Tidings of comfort and joy!"

I shall speak to Boz, Marley thought, an excitement beginning to fill his spirit. That is what I promised. But *I* shall choose the tale. It shall be *my* tale.

Marley bent close to the sleeping man's ear. He paused for several moments before he spoke. Then he began.

"Marley was dead," the ghost whispered. "This must be clearly understood or nothing wonderful can come from the tale I am about to relate..."

*****

When Marley finished his story, dawn grasped the edges of the horizon. Marley walked to the window of the outer doors and saw the first streamers of sunlight lance upward from the east like the spikes of a crown. No clouds blocked the view and the low sky took on a vivid red and gold sheen.

Marley passed through the doors to the balcony outside. He looked down into the walled garden, still dark with morning shadows.

As he bent forward over the rail, the darkness below seemed to deepen, then suddenly expand outward, becoming a vast void that swallowed the earth around it.

Marley felt the chasm lunge at him, clawing and clutching at his hips as though it were an animate being, pulling him off the ledge. Marley grabbed the rail tightly; his chest pounded. He tried to hold onto the rail and concentrate on the feel of its cold ironwork against his fingers. Then everything slipped away.

Marley tumbled, enveloped in blackness. At first he felt the fearful rush of falling, then that passed, leaving behind an empty feeling of simply having no weight at all, of floating.

Dreamlike. Something between dreaming and waking. Then Marley felt rock beneath his feet.

Slowly, Marley stood, still encased in darkness. He tested his footing. He felt heat in the atmosphere around him, a stifling thickness of air choked with dust and the smell of sweating men. He smelled ammonia and manure. Marley knew the place. Elizabeth's Furnace.

A voice made Marley flinch. Its sound began slowly, deep and rough like a growl, its words becoming intelligible only after a time, as though they evolved, lifting themselves from a primordial depth. When the words finally sharpened and became clear, Marley heard the voice say, "Let there be light."

A small glow appeared an indeterminate distance away. It hovered above the ghost's line of vision, unmoving, illuminating nothing but itself. From the light came a different voice, but one familiar to Marley: a beautiful—though melancholy—sound. It spoke in verses and Marley listened to its hushed and halting rhythm, as though it created each image as it went. It sounded both despondent and threatening: the voice of someone reflecting on a wrong and contemplating retribution. It mused:

"The flesh of ages,
of beasts long dead,
is the coal of England.
Begetting the mines and mills,
fuel, and heat, the light of steel.
A dragon becomes a sword.

"Bone-tired miners,
Stripping dragons in deep lairs,
Burn their scales for heat.
The burning dragon: a shield from cold and damp,

Becomes, enlightened, a lamp.

"In a miner's den, a pen, moving at night,
Consumes the light of lifted dragons,
And examines the tailings of worked-out souls.
There, on paper, the beast and man meet,
On pages lighted by each,
They burn through the night."

The voice repeated the phrase, "burn through the night," the way one does when considering an idea. When the voice stopped, the luminous globe expanded and lighted the inner roads of the mine, revealing the workings' scarred walls and sagging timbers. There, near the junction of two tunnels, Lucifer sat on a turned-over wagon: the light that illuminated the mine emanated from him.

"You did not carry out our agreement," the angel said, his voice dropping for a moment back into the tone of the growl.

"I carried it out to the letter," Marley said hesitantly.

"But not to the spirit of it," Lucifer said.

Lucifer took a step toward Marley then stopped. Marley watched, transfixed by a growing horror, as the angel took on a deeper glow, a hot orange sheen, like the bars of a coal grate. Lucifer's features, once perfectly black and white, now reddened, radiating heat.

Slowly Lucifer raised his arms and pressed his hands against the ceiling of rock, coal and earth above them. His arms trembled.

"Man!" Lucifer suddenly roared.

Coal dust began to flutter down from the ceiling; timbers whined and squealed. Marley heard the sounds and felt the tremors that always preceded massive collapses of tunnels. Marley's legs gave out and he sank to his knees.

"Man!" Lucifer cried again, his face pointed toward the ceiling, as if someone on the surface could hear him. "You defeat yourselves. You foolish children. What must I do to convince you?!"

With a weak cry of disgust, the angel gave one last shove at the ceiling and then dropped his arms. Marley ducked his head, expecting that the ceiling would follow, rushing in on him, smothering him into an airless, lightless void for all eternity. But ceiling remained fixed.

Marley raised his head slowly, looking first at the sagging beams and then at Lucifer. Marley's voice wavered. "Is this place your revenge?" he said. "Is this my hell?"

Lucifer's coloring cooled rapidly. He regained his white luminescence. The angel sighed and waved his hand in a dismissive manner.

"You hedged your bet. I am disappointed," he said, suddenly weary like the father of a disordered child. "But I suppose it's no great matter after all. Perhaps something will come of it someday, regardless. And if not, there are always more Jacob Marleys and more writers and more, much more time."

"Is this hell?" Marley asked again.

Lucifer shook his head. "It *was* your hell," he said. "A long time ago. You're well beyond that now."

Marley persisted. "Why are we here?"

"I'm taking you back," Lucifer said.

"Back to where?"

"Home, of course," the angel said. He added, "I'll miss you."

Lucifer turned, motioned for Marley to follow, then crouched almost to his knees and bent into the left-hand tunnel.

Marley followed the glowing angel down the passage, and from there walked through tunnel after tunnel, turn after turn. Marley could not be sure, but he sensed a slight upward grade as they walked.

Marley followed Lucifer's light, realizing that he could no longer see the shape of the angel, lost in its own brilliance.

After what seemed like hours, the light ahead stopped moving. As Marley gained on it, the glowing circle grew larger.

When almost upon it, Marley realized that the ball of light he'd been following had changed; it ceased being that of Lucifer; Marley now viewed the greater brilliance of real sunlight.

Marley emerged from the mine on the side of a hill. He stepped out of the cave into the light and breathed deeply.

The air tasted warm and sweet, like that of summer. Marley walked out onto a grassy slope under a mid-day sun that pressed its warm weight upon him. He came to a meadow and lay down on its warm grass, a gentle breeze blowing across his face. Below him a large, glassy pond mirrored a blue sky. The scent of mown hay filled his nostrils. He heard birdsongs and the laughter of children.

One of the young voices called to him: "Jake come play."

Jake rose to a sitting posture and smiled, putting one hand to his brow to act as a visor. A game of hide-and-seek scurried through the meadow. He could see all the players: boys and girls of his own age. He recognized them all. He waved toward the boy who had hailed him and, squinting, saw the familiar face against the backlight of the sun.

A girl sang. Her voice trilled familiar sounds. Her high and lisping words came from the meadow and Jake stepped toward them. The girl sang:

"'Old Christmas time was drawing near/ With the nights so dark and long/ The sons' bright ghosts came walking home/ Walking by the light of the sun/ As soon as they reached their own mother's gate/ So loud did the bell they ring/ There's none so ready as their own mother dear/ To bring these children in.'"

Jake Turner took off his shoes and ran down the hill toward his friends. Summer lay warm upon them, bright and fragrant. There would be time enough to embrace them all: everyone.

Jake ran on, the light of the sun growing brighter with every step. Summer. Bright. White. Brilliant. All contrasts burned away until nothing else remained. Only light.

Author's note:

On October 5, 1843, an idea for a new novel surfaced in the mind of English writer Charles Dickens. "A strange mastery...seized him," Dickens' friend and biographer, John Forster wrote, recalling how the idea gripped the writer. Dickens worked on the book at a feverish pace. *A Christmas Carol* emerged "almost ready-made," six weeks after Dickens began—in time for the holiday.

Charles Dickens (a.k.a. "Boz") later attributed parts of the novel to dreams he'd had that year.